ELKHORN DIVIDE

Other novels by Alfred Dennis

Chiricahua
Lone Eagle
Brant's Fort
Catamount
The Mustangers
Yuma
Rover
Yellowstone Brigade
Sandigras Canyon
Shawnee Trail
Fort Reno

ELKHORN DIVIDE

Alfred Dennis

Walnut Creek Publishing
Tuskahoma, Oklahoma

This book is dedicated to and in memory
of my great friend Robert Bob Conklin of
Walton, New York

Chapter 1

The cannon and musket fire was quiet now, the war finally ran its course. The pride of America, both Blue and Grey, left their life's bloodshed on many a battlefield across this beautiful land. In vain, many wondered; would they do it again? Yes, it was man's destiny to fight for what he believed in, and these young men, no matter what side they were on, were dedicated to their country and their families. Their pride would not let them do otherwise.

Soldiers in grey and butternut filed silently by the tall, dark haired man standing alongside the dusty road. Some salute, others only nod. Tired, hungry and beaten, they shuffle slowly to the south.

The officer drops his eyes. He cannot look into the eyes of these once proud men. Where did the fire and fierce pride go? This was an army that outfought and outmaneuvered the Yankees, from Bull Run to Chancellorsville. What happened?

Courage and pride was not enough. Sheer numbers and lack of supplies finally beat them down. Only three years past, the army marched down the same road singing, then cheering when they spotted their beloved General Bobby Lee, sitting on his grey horse, Traveler.

How did they lose? The tall Colonel turns his sorrel gelding. Finding it hard to leave his men, he turns back for one final look. Fire flashes from the dark eyes as they spot a Yankee patrol approaching. General Lee surrendered only two days prior, and already the Yankees were pushing south. Defeat is bitter in any man with pride and Matt Tillman has more than his fair share of pride. However, the old saying, "pride goes before a fall," is hitting close to home, where he is concerned.

A scarecrow of a soldier looks to where the officer sits his horse. "Lead us Colonel, Sir, and we'll fight them blue coats."

"No, the war's over son. Go home, plant your crops, raise your families and help put the south back on its feet again." The voice coming from the handsome Colonel was slow and soft, but strong. He called the soldier son, yet he was no older. The war aged him though, making him older than his actual twenty-six years. Four years earlier, he was a smart aleck, wet behind the ears kid. No longer than four long years of seeing his friends and comrades killed, it took the arrogance of youth away from him. Accomplishing what most people, including Jessie, thought would never happen, as he became a man.

The dark hair is already sprinkled with a little grey, but the fire is still there. The war only honed his senses, making him stronger, maybe even meaner. Four years of fighting, hunger, and seeing men killed, left its mark, making him bitter.

Reaching inside his grey tunic, he pulls forth a wrinkled letter. Once again the letter was unfolded. The worn pages spread open to reveal the neat handwriting; her handwriting; Jessie's handwriting. They say you can tell many things about a person by their handwriting. He smiles, perhaps the saying is true. The letter was like her, prim and proper, and the letters were formed beautifully. Yes, she was all these things. Why did she quit loving him and marry Cage so quickly after he left?

His black eyes study the words. His uncle, Matt Tillman was dead. The huge Elkhorn Ranch, somewhere out west in Colorado Territory, was left to his two nephews, the only living heirs. Tillman founded the huge ranch and held it together by fighting Indians, rustlers, sickness and the elements. One half went to Cage, his older brother, and one half to him, Matt Tillman, his namesake, who was named after the hard-bitten old man, whom some said his nephew took after. The older Tillman left Texas, two jumps ahead of the law, with over a thousand head of longhorns. Some say Tillman might not have legal and proper ownership to them but no one dared say it to the old man's face. Several deceased men, lying scattered about west Texas, would testify to the fact that Tillman was a tough character, and greased lightning with a pistol.

The Colonel read the handwriting, neat and proper, the way Jessie was. Now she belonged to another. Cage took her from him, marrying her as soon as he left for the war. Now they were somewhere in Colorado Territory on a ranch called the Elkhorn. He will get half the ranch. Yes, his brother is an honest man, but he will not get Jessie, the only one he ever loved.

His left hand balls into a clenched fist without him realizing it. Jessie was his, even from the time they were children on neighboring farms, but he was wild; too wild. She was just the opposite. Being the gentle person she is, she wanted him to settle down and when he left for the war, she married Cage. Yes, he truly loves her, but the south was in a war, fighting for its very existence; fighting for a way of life the north wanted to change. The south needed all of her sons. He would have come back to Jessie when the war was over. Now, it is too late. She belongs to another. Matt's face grows red with rage, thinking of his Jessie belonging to his brother Cage.

The letter he studies is three years old now. He received it after the second Battle of Bull Run. Riding with Jeb Stuart for four years, his bravery under fire, and the ability to lead men, brought him the rank of Colonel; a gentleman, in the midst of all the blood and gore. He refolds the letter and replaces it inside his blouse. What the hell is a gentleman?

"We's goin' home, Masta Matt?" The dark eyes shift to the huge black man behind him. "I told you Hob, you're free; now git."

"Yassa Masta, but is we goin' home?"

Shrugging his shoulders, his eyes settle on the black face looking up at him. Both men, white and black, were the same age. A black baby, born into the world, was named Hob because he was no bigger than a hobnail at birth, but this hobnail had grown to be the biggest black man in the county.

They had been together since they were babies. Hob's mother breast-fed both babies after Matt's mother died in childbirth. His father was distraught and never remarried. Matt ran free with his older brother Cage and the young black that he looked on more as a brother than a slave. They were inseparable as kids, then as young men. No three grown men in the county could whip them in a rough and tumble fight, which was as common then as eating. Matt's father would rant and rave that he was going to sell Hob, if they caused any more problems. Matt only laughed, knowing full well the older Tillman was just bluffing. Of course, now he knows Matt was the one who started the trouble and Hob was pulled into it, but he thought fighting was giving the Tillmans a bad name. Secretly, out of sight of the young men, he would grin and slap one of the servants on the back and laugh. He would not let them know but he was proud of both of them.

All through the hell and fires of battle, they watched each other's back. Hob did not particularly have a feeling about the south or the war, but he loved Matt and Cage; Matt more so, as he was the youngest. Cage yes, but Cage was steadier, more mature, and did not need Hob as Matt did.

"You're free."

"Yassa, Masta Matt, I is free to go with you." Hob was with the Colonel, fighting through every battle, even after Abe Lincoln freed the slaves.

"What about April and the children? I'm headed west, Hob; west to Colorado." Matt looks exasperated at Hob. Yes, Hob technically, had been a slave, but Matt never thought of him as such; more of a friend; a companion. Since birth, they were together, hardly ever out of each other's sight.

"We can take 'em with us Masta."

Both men look at each other. A bond exists between them, maybe a bond even stronger than brothers. They went through so many battles and survived. Even when they were children, Matt could not deny Hob anything. Shaking his head, he nods and gives up.

"Mount up then, let's go after them." The Colonel looks one last time at the backs of his retreating men and turns west into the afternoon sun. "We'll pick up the stallion and mares on the way."

"You speck they'll still be where we put 'em?"

"Should be; with the war, nobody's been back in those mountains for a spell."

"Yassa," Hob nods slowly, his dark eyes looking toward the south and home.

Chapter 2

The town of Elk Springs is not much, just a couple of stores, one saloon, and a few ramshackle buildings thrown together, forming a small, dusty street. The barbershop doubles as the office for the dentist, and undertaker, who happen to be the same person. Matt was surprised that he wasn't the doctor also, but he notices another sign down the street: Doctor William Wallace, M.D. Elk Springs, survives solely on the trade the local ranchers brought in, and the cowboys coming to town on Saturday night, to blow off steam from a hard weeks work. The saloon, which receives most of their attention, is the most lucrative of all the businesses in Elk Springs. Of course, Matt knows that any self-respecting cowboy, worth his salt, has to have a nip now and then, and some nip more than others. Some men proclaim a man that does not take a nip now and then, cannot be trusted. Not so, Matt grins. U.S. Grant took more than a nip, and Matt sure didn't trust that old heathen. About the time we thought we had him whipped, he came roaring back and sent us packing. "No," Matt mused. "General Grant could be trusted; he was a good man and a great General.

All eyes gawk at the strange sight of the tall white man in a confederate uniform. This is the west and plenty of ex-confederate soldiers passed through, but none were followed by a black woman and two young boys. Tied behind the wagon is a blood bay stallion, thoroughbred by the looks of him, and three mares. However, the people up and down the street are not gawking at the horses. No sir, Hob has their attention. They never saw a black man as big as him, and certainly not one dressed in confederate grey. Studying the faces of the town people, as they ride down the small street, Matt grins inwardly. He knows Hob fascinates people, not just his size but also the dark blackness of his skin. Every town they passed through on their way to Colorado is the same.

Not much of a place, Matthew Tillman thought, surveying the length of the town and the unpainted board structures lining the street. It feels good to finally arrive in Elk Springs, the town the Elkhorn Ranch was named after. It was two weeks since they passed through a settlement. Their supplies are getting low and this is the town Jessie calls home. Their journey is over. Now he can forget the war and build something; something as his uncle, Matt did, and maybe he can forget the war and her. No, forget is the wrong word. He will never forget her but perhaps he can finally find peace without her.

Pulling up in front of the only general store, in town, he waits until Hob rides up beside him and then motions at the saloon. "Reckon we found civilization Hobnail; at least a real saloon."

"Yassa, and trouble too, I think!"

"Now, you wouldn't deny me a drink, would you?" Matt laughs.

"Weren't the drink I mind Masta Matt. It be them folks looking. They don't seem real friendly."

Grinning, Matt dismounts and ties his gelding to the hitch rail. Motioning for Hob to follow, he pushes open the door of the general store and steps into the cool interior. The shelves, lining the floor and walls, hold every imaginable item of clothing, harness, or tin goods, a man will ever need. Looking at the cracker barrels, and pickle barrels, Matt can hardly believe his eyes. Never since the war has he seen a store so well stocked. The big room also has a shelf of books, something most western folks have little use for.

"Be right with …." The young store clerk stops in midsentence, when the imposing figure of Hob comes through the door.

"He's black alright and downright homely to boot," Matt shakes his head sadly.

The young man turns beet red then stammers, "I'm sorry Mister, we don't see many black folks here in Elk Springs and especially one that big."

"Well, he's big alright. Now, we need supplies and some information."

"We've got the supplies; don't know about the info." The clerk cannot take his eyes from Hob.

Matt lays a list, he prepared, on the counter and turns, looking around the store. Picking up the paper, the clerk studies it, but his attention is on the big man in front of him. The man wears the uniform of the confederacy. Even though the insignia was removed, the clerk knows he was an officer, but what is he now? He is not a rancher or a cowboy, no sir, maybe a gunfighter or lawman. He is almost as big as the black man. At least six foot two, around one ninety, and heavily muscled in his chest and arms, powerful looking. No, this one is no ordinary cowman.

Bounty hunters found a new occupation since the war, with all the outlaws running amuck. The young clerk's imagination runs wild. That could be it alright; a bounty hunter. Looking back at the list, the clerk begins piling items on the scarred, wooden counter. His eyes wander curiously back to the man. He seems older than his face shows, and for some reason, even though the tall man seems friendly enough, the store man feels he is dangerous. It's not just the gun strapped to his side. Maybe it's the way he watches everything, as a coiled mountain cat ready to spring at the least provocation. Whatever the reason, for him being here, it probably is not to anybody's benefit.

Laying a slab of bacon on the counter, his eyes look toward the door, where the big black man stands, waiting patiently; a Spencer Carbine resting on his arm. Nothing seems to get by the black. His dark eyes take in everything. "Well Sir, that's everything on the list," the clerk announces nervously.

"Add a couple more boxes of forty fours to that pile, if you don't mind."

"Yes sir."

"And two bags of hard candy." Matt lays a twenty dollar gold piece on the counter. Hob walks to the counter and picks up the supplies, retreating out the door. "Now, young man, I'm Matt Tillman and we're looking for the Elkhorn Ranch."

"That's it!" The clerk smiles, relieved. "You're Cage Tillman's brother."

"I'm guilty."

"He mentioned you'd be coming soon. Said to tell you he'd wait at the Divide, north of here."

"Divide?"

"Yes Sir, Mister Tillman. That's where the ranch splits. Right fork goes to the ranch house and the lower valleys. The left fork goes to the upper ranch land and the high meadows."

"I see." Matt picks up the two bags of candy.

"Mister," the clerk shifts uneasily. "Mister Tillman said for you not to come to the ranch house."

"He did, did he? Well alright."

"Ain't you two brothers?"

"We are, but in blood only."

"I see." The clerk counts out the big man's change. "And, just when does my brother intend to meet me at the Divide?"

"He keeps a man over at the saloon; has now for several days. He'll ride for Mister Tillman. I'll go right over and tell him you're here." The clerk starts around the counter toward the door, as Matt's long arm shoots out, stopping him.

"No, you mind the store, young feller, so no one steals you blind. I'm in need of a drink to wash down the trail dust. I'll tell him."

"Yes Sir, Mister Tillman."

"What's your name?" Matt looks closely at the young man.

"Bailey, Mister Tillman; Bailey Howard."

"Well now, Bailey Howard. We can't have two Mister Tillmans in the same town, now can we?"

"No Sir, I reckon not."

"Good. From now on you call me Matt. That'll shorten things down a mite and save a lot of confusion."

"Yes Sir." A look of relief spread across the young man's face. "May I ask you a question, Matt?"

"Alright," Matt waits. "Providing of course it's nothing personal."

"You're a bounty hunter and you're after somebody around here, ain't you?"

"Just this hard candy," Matt said as he raises the two bags of candy and nods to the youngster.

Passing through the front door of the store, Matt tips his hat to two women and steps to the side so they can enter. The younger of the women turns and stares at the tall frame of the stranger until the older woman pushes her on inside.

"Who was that?" The youngest woman shot a wide eyed look at the young clerk.

"Matt Tillman!" The clerk said. "And you stay away from him."

"You're not my boss, Bailey Howard."

"He's a dangerous man, Sis." Bailey set down a can of snuff he was dusting. "He's not like his brother Cage. I don't know why but I think he's as dangerous as a grizzly bear."

"I don't know if he's dangerous but he's sure handsome."

"That'll be enough Abigail." The older of the women said, frowning at the young girl. "I swear I don't know what has come over you lately.

"Oh Kate, I was just looking," Abigail pouts. "Don't do a body no harm to look. Besides, I saw you looking too."

Handing the younger woman a broom, she pointed to the floor. "It doesn't hurt a body to work either, little sister."

Bailey laughs from behind the counter. "That's telling her Sis. She's already got all the men around here drooling over her."

"That'll be enough out of you too, Bailey Howard." Kate Howard raised her sister and brother, since their folks were killed in sixty-one, by a runaway wagon. They were traveling west with a wagon train when the accident took their parents. All three children stayed with the train until they reached Elk Springs. Old Mathew Tillman took them under his wing, helping them buy the general store and restocking it. Money is still owed on the store, from the loan he made her, money she keeps in her safe, waiting for the other Tillman brother to arrive.

Turning back to the window, she studies the tall man as he disappears into Slocum's Saloon. So this is the younger Tillman. He is taller than his uncle but he has the same square shoulders when he walks, with an easy way of carrying himself. Yes, he is handsome. Dangerous, she does not know, but he is definitely handsome. She noticed how the big black man, shadows the younger Tillman brother, hanging back just a few feet. She senses somehow, the two belong together. She can almost see the bond between them. Bailey might be right. If they are not dangerous, they are very careful.

Turning, Kate bumps into her younger sister. "You think he's cute too, huh?" Abigail smiles mischievously.

Kate Howard is a beautiful woman in her own way; not like the younger blond headed Abigail, who the local cowboys were all in love with. No, Kate does not have Abigail's beauty. She is more mature and stronger because she had to raise her younger siblings. Dark headed, tall and straight, with dark brown eyes, she has the inner quietness of an older woman. Her carriage and poise, shows her to be a person of strength and character. No nonsense in this one. She is not quick to smile or be taken in by the locals, who were always hanging around the store when they managed to sneak off, from their work.

Matt walks into the dark saloon and quickly steps to the side of the swinging doors, out of the light, coming in from the street. He waits until his eyes adjust to the dimness, while Hob waits, just outside, on the wooden walkway. Midafternoon finds only a few loafers, sitting around the tables, playing cards. The only one wearing the mark of a cowman is sitting at a table, playing checkers with the barkeep. Matt notices how the man looks him over, as he enters. No animosity, just a man watching his back; a careful man.

Walking up to the bar, he orders a whiskey as the barkeep, wearing a checkered apron, quit the game and walks behind the counter. Turning, Matt lets his eyes travel the length of the room, as they settle easily on the young cowboy. Holding his whiskey in his left hand, he lets his right rest easily; his big thumb hooked into the rig of his holster, inches from the handle grip of his big horse pistol. Studying each man around the room, he guesses the cowboy at the checkerboard table to be the Elkhorn rider.

"I'm looking for an Elkhorn rider." The remark is short and crisp. Matt tosses down his drink and shakes his head. "Boy over at the store told me there was one here."

"Hard stuff, ain't it Mister Tillman?" The Elkhorn rider grins, pushing back his big felt hat. "That'll be me. I'm Elkhorn."

"What's your name?"

"Jim Cloud." The man put out his hand, which Matt ignores. Pulling his hand back, the cowboy takes a longer look at Matt.

"Well now, seems you already know who I am, so why don't you skedaddle out of here and tell your boss I'm in town."

"I'll do that; reckon Bailey told you where your brother said he'd meet you?" The rider named Cloud questions.

"That's a fact. I'll be there come sunup." Matt's voice is hard as nails. "You tell Cage I'm coming after what's mine."

"You want another?" The barkeep motions at Matt's empty glass.

"You hear me ask for one?" Turning, Matt pushes through the doors, back into the bright sunshine.

"Friendly cuss," the barkeeper said, sarcastically, shaking his head.

"Mister Tillman said he's a pretty tough customer." Jim Cloud said, as he watches the tall man walk down the street, "and I'm inclined to believe it now. I've seen friendlier looking rattlesnakes," as he looks at the black man with him.

The barkeep grins as he picks up Matt's empty glass. "It might just get downright interesting around here, when Mister Matt Tillman and Wylie Palette meet. Sure don't want to miss that little set to."

Nodding, the cowboy walks to the swinging doors, his eyes following the tall man across the street. "It'll probably be a good show but I wouldn't bet on Wylie if'n I was you; that is, if you don't want to lose your money."

Kate Howard steps from the store's porch and follows Matt as he walks toward the waiting wagon. Passing the two sacks of candy up to the young boys, he grins as they yelp with joy. She notices how white and even his teeth are and how he softens around the children. Stepping up beside him, she notices too, how tall he is. The dark eyes seem to bore through her as they look down at her. "Mister Tillman, I'm Kate Howard, I own this store."

"Yes ma'am." The Elkhorn rider passes them as they speak, loping his horse easily down the dusty street. Matt can tell he knows horses by the way he sits his saddle, his body in fluid motion with the rough gait of the horse. A man has to spend a lot of time in the saddle to ride a horse with the smooth, effortless motion, this rider has.

"He's Jim Cloud; rides for your brother." She notices the rapt attention Matt paid the horse and rider, as he lopes out of town.

"I met him in the saloon."

"I see but you don't know him. He's a good man; one half Arapaho, I understand." She waits, letting her words sink in. "If you are ever in need of a good hand, he's as dependable and honest as they come.

"Miss Howard, I'm a fair hand at judging men and I do my own hiring. Now, what exactly can I do for you?"

She studies his face. "I see you are a busy man. I'll get to the point. Your uncle Matt lent me money when I came here. He died before I could repay him. Here it is; half belongs to your brother. If you will sign this paper, settling my debt, I will not trouble you further." She pushes the receipt at him.

"Why didn't you just pay my brother?"

"Because, Mister Tillman, I wanted you to get your half."

"Cage is an honest man."

"Yes, he is; are you?"

Taking the paper and pencil from her outstretched hand, Matt studies the document and signs his name to it. "Yes ma'am, at least I don't steal other men's property."

"Meaning your brother does?" She studies the hard set to his face then hands him the money.

"Good day, Miss Howard." Matt mounts his sorrel and with an automatic gesture, he motions the wagon forward, toward the road leading northwest to the Elkhorn Ranch.

Kate watches him ride away, his back ramrod straight, sitting his saddle like he was born to it. Hard as nails, proud, and maybe even arrogant, but she has to admit, he cut a fine figure of a man. Maybe Bailey is right, the man is cold and hard as nails.

"He's handsome, isn't he?" Abigail comes up quietly, as Kate watches Matt ride down the street.

"Yes, he is."

"Bailey said he isn't allowed to come to Mister Tillman's ranch house; wonder why?"

"That's none of our business."

CHAPTER 3

Matt judges they traveled about six miles when they pull the wagon into a small grove of trees, making camp for the night. The Divide, Bailey Howard mentioned, should be only a mile or two from the creek crossing where they are camping.

Hob's boys, Jacob and Isaac, are already splashing happily in the water. April is busy starting a fire, to cook her famous biscuits, in the darkened Dutch-oven. Matt watches the boys and smiles. It seems only yesterday that Cage, Hob, and himself, played the same way. A close-knit family then but now, they are grown men with a ranch to split, and a woman they both want.

How old are the boys? They had been gone to the war four years and the boys were about three and four years old when they left. Time does have a way of passing. If he is not careful, he will be an old man in a few years. Shucks, he is already an old man. The years got away from him. He barely remembers when his Uncle Matt visited that one time, from Texas.

"We's gonna have trouble tomorrow, Masta?"

Looking up at the black face, Matt shakes his head. "No, we're gonna say howdy and that's all."

"Yassa Masta," Hob studies the ground. "She belong to Cage now. She his wife. Maybe we should go on somewhere else. You got some money and them fine horses. Let's move on out west; maybe the place I hear them call Oregon."

"No!" Matt's loud voice makes April look up from her cooking. "Hob," Matt starts to say more, but he knows Hob is right, they should go on.

"Yassa."

"There will be no trouble. The land is ours. We will stay here. Besides, we're gonna start us a fine horse ranch, ain't we?" Matt studies Hob's face. "The young ones and April are tired, and winter is coming on."

The big black head bobs slowly, up and down, but doubt shows in the dark eyes, as he watches the man across from him. Hob alone, knows the violence in the man, the only man he ever completely trusted. Even as a boy, he was wild, but now with the loss of Jessie, and the war, something replaced the wildness and changed it into coldness; a coldness that makes the black man worry.

If they stay, there might be trouble. Jessie is too close, too near. Hob knows both brothers are good men. When they were all youngsters, Cage was bigger, stronger, able to win at anything they tried; but now? No, Cage does not stand a chance against young Matt now. Lightning fast with the handgun, he carries. However, the war made him unpredictable, except for one thing; he knows how to kill and he would. When Jessie married Cage, it took something out of Matt and replaced it with coldness.

Only with April and the boys, Matt shows any softness or compassion. Has he forgotten how to love? Could one woman, turn a good man so completely, or had it been the war? No, many men fought the war. Hob knows his friend. Jessie turned him bitter. Sighing, he picks up the large coffeepot. If they stay here, there will be trouble, but Matt is hardheaded, when his mind is set on something. He is also like a brother to Hob. Not even April can come between them. No, whatever is to come, Hob will be where he has always been, at Matt's side. He remembers the last thing his aging mother asked him before she passed. Her words come back to him as if they were spoken yesterday. She asked him to stay with Matt and help him. She knew Matt. She knew the wildness that was in him. In time, she said his good side will win but it will take time. He made her a promise, there on his knees beside her bed. He would stick to that promise, no matter what.

Matt can sense the uneasiness in his friend, as he takes the hot coffee from the outstretched hand. "We've got to stay. We have the horses, but not enough money to go further. It takes money to travel and set up."

"We'es got money."

"What money? Confound it Hob, I've got less than one hundred dollars to get us through the winter."

"No Sir, you've got lots of money."

"What the dickens are you talking about?" Matt studies the dark face. "Where is all this money?"

"You remember when we took that studhorse from that big Yankee General you shot at the fight around Malvern Crossing?"

"I remember."

"Yassa, you remember you asked me what was in them saddlebags on that horse. You told me to look and throw it away."

"Yes."

"When we hid those horses, back in the mountains, I hid both them bags. I knew you'd turn it in to them army folks, and we'd lose it if'n I gave it to you, so I buried 'em near where we put the stallion and mares."

"Money was in those bags?"

"Yes Sir, gold money, a whole lot of these." Hob produces several gold pieces and hands them to Matt. Matt's mouth drops open as he takes the twenty dollar gold piece from Hob.

"How many are there?"

"You knows I can't count, but them bags are real heavy."

"Where are they?"

"Hidden in the wagon under the bedding."

Matt sits stupefied, slowly turning the gold piece in his hand. Yes, while the war was raging, he would have turned the gold into the confederacy. Now to turn it in, would only give it to the Yankee blue coats. Nodding his head slowly, he absently sips at his coffee. Money never meant much to him, but now, at least they have enough to see them through, until the ranch starts paying for itself. If he had known of the money before Lee's surrender, he would have considered it stealing, but not now. He wasn't about to give money to the blue coats for them to line their pockets and live in luxury.

"Did I do right?"

"The war is lost now Hob. Yes you did right. A few dollars more would have only extended the war and gotten a few more men killed."

"Do you want to see the money?"

"Not tonight. Leave it where it is."

Five riders sit their horses across the trail as they approach. Matt figures this fork, heading east and west, has to be what Bailey Howard calls the Divide. A deep worn path, winds off to the left, beaten down by what appears to be cattle and horse tracks. Recognizing his brother and the rider from the saloon, Matt absently slips his tie down thong, from the hammer of his pistol. Cage will not start anything but Matt does not know about the men with him. Motioning for April to hold the wagon where she is, Matt and Hob ride forward. Anything can happen and he wants her and the children out of harm's way.

"Good to see you brother." Cage Tillman is five years older and twenty pounds heavier than Matt. "Hob, is that you?"

"Yassa, Mister Cage."

"That's April and the young ones. My, how them young'uns have grown." Cage Tillman smiles and waves at the wagon.

"Yassa."

"Well, let's get on with it brother." Cage brings his attention back to Matt. "That trail there, starts your half of the ranch, just like Uncle Matt intended. I've had the papers fixed up all legal. You've got more range, but as I am married, I took the ranch house and the lower valleys." Cage left no room for argument. "I felt that would be fair, as Uncle Matt didn't stipulate how we were to divide the ranch."

"Alright."

Cage kicks his horse closer to Matt and hands over an envelope containing the deed to the upper Elkhorn. "One other thing, Matt."

Looking at the envelope, Matt let his eyes settle on Cage. "What's that?"

"She's mine now. Don't forget it. For now, I want you to stay on your side of the Divide and away from mine."

"Is that Jessie talking or you?"

"Both of us, we think it'd be best, for a while anyway."

"We? What if you weren't around?"

"What do you mean? Would you kill me, Matt, your own brother?" Cage studies Matt's face.

"It's on my mind Cage. You took her from me and you did it behind my back."

"Masta Matt." Hob pushes his horse next to Matt's.

"Stay back Hob, this is between me and Cage."

"You'd shoot me, Matt?"

"I aim to right now."

"Has the war made you that sour?" Cage looks incredulously at Matt. "That, you'd shoot me; your own brother?"

"A brother doesn't take what ain't his."

Cage looks into the dark, hate filled eyes, of a brother he no longer knows. Death looks back at him and he can feel it, clean to his boots. The man across from him is coiled like a rattlesnake, ready to strike. Matt's hand is poised over his big forty-four and his face is hard as ashen granite. Only a drop of an eyelash and someone will die, maybe both brothers.

Only seconds pass as the men sit their horses but it seems like hours to Hob. Cloud and the Elkhorn riders watch as both men sit poised, their hands only inches from their pistols and death. The men know this has to be settled between the two brothers. Wylie Palette wants to interfere, but he knows Cage will lose face if he does.

"Wait, Matt!"

"I'm gonna kill you Cage. I'm through talking." A viselike hold clamps down on Matt's hand before he can draw. "Let go, Hob."

"Masta Matt, I can't."

"Hob!" The voice is as cold as a blue northern, from the mountains.

"Alright Matt, you win." Cage places both of his hands on his saddle horn. "I'll not fight you over this, at least until you and Jessie have spoken. I'll bring Jessie to town in two weeks and you and she can have a talk. But, if she says so; it's finished!"

"If you don't," Matt left the threat unsaid.

"She'll be there."

"Alright Cage." The tenseness leaves Matt as quickly as the anger came. "You bring her in and let her tell me. Then, it'll be finished."

"Matt, don't think I'm scared of you 'cause I ain't, but. . ." Cage let it drop.

Sweat beads on Hob's brow, as he feels Matt's hand relax on the butt of his forty-four. Removing his huge hand, he looks guiltily down at the ground. Time seems to stand still until Cage turns his attention on Hob.

"You and April come and work for me Hob. Winter's coming and the high country will be plenty cold."

"No Sir, we'll stay with Masta Matt."

"Same old Hob, loyal to a fault," Cage smiles. "You're always welcome. Come to visit. I've got some good fishing holes, down lower."

"Thank you Masta Cage."

"Seems you'd tell him he's free, no more Mastas." Cage looks at Matt.

"He knows but old habits are just hard to break."

"I'm sending a rider with you as far as the line camp and then you're on your own." Cage looks around and waves Jim Cloud forward.

"No need." Matt drops the ranch deed into a saddlebag. "We can find our way a few more miles. We've come this far."

Cage ignores Matt, as the dark rider from the saloon rides up alongside. "This is Jim Cloud. He'll see you over the mountain."

Matt studies Cloud then turns his attention back to Cage, as his brother rides over to the wagon and leans over to hug April. It seems like old times. They are all back together, except for Jessie. Everything has changed. Nothing will ever be the same again.

Cage starts his horse down the trail to the lower valley with all but one of his riders following. A short slender cowboy rides to within ten feet of Matt and halts his buckskin gelding. Matt can tell, by the way the man wears his holster, this is no ordinary saddle tramp. Here is the real McCoy, a Texas gunfighter, and a man to be reckoned with. There will be no back up in the man. He will not run or back shoot you and he will be hard to kill. Here sits a real curly wolf and he is on the prod.

"You might have buffaloed your brother but next time it will be me."

 "What's wrong with right now?"

Hob backs his gelding out of the line of fire. This time he does not interfere. Sooner or later, these two will tangle and it might as well be now.

"Next time will do. There's no hurry." Looking Matt over carefully, the man nods coldly and turns his horse after the others. Hob rides his horse closer to Matt and watches as the gunman catches up to the others.

"He's a bad 'un." Hob speaks as the gunman rides off.

Matt takes in the tied down gun on the man's hip and the well-oiled holster that holds it. The cold, blue-grey eyes seem to bore through a man when he looks at you. The thin lips snarl like a rabid wolf. Yes, Matt has to agree, this one is a bad one and he knows that is a bona fide fact.

"His name's Wylie Palette, and your man's right, he's a bad one."

"Hob's not my man, Mister Cloud. He's as free as we are. Now let's ride." Matt waves April forward and they turn on to the fork that leads to the upper Elkhorn Range.

The climb into the mountains is a hard pull on the team. They top out steep mountain passes that lead back down into huge valleys. Several times, Matt and Hob has to tie onto the wagon tongue to help the laboring horses. The scenery is majestic, the mountains beautiful, and the air is as fresh and sweet as any he has smelled since the Shenandoah Valley.

Aspen, pine, cedar, and box elder, grows everywhere. Flowers of all colors grow along the trail, accounting for the sweet fragrance in the air. Small streams coming down the mountains, run clear and cold across the trail. Matt cannot believe his good fortune. He actually inherited all of this. No wonder

Uncle Matt fought so hard to hang onto this magnificent country. All a man has to do is put a little labor into this and it will reward him. The road, if that is what it can be called, rolls on due west. Cattle dot the plentiful valleys, running away as they pass through. Small herds of buffalo raise their heads and watch as the riders climb out of each valley.

Somewhere up ahead, Jim Cloud said they would pass through one more mountain pass and come into a larger valley. At the far end, near the head of a large lake, sits a line shack. The Elkhorn riders lived in it, riding herd on his brother's cattle, during the long cold winters that were notorious in these high mountains. Once the snows set in, the line riders have to keep the cattle pushed back into the valleys and not let them drift with the hard blowing snowstorms. It gets so cold in these mountains, ice has to be broken daily for the cattle to drink. Sometimes it takes an hour to open a water hole that freezes back in minutes.

"If you get tired of beef, Mister Tillman, there's still buffalo and plenty of elk left up here."

Matt does not answer and the rider let it go. Cloud can tell conversation is not one of this Tillman's long suits. Coming through the last pass, Matt's eyes take in the wide valley, covered in grass, belly deep on a horse. Cattle graze the rolling slopes, leading down toward the huge natural lake that covers the far end of the valley. The valley is large, running at least five miles before being obscured by a deep stand of cedars and pines. Flowers grow everywhere on the slopes and alongside the lake. Pines and cedars grow on the hillside, while aspens and willows grow along the edge of the lake.

"Kinda takes your breath away, don't it?"

This time Matt answers the man. "Yes Sir, it does."

Smoke drifts from the small line shack, taking Matt's attention away from the lake and surrounding countryside. Riding in closer to the cabin, he reins in his sorrel and studies the layout of the buildings. Two horses, standing in the corral, pick their ears up, nickering at the approaching horsemen. One other building, larger than the cabin, stands adjacent to the corral, probably a barn. In this high country, horses or cattle would freeze to death, left out in an open corral, with nothing to block the wind.

The place is well kept. It has been here awhile and someone has taken care to replace corral poles and boards that rotted from the barn. The cabin is a typical log structure that was built to withstand the rigors of a cold, harsh winter. Matt can tell by the chimneys, the little cabin has two stoves in it.

Nudging his horse forward, Matt rides almost to the door of the cabin.

Whoever is inside has to have heard the jangling trace chains and the squeaking wagon wheels, which were in need of a good greasing. Matt let his hand settle easily over his side gun. Whoever waits inside the cabin does not seem too hospitable.

"Take it easy, Mister Tillman. That's Tinker Jackson's pinto standing in the corral. He's been waiting for you to show for several months." Jim Cloud hallooed the cabin. "It's me you old goat, Jim Cloud, and your new boss."

A grizzled old-timer, steps from the door, a cocked Sharps buffalo gun, cradles lightly in the crook of his arm. Matt studies the bowlegged old man. He is probably older than dirt, wiry as a bobcat, and bad tempered as well. He had seen the type in the war. No one with a lick of sense should misjudge one of them, that is, if he wants to keep on living. No, these old-timers were a breed apart.

"Howdy, Old-Timer," Matt speaks easily.

Only a nod comes from the old man as his deep blue eyes study everything from Matt, down to the boys. "Howdy."

"I'm Matt Tillman, and I reckon you already know Jim Cloud here."

"Been waitin' fer ya." The old eyes settle again on Hob. "You're a mite late."

"How's that?"

"Bout four year I 'spect, but you're here now and that's all that matters."

"You know me?" Matt questions the man.

"Not personal, no; but I knowed your uncle Matt. Rode Segundo for him since we came up the trail from Texas, more'n twenty-five year ago. We cleared this country of injuns, bears, even skunks, if'n they got in our way. I'm all that's left of the old bunch. Rest of 'em have gone under." The old man's voice trails off.

"What's your name?"

"Tinker Jackson, but everyone calls me Tin Cup." The man pats a copper cup hanging from his belt. "Cheyenne warrior shot a hole right through the dang thing, nigh on ten year ago. Wouldn't hold nothin', nope, nary a dribble. Old Matt shot the smart aleck then fixed my cup. That's why they call me Tin Cup."

Matt nods. "Shot missed you, huh?"

"Didn't say that, took off my little finger clean as a whistle. Matt couldn't put the danged thing back on." Tin Cup holds up his left hand to show the nub of his missing pinky finger.

"Guess you miss a finger?"

"Did, but I got nine more, just like it. Ya'll light, 'spect you're tired and hungry. You've come a ways over the mountains."

Matt nods. Here is one of the salty old mossy horns, still full of fire. "You heard the man, Hob."

Hob looks suspiciously at the buffalo gun in the old man's arm. Turning his horse to where it will be between him and the gun, he steps easily to the ground. Peering over the saddle horn at the man, Hob waits to see if the old man was going to un-cock the Sharps or at least turn it in another direction.

"Kinda distrustful fella, ain't he?"

"Kinda," Matt agrees. "War does it to you."

"Your Uncle Matt said ya'll owned slaves. Thought Mister Lincoln freed 'em."

"He did; with the war lost now he owns me." Matt grins at the look on Tin Cup's face then dismounts.

"Reckon I'll be riding back, Mister Tillman," Jim Cloud speaks up, turning his horse. "Wish ya'll good luck over the winter."

"Names Matt; unsaddle and stay the night. April cooks up some mighty tasty vittles and you're welcome."

"Alright Matt." The rider steps down offering his hand once again. This time, to his surprise, Matt takes it.

Looking where Hob came from, behind his gelding, Matt nods at the big man. "This is Hobnail. That's his wife April and their boys."

Cloud nods at Hob and April and leads his horse toward the corral. The wagon is left where it sits by the cabin. The bay stallion is put in a smaller corral by himself, while the mares are turned into the larger corral with the tired team and saddle stock. Tin Cup, somehow manages to bring in a supply of oats from town. Hay is forked down to the hungry horses from the ample loft in the barn. Cage always has his riders cut plenty of hay from the lake meadow to fill the barn. When the snowdrifts get deep, the snow sled would be hitched up and hay taken out to the cattle. This helps them through the long cold winter and keeps them from drifting so much.

April, with the boy's help, unloads the wagon and starts supper when the men return from unharnessing the team. It had been a long haul from town and Matt feels his stomach grumble. The men pull out their tobacco pouch and paper, rolling themselves a smoke while they wait.

"How'd he get the oats up here?" Matt is curious.

"Brought 'em the closer way, through widow Gorman's Ranch." Cloud blows smoke through his nose. "Better road, too."

"How much closer?"

"Reckon five miles or better."

"Five." Tin Cup sits down on a broken back chair and leans against the cabin. "It'll save you a half days ride with a wagon."

"Tell me, Tin Cup, why didn't you stay down below with Cage, instead of waiting alone up here?" Matt asks studying the old man.

"Simple, that no-account Wylie ran me off the ranch." Tin Cup spits. "Maybe your brother didn't know it; maybe he did. Anyway, I got kicked off the place."

"He didn't try to run you out of here?"

"He tried alright but my old Sharps will reach a long way. I may be old and brittle son, but these eyes can still see."

"How much land does the Elkhorn have in these mountains?" Matt is curious, as the valley seems to run deep into the western mountains.

"Can't say in acres, but it runs clean to them high mountains back there, maybe ten miles or so. Then it borders on the Gorman spread to the south, your brother's place to the east, and the Arapaho claim everything west of here. It'll let you run all the cattle and horses you want, not counting the buffalo and wild critters."

"Arapaho?" Matt is curious.

"Whole passel of 'em, kin to Jim here. Government gave 'em the land, if they would stay peaceable."

"Are they peaceable?"

"The southern bands are. The northern bands ride with the Sioux." Jim Cloud flips his burned cigarette away. "Treat them right and they'll leave you alone. They're just like us; live and let live."

"Old Matt and me, been here a long spell, never had much trouble with 'em, 'cept for a missing cow now and again, when the snows were bad. Jim's right; leave 'em alone and they'll do likewise." Tin Cup adds.

"Sounds like good advice," Matt said.

"What's his name; Hobnail?" Tin Cup motions at Hob. "He don't talk much or can he talk at all?"

"Can't."

"Can't, what you mean he can't?"

"Weak? We ain't had a good feed since the war began," Matt laughs.

"Yea, he looks weak," Jim Cloud adds.

April sticks her head from the cabin and frowns at Matt. "If'n you don't stop your lyin' ways, Matt Tillman, you may just starve to death, cause I'll stop cookin'. Look what you're teaching my young'uns."

"Huh-oh boss, she done heard you." Hob looks to where April stands grinning.

"It's the truth, so help me," Matt swears, raising his hand.

"Ya'll come get it," April hollers, her white teeth shining in the evening dusk.

Supper finished, Matt walks down to where Cloud is looking at the stallion. Full of oats, the horse is showing off in the small corral, charging at the cedar pole fence, every time one of the geldings comes near it. He is putting on quite a show. He is a blood bay with black legs, clean to his knees. Sixteen hands at the shoulder and deep in the girth area, he is a thing of beauty. Heavier in the hindquarters than most thoroughbreds, he still has the long smooth muscles that won't tie up or give out on a long haul. Matt knows when he breeds this stud over some good mares; he will have the finest Cavalry horses the army will want. Mounted on his offspring, the northern Indians are going to have their hands full, just keeping out of reach of the army.

"He's a beauty," Jim Cloud marvels as Matt walks up.

"Thoroughbred; came from Kentucky. The mares are thoroughbred too."

"Must of cost quite a penny?"

Matt thought back to the dead Yankee General at Malvern Crossing, and the day he left Jessie for the war. "Yes, he cost me quite a lot."

"What you gonna do with him?"

"I'm going to breed Cavalry horses. The army needs good horses. Now that the war is over, they will turn west and they'll be wanting big, stout horses to carry their soldiers. Soon as I can round up some mares, I'll have horses that'll run down anything they're after."

"Sounds good. With the cattle you've already got, the ranch should make money."

"How many head of cattle are up here?"

Cloud looks off toward the mountains. "Mister Tillman said not to drive any out of here. What are here is yours. I figure, maybe three hundred mama cows, give or take a few, some with calves."

"Yeah, my brother is an honest man."

"Yes Sir, he is; one of the best men I ever worked for."

"How is she, Mister Cloud?"

The cowboy looks sideways at the tall man. "She's fine, as far as I can tell. We don't see much of her, except on Saturdays, when they go into town. Mister Tillman always wants a guard on the wagon."

"Why a guard?"

"Few months back, men shot Miss Tillman's driver, spooked the horses and turned the wagon over. Luckily, she wasn't hurt but Mister Tillman wouldn't let her go into town for a long time. Now he goes with her and with several outriders."

"Who did the shooting?"

"Don't rightly know. Mister Tillman thinks it was outlaws, down from the high country, but I couldn't tell you for sure."

"And you, Mister Cloud; do you have a guess?"

"Not my place to speculate."

"I'm asking."

"Alright, I think it was a grudge shooting. Saul Jones, Miss Tillman's driver gave one of the Gorman hands a bad beating a week earlier. Jones and Wylie Palette are friends and mean as snakes. Wylie put him up to it. I think Jones was killed because of that."

"Who got the beating?" Anger flares from Matt's face.

"His name's Doyle, Nate Doyle." Looking at the fire in Matt's eyes, Cloud turns away. "I don't know anything for sure. Could be as Mister Tillman says outlaws. Anyway there's always a guard now when they travel to town."

"Saturday week, I've got business in Elk Springs. We'll ride to town, through the Gorman place. I want to talk to Mister Doyle."

"We?"

"I need hands Mister Cloud. You want a job?"

"Two conditions; my name's Jim or Cloud, and I have to ride over tomorrow and settle with your brother."

"Alright, Jim." Matt reaches out and shakes the cowboy's hand. "You're hired. Take whatever time you need."

"Better take Tin Cup with you to town. Widow Gorman has some tough boys riding for her and she don't cotton to trespassers."

"You're not going?"

"Doubt I'll make it back before Saturday. I'll meet you in town and ride back with you."

"What happened to her husband?"

"Wylie Palette, he's sudden death with a handgun."

"What'd they fight about?"

Jim Cloud looks away, dropping his eyes. "Couldn't say, all I know is Mister Gorman come up on the short end of Wylie's gun."

"This Palette, you scared of him?"

"Let's just say I'm not in his class with a pistol but with these I'm better." Cloud raises his fists.

"They'll do," Matt notes. "Any pistol play to be done, I'll do it."

Hob walks out where the two men stand talking and puts his foot up on the bottom rail. Reaching out, he strokes the stud as he walks up. From out of his pocket, he produces an apple. Feeding the stallion, he laughs when the horse takes a playful nip at him.

"You've got him spoiled, Hob."

"Yassa, he be that."

"Hob, Jim here is working for us now."

"Yassa,"

"I aim to close off the gap, from the Divide. If I can talk Miss Gorman into it, we'll use the closer road into town through her ranch. That way we won't have to be wasting so much time traveling the long way around. Too time consuming and we're going to have our hands full with the horses and cattle."

"There's a canyon below the lake that will hold the stud and mares. It's a nice little valley. Old Matt has a fence up across the mouth. He used to keep his yearlings there. We'll have to mend on it a little, but it's got plenty of water and grass. It should hold them all winter, if we don't overload it." Cloud motions across the lake.

"Good, we'll have a look in the morning."

Hob studies Matt's back as he walks toward the cabin. He almost seems like his old self, the tightness gone from his shoulders, and the hard look missing from his eyes. Maybe the ranch will settle him and just maybe, he found something to replace her. Patting the stud one last time, he turns toward the wagon. Only time will tell.

Chapter 4

Matt leads the stallion, while Hob pushes the mares toward the box canyon they scouted earlier in the morning. It is exactly as Jim described it, a natural box canyon with steep sides, too rough and high, for the horses to climb. The abundant supply of water and good grass in the valley will hold them year round. The old fence was a problem, as it needs considerable mending. Cedar poles are cut and brought to the small mouth of the canyon replacing the broken and rotted ones. The mares are already in the enclosure and the stallion is prancing on the end of the lead rope, raring to go.

Bear and cougar tracks are found along the small creek that springs from the ground, deep into the lush meadow. They were probably feeding on the abundant deer and small game that jumped up under the feet of their horses, Matt thought. Later, when the colts are born, they will have to do something about the cougars, but for now, the grown horses will be safe.

Turning the stud loose, Matt watches, as the stallion races down the flat meadow; the mares running full out ahead of him. His neck snakes out, as he nips at the running mares, playfully. He is a thing of beauty. His tail stuck straight out with his muscles rippling, every stride. Yes, he is going to produce the finest Cavalry remounts, the army could want. The horses are free here in their natural environment; free to run and they feel it.

Soon as his business in town is finished, he will ride west to Arapaho country. He will try to trade for some good mares to breed with the stallion, but for now, he has other things on his mind. Tomorrow the men will start on the new house. Bad weather is coming and they need shelter bad. Later, he will ride to Elk Springs and stop at the Gorman Ranch, along the way. He wants to talk to Nate Doyle and see what he knew about the shooting. The man will probably admit nothing but he will ask anyway. Matt sits his horse, waiting for Hob, who is busy pulling the gate poles across the entrance to the canyon, closing it off. Uncle Matt built the fence high and strong; tall enough so a horse could not jump it and strong enough so cattle would not push through it. He will have one of the hands check on the stallion every day until they turn him out on the open range.

Jim Cloud left earlier in the morning, riding back to the lower Elkhorn to speak with Cage. Matt liked the man. Even Hob takes to Cloud, which is something, as Hob trusts hardly anyone.

"We'es ready Boss."

"Let's head home then." Matt turns his horse toward the small cabin. It was a good day's work and he is ready for supper.

The rest of the week they will lay the groundwork for the bigger cabin, Matt plans. He knows government buyers will eventually stay here as his horse herd grows and he wants a house large enough to accommodate them. Plenty of pine trees stand at the far end of the valley and the mountains are full of flat rock, for the floor and fireplaces. Next week, he will have the men start cutting and snaking the logs in. Hob and April took over the smaller cabin. The cold weather will come soon so they have to hurry.

Matt leaves the men working on the house and rides out alone toward the lake. Sitting his gelding, his eyes gaze across the beautiful valley towards the lake, he knows he will be content here. Everything he ever wanted is here, everything but her. All the ranch needs is a little hard work.

Riding back, he passes cattle, grazing in small bunches. He can remember his uncle's one visit back east, laughing about the times he had, running these very cattle. Turning the gelding toward the ranch, he lets his eyes rove over the beautiful valley one more time before kicking the gelding into a lope for home.

Saturday morning finds them riding south toward the Gorman Ranch. Tin Cup, with his big Sharps resting across his lap, leads the way on his pinto. The old man is slow on the ground but on a horse, he comes alive. His horse can flat walk a hole in the wind. Only one other horse, Matt saw, had as fast a running walk as the pinto, and that was General Jackson's horse, Little Sorrel. Tin Cup's old eyes take in everything, as they make their way along the dusty trail that passes as a road. April and the boys laugh and talk continually as the wagon bounces and clangs across the rough ground. Hob, as usual, follows the wagon at a distance, seemingly nonchalant, but his sharp eyes miss nothing. Many times on patrol, he found the enemy before Matt's soldiers rode into an ambush.

The boundary where the two ranches border was marked by a signpost that stands where they pass through a small draw. No fences separate the two ranches. When a rider finds stray cattle wandering onto the wrong range, they drive them back home. A little more work is involved but Uncle Matt hated the newfangled barbwire. He saw a man and horse cut all to pieces after they accidentally ran into a wire fence. Trouble was, cattle and buffalo completely ignore the pole fences and either run through or jump over them, whichever struck their fancy.

Matt pulls up, studying the mouth of the draw separating the ranches. When he brings in his mares, he knows he will have to build a fence. Good horses are too tempting for a rustler or a horse thief with sticky fingers, especially horses wandering too far from home. Horses roam over a large area. It is their natural instinct and he does not want to expend the manpower watching over them continually.

Tin Cup reins his pinto down, letting Matt catch up. "We got company."

"Where?" Matt's eyes focus on the road ahead, as if they are just talking.

Tin Cup nods, "behind that small stand of cedars, about a hundred yards, yonder. It's probably Gorman riders but you never know."

Matt turns slowly and waves at April and the boys but he is really motioning to Hob, giving him their old warning signal. Hob nods, as he is already aware of whatever Tin Cup saw. Silently, two riders appear from their place of concealment and wait in the middle of the road. Henry repeaters rest across the swells of their saddles.

"Howdy boys," Tin Cup smiles and nods.

"Howdy Tin Cup. What you got here?" The smaller of the riders nods at the wagon.

"This be Matt Tillman and his hired man and family."

"Heard he was coming but not so much of him." The man looks at Matt's size and then looks to where Hob rides up behind the wagon, his Spencer rifle pointing right in their direction. His dark eyes miss nothing, as he rides closer to the strangers.

Matt nods slowly. Whoever the riders are they do not rattle easily. Kicking his horse, Matt moves closer to the riders. "What can I do for you boys?"

"You happen to be on Gorman range and Miss Gorman don't take kindly to trespassing." The older of the riders spit a stream of tobacco.

"Matter of fact, we're on our way to pay our respects to your boss."

"In that case, Mister Tillman, we'll ride along with you to the ranch."

"What you boys doing up here?" Tin Cup asks, biting off a chaw of tobacco.

"Some feller named Tillman got himself an old geezer named Tin Cup. He can't keep his boss's cows home, so we have to push 'em back," the younger rider laughs, his bright blue eyes lighting up.

"Tom Ward, you've always played the smart aleck." Tin Cup spit a stream at the rider's horse.

The Gorman Ranch is neat, as only a woman would keep it. The house, barn, and corrals were all painted red. Everything is in order, not even a single pile of horse droppings litter the flat ground. Maybe they don't crap, Matt thought to himself. Looking over at Ward, the Gorman rider grins his youthful smile and looks toward the ranch house.

"She's got a rider that picks up the droppings as soon as they hit the ground," the youngster answers his unasked question.

"That's all he does?"

"Just about. Miss Gorman fired a feller once for shirking his duty, she surely did. She hates anything out of place."

"And horse droppings on the ground are out of place?" Matt asks incredulously.

"Speck so, Mister Tillman," the rider laughs. "Anyhoo, she up and fired him."

"Well, I've heard it all now. You hear that Hob? Best buy you a good shovel, cause we're gonna have a considerable amount of work for you to do," Matt laughs aloud. Something sounds good to Hob, who actually smiles too.

"Yas suh."

"I'll tell you, that's where I draw the line and Miss Gorman knows it. Yes Sir, she handed me that shovel once," the older rider said, as he leans over and spits a stream of tobacco at Tin Cup's paint horse.

"What did you do?"

"He cleaned up horse droppings, that's what he did," Tin Cup laughs, slapping the rider across the back.

"Miss Gorman is kinda set in her ways," the cowboy grins sheepishly. "Told me it were unsanitary, whatever that means."

Reining in front of the house, Matt is surprised at the woman who comes out on the porch. Expecting an older woman, instead he finds before him a woman barely older than himself. Slender build, the dress she is wearing can barely conceal her well-rounded figure. Black hair frames her oval face, a beautiful face. A face time seems to pass over, untouched from childhood. A friendly smile crosses her face as she recognizes Tin Cup. Stepping to the railing, she looks across at Matt.

"Miss Gorman, this be Matt Tillman, your new neighbor." Tin Cup makes the introductions, nodding at Matt.

"Yes, I heard you were coming. Tin Cup wouldn't give up on you. Won't you and your people get down and come in for some coffee?" She looks across at Hob and April.

"No, thank you just the same. We need to get into town and back before dark."

"Very well, maybe you'll have more time on your next trip."

"Yes ma'am; it'll be my pleasure. I just stopped by to introduce myself and get your permission to cross your range on my trips to town."

The young woman looks Matt over appreciatively, nodding her head. "Your uncle was always welcome to cross my land. You're welcome too. It's a lot closer to town and perhaps we can visit sometime."

"I thank you ma'am. It'll be a lot handier for sure. One other thing, you've got a rider riding for you, Nate Doyle I believe." Matt is taken with her friendliness.

"Nate rides for me." She looks over at Tin Cup. "Is there a problem?"

"No Ma'am, no problem," Matt shakes his head. "I'd like a word with him, that's all."

"Well, you're riding the right direction, Mister Tillman. He's in town. You'll probably find him at the saloon."

"Thank you, Miss Gorman, and the name's Matt."

"Matt it is, and your friends?" Vickie Gorman looks at Hob.

"His name is Hob, and his wife April, and their boys."

"Well then, you all come back when you're not in such a hurry."

"We'll do that Miss Gorman." Matt tips his hat and Tin Cup leads out east, toward town. Matt looks back once, to see Vickie Gorman watching them from the porch.

Elk Springs is quiet for a Saturday but it isn't quite noon yet. Matt rides ahead of Tin Cup and pulls up in front of the general store. Stepping down, he stretches slowly letting his eyes drift across the dusty street. Several horses stand hipshot, in front of the saloon. He recognizes the Elkhorn and Gorman brands but the other brands are all new to him. He notes them mentally in his mind.

"Well Matt, while you're stocking up, I'll drift over to the saloon and stock up a little myself," Tin Cup grins, licking his lips. "Been a dry spell. You were late getting to where you were supposed to be going."

"Little early in the day, isn't it?"

"Early? Nah, I figure I'm getting a late start. The place is already filled up. Sure hope they ain't drunk her dry."

Matt watches the old man climb the steps slowly and disappear inside. He turns into the store with Hob, April, and the boys close behind. Kate and Bailey Howard are working behind the counter as they enter. Matt notices Kate does not break a smile as she studies him from the ladder she is standing on. Matt averts his eyes as she stocks the high shelves that run the length of the store.

"Proud woman," Matt thinks to himself as she climbs down and a mighty attractive one. Well, he hadn't been any too friendly on their last meeting himself. Laying the list he made on the counter, he walks to where the handguns are kept. He busies himself, looking over the new Texas rigged, holsters and belts. His own is well used from the many years of hardships and rain it endured. Occasionally looking to where she fills his order, he notices she is completely ignoring him.

"These holsters got a cutaway, so your trigger is open to grab quicker." Hob scratches his head, as Matt explains the reason for the cut away holsters. Running his fingers admiringly, across the smooth leather of the new belts, Hob places it back on the shelf.

"Want one?" Matt picks the fancy holster up.

"Shucks, suh, what would I be doing with one of them things. You knows I can't hit nothing with a short gun."

"You could learn."

"No suh, I'll stick to this old Spencer." Hob lifts the rifle that rests lightly in his hand.

"Suit yourself but handguns are easier to carry horseback."

"Not for me. Might as well be carrying rocks to throw at something," Hob grins, removing his hat as Kate approaches.

"Will there be anything else, Mister Tillman?"

Matt can sense the coldness in her voice. "Yes ma'am, I'll take this gun belt. His hand stops in midair, as he hands the belt to her, his attention rivets on the front window and the buckboard passing the store's front porch.

It's her, Jessie, sitting high on the seat beside the driver with her shoulders as straight as an arrow. Matt's heart skips a beat as he takes in the beautiful face he remembers so well. The face of his Jessie, a little older perhaps, but the beauty is still there. Yes, she is as beautiful as ever and perhaps more. Absently handing Kate the holster, Matt starts for the door.

"Masta Matt!"

"It's alright Hob, I'm just gonna talk," Matt assures the worrying Hob, as he passes through the door.

"Please Masta!" Hob hurries after Matt, checking the load in his Spencer as he leaves the store. Kate watches, as Hob moves between Matt and the Elkhorn riders that are following the wagon into town.

Did the black call the younger Tillman, master? Kate steps from the door curiosity spurring her forward. Why did Hob check his rifle? She can smell the excitement in the air, will there be trouble?

She watches as Cage Tillman reins his horse around to intercept the younger Tillman. She can read the eagerness in Matt's stride and she can see the hard look in the older Tillman's face. She does not know how but she can sense trouble only a breath away. She watches with anticipation growing in her breast. She's afraid for the younger Tillman brother, yet she barely knows him. Her eyes stare, transfixed to the scene on the street, as the two brothers, both tall and handsome, near each other. Death waits, the wrong move or the wrong words as she can feel the electricity in the air. What could cause two brothers to hate each other? Then she looks at Jessie Tillman sitting on the wagon seat, and she knows.

"You've got ten minutes, that's all." Cage's hand rests on the butt of his pistol.

"That'll be plenty." Matt brushes around Cage's horse and walks toward the buckboard, not looking back at Cage or the Elkhorn crew. The driver steps from the wagon as Matt approaches, leaving Jessie alone on the seat. Cage stays discreetly out of hearing. Kate notices, Matt completely dismisses his brother and turns his entire attention on his brother's wife. She knows there is more to this meeting than a family reunion. Matt looks up into the beautiful face that he remembers so well. Jessie seems troubled, almost scared. Surely, he thought, she isn't afraid of him. They had been so close and so much in love. Surely, she does not fear him. His mouth starts to reassure her when a small head looks around her. The dark eyes, dark complexion, and ringlets of curls over his ears, take the words from his mouth.

"Yes Matt, he's four years old."

"Jess, I didn't know," Matt stammers, truly shocked.

"I know, but I didn't know either when you'd be back from your infernal war! What was I to do? You were gone, I was in...." She let the words pass.

"I'm back now."

"No!" The words hiss out of her mouth. "It's too late Matt. I loved you as I will never love another, but I'm married to Cage now. He is the boy's father, and if you ever cared for me, you will let it lie."

"And the boy?"

"We named him Michael, after your father."

"A good name, Dad would have liked that."

"Matt, the boy needs his father as I need my husband. I'm begging you, please, let us alone and forget me."

"Are you sure?"

"Yes I'm sure. Good-bye Matt. I hope you find happiness."

"Good-bye, Jessie." Matt turns and starts toward the saloon, staggering a little as he passes Cage Tillman.

"Matt!" Cage calls his name but gets no response. The shaken look on his brother's face says it all. Cage looks at Jessie then back at Matt, wondering what she told him.

"It's finished, there'll be no trouble." Matt never looks back, just speaks over his shoulder.

"Good heavens, Mister Matt!" Hob is still staring at the boy as Matt passed. "He's the spittin' image of you at that age."

"Hello Hobnail," Jessie speaks from the wagon, trying to stop the tears from coming.

"Miss Jessie," Hob nods, turning quickly to follow Matt.

Matt stops at the swinging doors of the saloon and watches as Cage climbs onto the wagon, making it groan under his weight. He watches as Jessie lays her small hand on his big arm and speaks to him. The hardness leaves Cage's face, as he clucks to the team and heads out of town.

"Let's go home boss," replies Jim Cloud who rode in tried to intercept Matt.

"I need a drink."

"Wylie is in there and he's been drinking."

"Good, I never liked to drink alone."

Cloud glances at Hob as Matt pushes through the swinging doors and steps toward the long counter. Wylie Palette is elbowed up to the bar, a whiskey clutched in his hand. Matt pushes his way between Palette and another Elkhorn rider, spilling their drinks. Furious, the man turns on Matt, while Palette, sensing the killing mood Matt is in, watches. The rider grabs for his pistol, his hand is only a blur. Matt outguesses the man and reacts quicker. Slamming his huge fist into the man's stomach, he takes the air from the rider's lungs, finishing him off with a hard right to the chin. Watching the man sink to the floor, Matt turns to where Palette waits, his hand poised above his holster.

"Now, Palette, does today suit you better?"

Palette wants to draw, but at this range both men would surely die. He isn't scared, but common sense takes over and he shrugs and turns back to the bar. Tillman wants to die and Palette can sense it. Palette is not a coward but he isn't a fool either.

"Not today, Mister Tillman." Palette places both hands on the bar.

"You don't have a choice. I'm calling you."

Hob watches from the doorway, the Spencer covering the room. He knows Matt's moods and he knows Palette is a dead man if he reaches for his gun.

What did she say to enrage Matt so much?

Palette turns and walks toward the back of the saloon, making space between him and Tillman.

Matt pulls and cocks his pistol. "I'm gonna kill you Palette, draw."

Palette never moves, as the bullet strikes the floor beside his boot. Seeing the man's back to him, Matt finally comes out of the killing rage that took hold of him. Holstering his weapon, he turns and walks from the saloon.

Kate watches as Matt and his riders, ride slowly out of town. Their grocery list and Nate Doyle are completely forgotten. Matt's shock, finding out about the boy, is too great. She watches as the riders from the lower Elkhorn help their fallen comrade from the saloon and onto his horse. Listening, as several men laugh about Palette getting his comeuppance and so easily at the hands of the young Tillman, she turns to where Matt rides. Yes, he is a dangerous man but he is a handsome, dangerous man.

"I'd never believe anybody could have backed Wylie down that easy." Cloud leans against the side of the barn, talking to Tin Cup and the two extra hands that Matt hired. Pulling hard on his cigarette, he shakes his hand and exhales smoke. "No Sir, if I hadn't have seen it, I wouldn't have believed it."

Tin Cup replies, "I've seen a few bad ones in my time and Matt stands tall with the best of them, except for one thing maybe."

"What's that?" One of the new hands speaks up.

"Well Sam, I'll tell you, he's not as mean, dangerous yes but not as mean."

"Doubt Wylie would agree with you there, old man," Cloud laughs. "I think Wylie seen the killing mood Matt was in and didn't like his chances."

"He'll have to kill Palette next time they meet," Sam adds.

"I didn't say he wouldn't, I just said he didn't have a mean streak in him," Tin Cup adds. "And I know Wylie, he wasn't afraid. Like Jim said, he didn't like his chances."

Two weeks passed since the rendezvous in town. The house walls are up and the men are finishing with the stone floor and fireplace. Two more weeks and the house will be livable. Matt steps from the barn into the early morning crispness. The sun is just beginning to show itself above the tall craggy mountains to the east. He can smell Tin Cup's old corncob pipe and knows the old man will be in his usual place, outside the smaller cabin, waiting for breakfast.

"You boys fall out, breakfast is on and we're wasting daylight." Matt looks into the shadow of the barn where Jim and the two new hands are rolling from their bedrolls. This high, even in the summer months, the mornings are cold.

"Morning Sir."

"Hob, Tin Cup, good morning to you," Matt greets the men as he nears the cabin.

"April will have breakfast most anytime now."

"No hurry." Matt pulls the sweat stained Cavalry hat from his head and hangs it on the peg outside the kitchen door. April hands him a steaming cup of hot coffee and disappears back inside. Nodding his thanks, he sips slowly then looks off to the north.

"I'm heading after the mares right after breakfast. If I don't get going, we may not be able to get through the passes till next spring, and that'll throw us another year behind."

"Yassa," Hob nods, studying his own coffee cup, as the other hands walk up.

"We got you boys a good start on the house. If it ain't ready before snow flies, we're all liable to be a little cramped in this cabin."

"We'll have it ready when you get back, boss," said Sam, one of the new hires, his big Adam's apple bobbing up and down with the motion of his chin. Tall and lean, he has the biggest set of hands Matt ever saw on a man. A carpenter by trade, he was a valuable asset as the house starts up.

"Jim will be going with me. Hob is in charge and will be running things."

"Whoa there, Boss," Rollie speaks up. "I don't know about taking orders from a black man."

"Take his orders or draw your pay." Matt stands up slowly. "Your choice."

"I'll give it a go."

"What about me?" Tin Cup asks sullenly.

"I want you to go into Elk Springs and hire me at least one more good hand, two if you can find them."

"What fer?" It's coming winter, won't be enough work around here to keep a billy goat busy."

"I need hay cut and stacked in the barn." Matt looks over at Hob. "I want that loft so full of grass, the seams are busting. If you want to do it yourself Tinker, go at it."

"Me?" Tin Cup looks incredulous at Matt. "Why, your old uncle would flip in his grave if'n he saw me with a sickle in my hands."

"What I figured. You go hire me some men that don't mind working."

After breakfast, Matt pulls Hob off to one side, out of earshot. Pulling his cinch tight, he speaks quietly to the big man. "You're running things here. Work on the house and watch after the stallion and mares, but stay close. And let Tin Cup think he's running the place unless it's serious."

Hob grins. "Yassa."

"Jim figures we'll be gone a couple weeks, maybe more."

"Yassa."

Jim rides up with the packhorse in tow as Matt steps easily into the saddle. "Stay close, Hob."

"I will suh, watch your backsides." Hob watches, worry showing in his face, as Jim leads the way, due west. He was never separated from Matt and never unable to watch his friend's back.

Jim takes the lead and keeps his sorrel gelding in a hard, ground eating trot almost all morning. Matt watches the looming mountain peaks ahead. Somewhere up high, Tin Cup tells him, there is a natural pass leading into Arapaho country. Not wide enough for a wagon but a saddle horse can navigate it easily. Jim, raised in these mountains, will know where it is and that is where they are heading.

The crispness of the morning passed and the horses begin to show sweat stains on their necks and flanks. Crossing several small creeks, Matt notices, the deep holes of water are chock full of speckled trout. Making a mental note, he will bring the boys back and take them fishing. These small streams are a paradise for fish. The water, crystal clear, running noisily over the pebbled bottoms, are a dream come true for a fisherman. How long has it been since he went fishing?

Iron shoes reverberate through the small canyon as they pass across the rocky ground. Topping out the trail, Matt is amazed as he stares across several mountain ranges and valleys. They seem to extend on forever, the tall pines covering each mountain as far as the eye can see.

"Arapaho land." Jim waves his arm across the vast sea of timber and grass.

"It's majestic!"

"Yes, it is that," Jim agrees, as he looks at Matt's amazed face. "I guess the government men didn't know what they were giving to the poor old red man."

Matt figures they went about twenty-five miles, when Jim pulls up in a stand of willows and poplar trees. "We'll camp here for the night."

"Good spot." Matt steps down from his dun gelding and starts unsaddling. "How much further?"

"Another days ride, unless they moved the village I'm looking for."

"Is there more than one village around here?"

"Several, but this particular village is friendlier than most and if we can trade with them the others will be easier."

"Sounds okay, to me."

"We'll go in at daybreak, that'll give us all day to do our trading and move on."

"You don't trust them much. Thought they were friendly?"

"The old ones are, but there's plenty of young bucks who have been hearing of the problems up north and want to join their brother's, the Sioux."

Chapter 5

Early morning finds Matt and Jim sitting their horses on a high ridge, studying a village that is cloudy with mist and vapors coming from the small river that splits the grass covered valley. The camp is not large, maybe forty lodges. Matt's eyes take in the horses that graze everywhere. The Arapaho might be poor but not in horses. Even from this distance, he can tell they are mostly the smaller mustangs. Smoke, from the early morning cook fires, curls lazily above the valley. The village appears asleep and unguarded, and it surprises Matt when several warriors gather in a group and point up at the ridge where they are observing the village. Matt watches, as the Arapaho people cluster around a large tepee in the center of the camp.

"Let's go, they spotted us." Jim clucks to his horse and starts him down the rocky trail.

As they ride past each band of horses, Matt studies them closely, picking out the few that will throw good heavy boned colts. It's almost midmorning when they finally ride into the village. Jim timed their arrival perfect as they finally come face to face with the elders of the camp. Dismounting in front of the chief's lodge, Jim speaks slowly in Arapaho to the warriors, motioning toward Matt on several occasions.

"The Chief says you are welcome in the village of the Arapaho and they are happy to meet the son of the Iron Man," Jim translates to Matt.

"Iron Man?" Matt is curious.

"The name they gave to your Uncle Matt."

"What is his name?" Matt motions to the leader.

"In your language, it is Singing Wind."

"Tell him I am happy to be here." Matt nods at the gathered men. With a signal from one of the elders he takes a seat where the man points to on the ground. Each warrior finds his own place in the circle. "They ask why you come here?" Jim translates to Matt.

"Tell them I come to trade for ponies."

"They say there are many ponies here. He wants to know what you will trade for them and how many ponies you will trade for."

"Tell him I will trade cattle, so when the snows come, their people will not starve. Also tell him I will trade for all the horses he has, that I like."

"He says no cattle; they have plenty of buffalo and elk to eat."

"What does he want?"

Again Jim speaks to the assembled men. "Guns, bullets, and blankets," they reply.

"Blankets I will send but no bullets or no guns." Matt spread his hand in a sign of refusal.

"He says no trade."

"Tell him I understand. Now we will go on to the next village." Matt stands, as if he is leaving.

"He says the guns are only to hunt the buffalo."

Matt turns. "He does not need guns to hunt the cattle I will send him. Tell the Chief I will not trade guns for the horses."

"He says you will not cross further into Arapaho lands. He says for you to go back and leave Arapaho lands."

Matt studies each face as he looks around the circle of warriors. Walking back to where he was sitting, he sits back down and stares hard into the face of Singing Wind. Several seconds pass as each man studies the other. Finally, Matt breaks the silence, again addressing the Arapaho Chief. "Tell the Chief I come to trade. Tell him I want to trade, but if he does not, I will ride on through Arapaho land until I find someone who will see the value of my trade."

"He wants to know if you look for a fight. He wants to know if you would die for the ponies. He wants to know why you no trade guns?"

"No, I do not wish to fight with the Arapaho. I wish to be friends but I will not trade guns that might fall into the hands of Crazy Horse and the Sioux, who are fighting my people. Also tell him I am going on to the other villages to get horses."

The old Chief looks into Matt's eyes for several seconds then smiles. "We will trade with the Little Iron Man."

Cloud lets out a sigh of relief as he translates the Chief's words to Matt. He thought the Arapaho were just trying to test Matt's courage but he was not sure.

Rising, Matt goes to his saddlebags and removes several twists of tobacco, which brings smiles of approval from the gathered men. Tobacco of the white man is relished by all the tribes.

Singing Wind calls to several younger boys and men. Soon anyone with a horse to trade starts bringing them in from the herds.

Cloud is specific about which ones to bring. They are to bring only sorrels and bays. The mares must be at least fifteen hands tall and around nine hundred pounds in weight. This is a tall order, as Indian horses are mostly smaller because they are raised only on the grasses of the land and there is little grass in winter. This causes most of them to be stunted. Matt knows with good grain and crossing with the thoroughbred stallion, their colts will grow to fit the army's needs.

With their mustang breeding, big horses are hard to find among the Indian herds. Occasionally, a horse stolen or lost from a white ranch or wagon train would mix into the bands and this is what Matt is looking for. The day wears on as Matt and Jim carefully cull anything that does not meet their standards. Most of the Arapaho horses do not because they have too much mustang blood in them. At the end of the day, Matt finds only five that are blemish free and of the size, he needs.

"There's an Iron Grey, picketed near the creek Matt, and she's a dandy," Cloud announces, walking to where Matt stands.

The men walk to where the mare is picketed. Matt runs his eyes and hands over the grey, appreciating her even more. Heavy boned for plenty of strength, she still has the finer qualities Matt is looking for in his mares. Small head and ears, arched short neck, and straight legged, the mare is indeed a thing of beauty. Only a small quarter crack in her right rear foot that reaches clean to her coronet band can be held against her, but it can easily be fixed in a couple of shoeins. Matt looks around at Jim and nods.

The owner sees the admiring looks in the white men's faces and steps nearer. He is as tall as Matt and well built but older. The muscles in his arms ripple whenever he raises them.

Jim speaks quietly to the man then turns to Matt. "She's not for sale."

"I want that mare at any price. Tell him to name it."

Cloud turns to the warrior and speaks to him for several minutes, finally turning back toward Matt. "He does not wish to trade or sell, but he wishes a favor from the son of the Iron Man, and for this he will give you the horse."

Curious, Matt looks closer at the warrior. "What does he want?"

Cloud converses with the warrior several minutes and then turns to Matt.

"Well boss, how bad do you want this grey horse?"

"What is it Jim?" Matt can see the amusement in Cloud's face, why would this warrior want to give him a horse of this quality?

"Near as I can tell, his wife's daughter is the favor. He promised his wife as she was dying he would bring the girl to your Uncle Matt. Old Iron Man was well thought of and respected and his wife wanted her daughter to be raised by him." Cloud grins. "Now that the old Iron Man is gone to live with his ancestors, the younger Iron Man will have to do."

"What?" Matt can't believe his ears. "Take his daughter?"

"He wants you to take the girl back with you and raise her as a white."

"You mean marry her?"

"No, no," Cloud laughs. "Nothing like that."

"What then?" Matt looks spooked. "Why raise her as a white? Ain't she an Arapaho? For Pete's sake, Jim!"

"Well, it seems this warrior Fox Tails, traded some horses to the Cheyenne for a white woman years ago. The woman was with child, a white child, and it turned out a girl. The girl, the one he's trying to get you to take. Now old Fox Tails here thought a whole lot of this woman and on her deathbed he promised her he would bring her to your Uncle Matt."

"That's it?"

"In a nutshell."

"Anything, else?"

"Well, she's white and we do need to help her, sides you are getting a good horse, and the little girl couldn't eat too much."

"You sure she's white?"

"She's white alright. All the elders here kinda agree to that."

"What do you mean, kinda agree?"

"Now that has me puzzled a little." Cloud scratches his chin. "Can't quite figure what they're after. Maybe they're just trying to do as they promised, but I can't put my finger on why they are so eager to be rid of her."

"A little girl couldn't eat that much, could she?" Matt looks at the mare.

"I wouldn't think so, but he seems in an awful hurry to get rid of the girl.

Said he'd throw in another horse, good as the grey." It seems like too good a deal, as Arapaho warriors are very fond of their horses, and would hardly ever part with one unless there was something wrong with it. Cloud cannot figure out the catch, but he knows there has to be one.

Matt turns, as they lead a red dun mare beside the grey. Except for their color, the mares are a perfect match. Cloud can almost see Matt's mouth watering, as he studies the mares, and so can Fox Tails.

"She's a beaut, Jim."

Fox Tails steps forward and offers the lead ropes to Matt.

"You take the ropes boss and you've given him your word to take the kid," Cloud speaks up. "And if you give your word there's no backing out, not if we want out of here with our hair."

"Like you said, Jim, she's white, and it's our Christian duty to help her." Matt takes the ropes and runs his hand down the dun's shoulder. "I need these mares. Man, they are beauties, as good as I've ever seen back east."

Fox Tails releases the ropes and grinning broadly he nods several times and retreats. Admiring the mares, Matt's attention focuses on the horses and he is not aware of the procession of warriors coming towards him.

"Ah, boss, I think your package is here."

Turning, Matt's eyes widen as big as Jim's, as they drag a dark haired, brown-eyed spitfire of a woman, wearing a doeskin dress, fighting and kicking toward them. Matt cannot understand what she is saying, but he knows by the way she is carrying on it isn't good. Two stout warriors hold her between them. Even with her hands tied by a leather thong and a rope encircling her slim waist, she is giving them all they can handle. The whole village is watching the show to see what the Iron Man will do.

Cloud shoots an apprehensive look over at Matt, whose mouth is gaped open. "I told you something was wrong with the deal, a man should never trade for a pig in a poke, you just never know what might jump out at you."

"Alright, alright." Matt studies the lunging young woman. "What's the matter with her, is she crazy?"

"No, she is Arapaho. She may be white outside, but inside she's pureblood bona fide red, and that boss, is a fact."

"If she's Arapaho, then why do they want to get rid of her so bad?" Matt is having second thoughts about taking the mares as he watches the young woman giving two stout warriors all they can handle.

"Told you, old Fox Tails there, gave his word to his dying woman, and with that temper, I doubt he figures he'll ever be able to marry her off," Jim laughs. "And now you know, Boss, it's our Christian duty to take her away from these heathens."

"Very funny. Tell Fox Tails or whatever his name is, the deals off." Matt starts toward the warrior.

Fox Tails backs away, shaking his head then turns his attention to Cloud. "He says no, you make trade; you give word; girl yours now. He says you're Iron Man now and you have to keep your promise to the poor Arapaho."

Matt can tell Cloud is having a good time at his expense. Almost tempted to take a swing at the man, Matt holds his temper and starts trying to figure his way out of the mess he accidentally stepped into.

"Girl? She's no girl. She's a full-grown woman." Matt is staring hard at the fighting girl, who will not give up. Matt hardly gets the words out, when she pulls out a skinning knife, hidden beneath her skirt. At the sight of the knife, the warriors holding her, release the ropes and dodge away from the crazy woman. Springing at Matt, as fast as a bobcat, she slashes him across the arm before he can move. She starts forward again, only to receive a hard slap to the face, knocking her to the ground. Matt kicks the knife away then lifts the girl to her feet. The girl glares at him, showing no fear, as he holds her at arm's length. Looking into her eyes, Matt remembers the many widows and orphans of the war that had the same look.

"Tell her I'm sorry I had to hit her, but she's going with us and tell her she'll be safe with us as long as she behaves herself."

"You still taking her?"

"Why not? You said yourself it's our Christian duty."

"You know Matt, she's really pretty when she's mad like that," Jim grins.

"I still think she's crazy." Matt looks at his bleeding arm. "If she's not, then I guess I am for taking her with us. She'll probably kill us all in our sleep that is if we get any sleep, which I doubt seriously."

"No, I'd say she may be a little upset but she's not crazy." Cloud is still grinning. "She get you deep with that little pigsticker?"

"I'll live but you may not if you don't quit grinning like a treed coon."

The hard slap seems to take the fight out of the girl for the moment. Fox Tails walks to where Matt is standing. "He says the girl's name is Little Flower," Cloud interprets.

Matt nods as the warrior hands him a rabbit skin with something wrapped in it. Untying the leather thong that holds the skin, he produces another skin with writing on it, a letter written in perfect English.

Matt studies the words and then looks at Jim. "It's from her mother."

Matt reads the letter aloud. "If you have this letter, then you have my little girl, and I will be dead from a stomach illness. She's now eighteen years old, near as I can remember. Her name is May Bell Williams. Her father was killed when I was captured. His name was Elias Williams. She is a good girl, but does not want to go back to the whites, but I feel it is best for her. My husband, Fox Tails, has been good to us. I made him promise to return May Bell to her own people. She has no living relatives, so I beg of you to give my baby a good home. She is a little headstrong but she is a good girl. Please take care of her."

"A little headstrong!" Matt mutters under his breath as he finishes the letter and refolds it. "She sure ain't no baby and I agree with you lady, she's definitely headstrong."

"She's your problem, Mister Cloud." Matt tosses the rope holding the girl to Jim and then grins as Cloud looks at him in shock. "You said she was pretty, didn't you?"

"I did, but I don't know anything about baby-sitting."

"You'll do fine," Matt laughs. "Just dandy."

Turning to the elders of the village Matt hands them a bundle of rolled tobacco. He has Cloud thank them and tell them to come to the ranch for their cattle whenever they want to. Matt walks away, leading the two mares to where several young Arapaho boys are holding the other five mares.

Twelve days find Matt, Jim, and May heading for home. Three young Arapaho warriors are hired to help drive Matt's herd of mares to the pass that separates the Elkhorn Ranch from Arapaho lands. It took almost ten days, traveling the mountains, to trade with the various villages, but Matt has his mares. Twenty-five sound broodmares that will be the start of his horse ranch. The pick of the Arapaho horse herds are in front of him, the foundation mares for his Elkhorn Horse Ranch, now he can sell remounts to the army, and Matt is elated. Now he can start his breeding program without further delay.

The woman finally settled down and quit trying to fight them. Matt thought that maybe she saw the futility of trying to escape so they quit watching her as closely. Jim knows better. Her wrists are free, but Jim still leads the mare she rides. He knows she is biding her time. At the right moment, she will leave out like a scalded dog with its tail afire. Making sure, she is on the slowest horse he can find, Jim knows eventually she will try to run. He watches her, his dark eyes never leaving her. Still, he has to admit, she is the prettiest thing he ever laid eyes on. He is in love even if she is white and a little bit contrary. He is smitten with her and he is not about to let her escape back to the Arapaho.

Noon finds them on the banks of the small but deep and fast flowing, Big Sandy River. The young warriors cross the mares first and have them heading for the far bank. Cloud's horse just reaches deep water when the girl bails from her horse, stroking hard, heading down stream. Cussing, Cloud removes his pistol and boots, strapping them to his saddle horn, diving into the water after her. The river narrows around a bend, causing the current to speed up. The hard pulling undercurrent is strong, taking the two swimmers by surprise. It sweeps Cloud and the girl downstream quickly. Cloud is a strong swimmer but to his amazement, he is not gaining on the bobbing, dark head of the hard stroking May Bell.

Intent on escaping from her pursuer, May Bell keeps turning to see if he is gaining on her. She does not see the heavy log, spinning in the water, until it is too late to dodge. The blow takes her fully on the side of the head, knocking her unconscious. Cloud watches, as the girl hesitates and then disappears under the cold water. Swimming with all his remaining strength, he dives quickly at the site she disappeared. Coming to the surface and gasping for air, he is about to dive again, when the under current pops her to the surface, almost within his grasp. Grabbing for her long hair, Cloud feels his fingers close around the wet mass. Pulling her into his arms, he lets the strong current carry them downstream into calmer water, where the stream widens.

A rope settles with a splat around both Cloud and the girl. Matt backs his horse from the cold water, pulling the soaked swimmers into the shallows of the river. Dismounting, he helps Jim pull the girl onto the sandy bank, where Jim starts trying to pump air into her almost lifeless body. Coughing and sputtering, the girl breathes deeply, looking up into Cloud's concerned eyes as he turns her over.

Confused from the water and the blow to the head, she stares quietly at him. "What happened?" She asks in English.

Matt and Jim look at each other surprised. In the time she has been with them, she spoke very little and only in Arapaho. Helping May to her feet, Jim holds onto her as she steadies herself.

"Log knocked you unconscious Ma'am, Jim here pulled you from the river." Matt nods at the stunned Jim. "If he hadn't, you'd be a drowned rat right about now."

The Indian boys are standing around grinning, letting the herd scatter until Jim hollers at them.

"Thank you. I'm sorry for the problems I have given you. I do thank you for saving me from drowning." The girl smiles, her gleaming white teeth shining in the afternoon sun.

"Yes Ma'am," Jim blushes as the girl stares directly into his eyes. Looking up at Matt she nods. "And I thank you, Iron Man. Now if you will let me go back to my people you will have no more trouble. Everybody will be happy and there will be no more delays."

"I don't think everybody will be happy, Miss," Matt looks at Jim. "No, I gave my word. You're going with us to the Elkhorn. Miss Williams, there will be no more trouble or I'll paddle you, myself."

Again, the smile leaves the pretty face and the beautiful dark eyes turn hard.

"You will not strike me and I will try to escape again."

"You do that young lady and I promise, I'll tan your backside myself, until you holler," Jim glares at the girl, heaving her bodily onto the mare the boys retrieved.

Matt laughs, turning his horse to the east and toward home. One more day's hard riding will find them near the canyon separating the Elkhorn and the Arapaho lands. Watching the herd drifting before them he is eager to get home. The mares are the beginning of his horse ranch. He is proud of them and can hardly wait for Hob to see them.

The small blaze of the fire flickers on the surrounding brush as the girl prepares their supper. Since the near drowning at the river, she pitched in and started helping.

With the Arapaho boys heading home, Matt tells Jim to turn her mare loose and let her help drive the herd toward the Elkhorn. Reluctantly, Jim hands her the lead rope. He is still not convinced she will not try to run, but Matt is the boss.

Only the popping of the dry sticks in the fire breaks the stillness as the men smoke and wait for their meal. May keeps looking worriedly into the surrounding shadows and then back at Jim. Something is bothering her. Shucks, he does not figure she will dare make a run for it on foot, but he is ready for anything from this little spitfire of a girl.

Rising, she walks to where Matt sits on a downed log. "We should put the fire out now, the food is ready."

"Why? I like looking into it," Matt looks up at the girl.

"A true warrior never looks directly into a fire," she scolds him then looks again into the surrounding darkness.

"Why?" Jim can feel the anxiety in her voice.

"It blinds him to his enemies. I will put the fire out." She turns to the flickering blaze.

"Wait," Matt stops her. "I don't want to eat in the dark."

"Maybe we better Boss. Something is spooking her." Jim starts toward the fire when several warriors appear at the edge of the clearing. These are not the friendly Arapaho they traded with recently. No, they are from the northern bands, the ones that ride with the fierce Sioux.

Six warriors walk from the woods toward the fire. The wavering light, gives them an eerie look as it cast shadows across their ruddy faces. Armed heavily with trade muskets and bows, the warriors are painted for war. Pitching his coffee cup to the ground, Matt comes easily to his feet, pulling the leather thong from his pistol. Looking quickly to where Jim rolled to his feet, Matt turns his attention to the warriors.

Jim steps to the front and raises his hand in greetings. Speaking in the guttural tone of the Arapaho, he gestures for them to come to the fire. Shaking his head, a large warrior motions for the girl to come to him. Jim grabs her by the arm as she starts to pass him.

"The white squaw is my woman!" The huge warrior steps forward, slashing his hand downward.

"She has been given to the Iron Man. She goes with us to the east."

"No!" The warrior makes another step forward, the fire throwing shadows on his huge chest. "She goes with me. I have spoken for her, and I now bring you the ponies I have offered her father Fox Tails."

"How are you called?" Cloud stalls for time.

"I am Yellow Bonnet, Northern Arapaho."

"I am Jim Cloud and this is the Iron Man," Cloud motions toward Matt.

"Half breed dog, I know of you," the warrior spit with contempt. "Your father was a dung eater from the north woods."

Cloud's hand rests lightly on the hilt of his knife. Matt cannot understand what is being said, but he can tell Cloud was insulted.

Stepping between the warrior and Cloud, he speaks easily to Cloud. "Tell this warrior, the girl is my property. I bought her and she stays with us.

Several horses are led into the light of the small fire. The warrior points his hand at the horses then speaks to Matt. "You trade for horses, these are good horses. You take, and I take girl."

Cloud interprets the warrior's words. "No!" Matt's hands went flat in a sweeping motion. "The girl stays with us."

"When the great one comes again, I, Yellow Bonnet, will come for the girl. You will take the horses and give me the girl, or the Iron Man will fight me for her." The words are hardly spoken when the warriors disappear into the night.

Cloud looks to where Matt is standing and refills his coffee cup. "I've heard of this warrior Boss, he's a rough one."

"The girl stays. Now let's get some sleep and we better tie her up for her own good." Matt produces a strip of leather from his saddle.

Breakfast consists of cold biscuits and river water as Matt wants to move the mares before the Arapaho return. The sun barely appears in the east when they discover the warriors ahead of them spread across the narrow trail. The huge figure of Yellow Bonnet sits his horse in front of the other warriors. Matt holds the mares up and watches, as the warrior leads the same horses he offered last night forward, motioning at May.

Shaking his head, Matt turns down the trade. The warrior slips from his horse armed only with his hunting knife.

"He aims to kill you, Boss." Cloud cocks his Henry repeater, laying it across his saddle horn.

"Is the Iron Man afraid and too weak to meet me, Yellow Bonnet, armed only with a knife?" The warrior sneers as he waits.

Matt steps from his horse and removes his pistol belt. Only the long blade of his bowie knife rests in his hands.

"You watch yourself Jim. If this goes bad, take my pistol. You'll have a fighting chance, maybe."

"He'll come at you fast." Cloud grabs May's arm as she steps forward. "Watch his empty hand."

"You don't have to fight. I'll go with him." May Bell steps forward.

"Is that what you want?" Matt asks watching her face.

Looking up at Cloud, she shakes her head. "No, I wish to stay here, but I have caused too much trouble already."

Matt looks the tall warrior over. He is indeed a formidable foe. Almost as tall as Matt, heavy muscled, he is very sure of himself. The warrior eases forward, reminding Matt of a mountain lion stalking his prey. He will have to be careful if he is going to live and start his ranch. With the speed of a cat, the warrior lunges forward and strikes with his knife, only to find his quarry spinning out of the way. Yellow Bonnet misses, but Matt leaves a thin trickle of blood running from the warriors back.

Surprise shows in the face of Yellow Bonnet as he turns to meet the white man. Circling, trying to get the advantage, each man watches the other's eyes, each trying to outguess the other. Matt charges forward swinging his knife in quick slashes, but only succeeding in driving the Arapaho backward across the trail. Yellow Bonnet counters with a belly thrust that would have disemboweled Matt if it succeeded.

For several minutes both men circle, craftily avoiding the other's menacing knife. With a quick lunge, the sharp knife of the warrior opens a furrow down Matt's arm. Again, the warrior comes forward, but this time Matt strikes first, leaving a shallow trail of blood across the man's chest. Matt rushes in as both men grab the other's wrists, putting their strength into trying to make the other's arm bend. Falling backwards, the Arapaho flips Matt over his head, throwing him hard to the ground. As Matt is rising, the warrior charges the shaken Matt, but the gravel and small rocks on the trail betray him. Losing his footing he falls hard on his back. Scrambling forward, Matt pounces on top of the fallen warrior, his foot pinioning Yellow Bonnet's knife hand to the ground, the point of his knife at the warrior's throat. Only contempt shows from the warrior's eyes as he looks up at death.

"You are a brave man. Only the slip of your foot allows me to win this day, I will not take a brave man's life." Matt steps away from the fallen warrior.

Cloud translates the words to Yellow Bonnet as the warrior stands up.

Stepping in front of Matt, the warrior extends his hand. "It is finished. The Iron Man gives me back my life. You and your people will always be welcome in my village."

"Tell him he will always have friends on the Elkhorn if he needs us," Matt replies as Cloud translates.

Yellow Bonnet takes one final look at May, mounts, and leads his warriors back toward Arapaho lands.

Matt mounts and turns his gelding toward the Elkhorn and home.

Chapter 6

The fight finished quickly. Maybe Matt made a friend among the Arapaho people. A year ago, he would have killed Yellow Bonnet with no compassion, but today he did not kill. Did he become soft, or maybe the gentleman in him, finally came out.

Passing the west end of the lake Matt can see smoke curling from the cabin's stovepipe. It is dusky dark and later than he expected to arrive back at the ranch. Two weeks on the trail took their toll on the mares. Some are sore footed from the rough ground, their feet worn down from the constant traveling with no shoes. Every mare is gaunt from lack of grazing. Two weeks of good grazing along the lake will put the weight back and give the soles of their hooves time to harden up. Matt smiles as he looks at the mares spreading out along the lake. Yes, the ranch is beginning to take shape.

Matt's dark eyes study the distant cabin, the light shining from the window is a beckoning call. Only a tired rider, heading home late at night knows the feeling upon seeing a light in a window. He knows the day's work is almost over and there is hot supper and rest waiting. A woman should be waiting, but Matt knows his woman waits for someone else now, but he can only blame himself.

Looking behind him where Cloud and May are bringing up the drag, driving the tired horses on, he smiles. At least Cloud has him a woman and they are in love. Since the crossing at the river and the trouble with Yellow

Bonnet, the girl clings to Cloud's side. Never leaving him for a second Cloud is not minding it at all. Yes, they are in love. Cloud is half Arapaho and that problem will have to be met, but watching the two of them together seems a match, which some people call "made in heaven." Anyway, they will cross that bridge when something happens. Matt knows people like Jim Cloud but the idea of a white woman marrying an Indian will not be welcomed by the white people. No matter, May being raised Arapaho makes it seem like a good match to him. Anyone wanting to argue the point will have to buck up against the Elkhorn.

"We'll leave the mares close to the lake tonight, I figure they're too tired to roam far," Matt said, nodding at the mares, as Cloud and May Bell ride up to him.

"Sounds like a good idea to me," Cloud answers.

Hallooing the cabin before getting too close, Matt sees the barrel of a rifle protrude from the window. "It's us, you old heathen, put that cannon away."

"How'd I know it were you?"

"Now who else were you expecting?"

Guns and men come alive from the cabin as Matt dismounts and shakes hands with Tin Cup.

"Dang, it's good to see you Matt. Thought maybe the Arapaho got you."

"They durn near did."

"We were just finishing our cornbread and fixin' when the boys heard you coming. Made 'em a mite nervous," Tin Cup spit.

"And you, you old goat?" Cloud slaps Tin Cup across the back and laughs.

"Nope, not me. I knew nobody but a Tillman, would be game enough to ride straight up to this cabin after dark." Tin Cup nods at the men coming out of the shadows armed to the teeth.

Matt studies the face of each man as he enters the light of the window. Sam and Rollie, he already knows. The other two men he never saw before.

"This is Mister Tillman, boys, your Boss." Tin Cup motions at Matt.

"Name's Matt. Mister Tillman lives at the other end of this ranch."

The two men step forward. "Name's Chink Howard and this is Lonnie Hall."

"Glad to have you boys on the payroll." Matt shakes hands with the men, turning to where Cloud and May stood. "This is Jim Cloud and May Bell Williams." Both men remove their hats and nod to May. Tin Cup looks the scared girl up and down then grins. "Arapaho, seen her once when she was a little snapper."

"You sure it was the same girl?" Cloud asks.

"Same girl, just smaller back when I seen her." Tin Cup is sure.

Hob steps forward and stands beside Matt, causing May to shrink back in fear. Never has she seen a black before. Her dark eyes widen in shock.

Matt laughs. "He's ugly, May, but he's friendly."

"Has he been painted black?" May speaks to Cloud in Arapaho, causing him to laugh.

"No, his wife is inside and she's black too." Cloud hardly gets the words out when April steps outside and walks to where May stood.

"Don't be scared Missy. You comes with me and we'll fill you up with some vittles." April ushers the nervous May inside the cabin and away from the men.

"You get the horses?" Hob asks.

"Sure did, the best horses in the Arapaho bands."

"Where are they?" Tin Cup's eyes scan the barn area.

"Left them grazing along the lake. You'll take Hob and Jim and put them in the box canyon with the stallion in the morning."

"Boss, the grass in that canyon won't hold that many horses for long," Cloud speaks up, "not a big enough pasture for all of them."

"I know we'll start fencing every pass out of this ranch tomorrow, as soon as I get back from the Gorman Ranch."

"What'cha going over there for?" Tin Cup grins slyly.

"Well, Mister Nosey, I do believe Mrs. Gorman would like to give her permission before we start slinging fences up, don't you?

"And your point is?" Tin Cup fires back at him.

"Sam, you work on the house. The rest of you boys start cutting more grass. I want the hay barn so full by first snow that it pops at the seams."

"Yes Sir." The tall lanky man's huge Adam's apple bobs up and down every time his head moves. Tin Cup swears the man looks like a tom turkey gobbling. Course now, he does not swear that where Sam can hear him.

April steps through the door and waits until she catches Matt's eye. "Mister Matt, your supper be getting cold. Ya'll best be coming to eat."

Supper finishes, Matt, Hob, and Tin Cup sit down outside the cabin when all hell breaks loose inside the barn where the men are sleeping. Suddenly, two bodies come barreling outside, barely visible in the dark. Jim Cloud and the new hired man, called Lonnie, are at it tooth and claw. Matt and Hob hurry over, but stop short of the fight as Sam waves them back. Matt cannot imagine what started it and eases over to where Sam stands; his eyes fixed on Cloud as he delivers a right to Lonnie's jaw.

"What's going on?"

"Lonnie said something about the girl being pretty and the fight was on," Sam grins as hard fists land with a thud on each man. "Weren't nothing bad, just a man admiring a pretty woman twas all."

"You want me to stop it Mister Matt?" Hob steps forward.

"Not yet, let 'em work it out a bit or they'll be back at it tomorrow."

Lonnie is bigger and stronger than Jim Cloud, but Cloud is faster and madder. In the dark, Matt cannot tell which man was getting the best of the battle, but he can hear them groan when a hard lick hits home. Neither man is willing to give an inch so Matt figures he best step in before they are too beat up to work. Matt grabs Jim Cloud and Hob hurls Lonnie several feet backward as he tries to reach Cloud with another haymaker. Lonnie isn't ready to quit yet, but with Hob standing in his path to Cloud, he doesn't have much choice.

"You boys settle down now, we've gotta work at daybreak." Matt releases Jim Cloud. "Shake hands and end it right here."

"I'll not have another word said about her!" Jim Cloud hisses.

"Not from me you won't." Lonnie tried to grin, feeling of his chin.

"Anybody else?"

"I think you've made your point, Jim; now let's turn in."

Daylight finds Matt inspecting the house. All it lacks to make it livable are the windows. The heavy oak door is already in place and the roof is fitted with new shakes. Sam is truly a good carpenter. Walking to the barn, he sees the men are busy there, too. The smell of fresh cut hay floats down from the loft, making him take a deep breath.

"Reminds me of home," Matt mumbles. "Nothing smells better."

"Nothing 'cept flapjacks and side meat Boss, let's go." Chink Howard was standing behind Matt while he was looking up into the loft.

"Sounds good to me." Matt follows the man towards the cabin. As soon as breakfast finishes, Tin Cup, with Hob and Jim Cloud following, ride out to push the mares into the box canyon with the stallion. They do not want them to drift too far and find their way off Elkhorn Range. Rollie, with the rest of the crew, heads back toward the hay meadows along the lake. Hob's oldest son, Jacob, drives the wagon. Big for his age, the boy has his chest thrown out, proud to be doing his share of the work, like the rest of the men. If he keeps growing at this rate, he will be bigger than Hob.

Matt catches a good-looking roan gelding from the corral and saddles him. Circling the horse, he lets him hump a little on the end of his lariat, before bridling him. Roans, broke to the saddle right are good, tough horses. Most have a little bronc in them and early in the morning, when they are fresh, they will try you. Leading the gelding outside, Matt pulls his head around to him and steps easily into the saddle. To his surprise, the roan rides off quietly.

Clearing the yard, he kicks the roan into a short, ground eating lope, and heads for the Gorman ranch. The gelding is tough and Matt enjoys the cool wind, fanning around his face. The morning is beautiful. Deer, buffalo, animals of all kinds, spook and run as he passes. The roan's shod hooves hardly make a sound in the soft sandy trail. Pulling the horse to a stop, he inspects the mouth of the canyon separating the two ranches. The new barbed wire would be a better and quicker fence, but Matt hates the stuff. He knows what can happen, if a horse accidentally got tangled in it. Well, he will let Mrs. Gorman decide what she wants, barbwire or a pole fence. The draw is close to a hundred paces across. He will have the fencing crew start here. Turning the roan, he heads on toward the Gorman spread.

Vickie Gorman is on the front porch, watering her flowers, when she spots Matt coming. Her eyes take in the tall frame and sunburned face, as he rides up to the house.

"Good morning, Miss Vickie."

"Why, Matt Tillman, what a pleasant surprise." She is genuinely surprised to see him so early in the morning. "Step down and I'll get you some coffee."

"Don't go to any trouble. I've come on business."

"Pssh, no trouble, come in." She holds the door open for him. He can smell the fragrance of her perfume as he slips by her and enters the house. His eyes take in the large sitting room, lavishly decorated with a woman's touch. Removing his hat he pushes back his thick black hair and turns to face her.

"Now you make yourself comfortable and I'll get us some coffee." She disappears into the kitchen.

Matt listens to the china rattling in the back of the house then looks around the lavish room. For some reason he is uncomfortable. He has lived too long outside under the stars and without the company of a woman. As he eases down onto the settee, it feels good to be in a room such as this, and in the company of a beautiful and charming woman.

"Here now, how do you like your coffee?" She smiles, placing the tray on a small table. "Black, or with cream and sugar?"

"Black will be fine."

"My husband, Thomas, took his coffee black."

"Yes Ma'am, I'm sorry to hear about his death."

"Yes, it was a shame. He was so young, too young to die. He shouldn't have drawn his gun and shot at Wylie that day." She pours the coffee, handing Matt a steaming cup. "We could have worked it out in time."

"Then you don't fault Palette for his death," Matt asks amazed.

"Yes, I do, and no, I don't."

"Ma'am?"

"My Thomas was no gun hand but he could be mean, and he was very jealous. He drew and fired at Wylie twice before Wylie fired back. He would have killed Wylie for no reason, other than a few words that passed between them. Like I said, my husband had a violent temper. Now let's talk about something more enjoyable."

Matt's coffee suddenly turns sour. He looks across at Vickie Gorman, seeing her in a new light. The beauty is still there, but for the first time, the coldness in her is apparent. Setting his cup back onto its saucer, Matt looks outside, wishing he could find an excuse to leave quickly.

"Miss Gorman."

"Vickie," she interrupts.

"Yes ma'am, I'll be turning my mares loose on the range and I need a fence between us to keep them turned back from your ranch."

"What kind of a fence, Matt?"

"I would prefer a pole fence. The new barbed wire is suicide if anything gets into it." Matt sips his coffee, hardly tasting it.

"A fence between our ranches seems like a barrier between us."

"Yes Ma'am, that's kinda the idea. We don't want my horses eating your graze now do we?" Matt studies the woman, but her words about her husband keep coming back to him, taking the beauty away from her. "Naturally, it'll have a gate."

"No, I suppose you are right."

"Will the pole fence be alright with you?"

"Why don't you speak with my foreman, Cody Pauly, he'll know more than I about such matters."

"And where will I find Mister Pauly?"

"You don't have to leave so soon?" She pretends to pout.

"Yes Ma'am, I do. I need to be getting back, plenty of work to do at the ranch." Matt places his cup back on the table and reaches for his hat as he stands. "Thank you for the coffee. I'm sorry to have barged in on you without advance warning."

Vickie Gorman smiles and moves closer to him as she rises from the settee. "Will I see you soon?"

"We'll stop on our way to town next Saturday."

"We?" Vickie seems disappointed.

Matt steps back automatically as she pushes closer to him. "Hob and his family will be with me."

"I see. This black man and his family, were they your slaves as people are saying?"

"Well ma'am, I don't know what people are saying, but Hob and his wife and children are as free as you are."

She can hear the defiance in his words. "Maybe more so, they have something that most of us don't, happiness and each other."

"Yes, yes, of course."

"Now, where can I find this foreman of yours?" Matt passes through the door.

"He'll be at the barn," she points with her chin.

Stepping up on the roan, Matt tips his hat and nods. "Much obliged for the coffee."

"You will be coming to the dance?" She places her hand gently on his knee and looks up at him.

"Dance?" Matt did not hear about a dance.

"The town has a fall dance every year, to celebrate the year's harvest. It'll be two weeks from Saturday." She smiles provocatively up at him. "I'll save my first dance for you. You will come, won't you?"

Looking down at her he nods slowly. "Barring fire and flood, I'll be there."

Vickie smiles. "Here we say barring snow and blizzards."

Matt turns toward the barn where two men watch him from an open window. The roan stirs up puffs of dust as he walks slowly across the ground separating the two buildings.

"Looks like you got yourself a rival, Wylie." The taller of the two men grin at the frowning face of Wylie Palette. He knows Palette saw the looks Vickie gave Matt and her hand was on the tall man's knee. The smaller man laid his hand easily on his pistol. "We'll see."

"Not here on the ranch. Take your killing somewhere else."

"Alright Cody; anything you say."

The foreman watches as Palette eases out the back door of the barn and mounts his horse. The tall man shakes his head. His dislike for the retreating gunfighter is as strong as a rabbit's dislike for a coyote. Along the same lines, he fears the man. A cold-blooded killer, Palette has loyalty for only one man, and that is Cage Tillman. Two things he never understood; Palette admiring the owner of the Elkhorn, and Vickie Gorman for letting the killer of her husband come calling on her.

Palette's visit this morning was interrupted by the sudden arrival of Matt Tillman. The foreman shakes his head and watches as Palette disappears from sight. He would have killed the young Tillman, without a second thought, if he did not stop him. Wylie Palette is meaner and far deadlier, than a coyote, and where a coyote was a coward, Palette has never shown yellow.

Stepping from the door, he watches as Matt steps softly to the ground. The barn was only a ways from the house, but young Tillman rides his horse over instead of walking. The mark of a real horseman, the foreman thought. He never knew a true horseman to walk when he could ride, no matter the distance, five feet or ten miles. It seems almost an embarrassment to most cowboys to be seen walking.

"Cody Pauly?"

"That'll be me, Mister Tillman."

Matt takes the offered hand and studies the tall man. "Reckon you already know me, Miss Gorman said to see you about stringing a fence between the ranches."

"Let's say, I have heard of you."

"Good, now about the fence."

Finishing their business, Pauly watches as Matt mounts the roan. "I'll send a crew to help you Monday morning at daybreak."

"We'll be there." Matt nods and kicks the roan into a lope, unaware of Vickie Gorman's eyes following his departure.

Pauly watches from the barn as Matt rides out of sight, knowing he should have warned the rancher about Palette, but he didn't want to get involved with the man. Scared or smart, or a little of both, he does not know which, but he does know Wylie Palette is a killer and he holds a grudge. He likes the young Tillman, though he just met him. Indecision takes hold of him or maybe guilt.

Matt is hardly out of sight of the Gorman Ranch when he hears the pounding of a hard running horse coming up fast behind him. Turning in his saddle, he is surprised to see Cody Pauly. Matt smiles to himself. The big foreman makes the small cow pony he was riding seem small. The man has to be at least a couple inches over six feet and the horse is about fourteen hands at the shoulder. Pauly's long legs almost reach the ground and his upper body rises over the horse gigantically.

"Thought I'd ride along with you and take a look see where you want to string this fence."

"Alright, I'm obliged for the company." Matt looks over the foreman's rig. A Henry repeating rifle, hangs from a scabbard on the horse and the man has a horse pistol strapped to his waist.

As they ride Matt notices Pauly scanning the trail ahead, as if he is watching for something or somebody. The hair on Matt's neck seems to stand up. Slowly, without letting Pauly see what he was doing, he flips the thong from his pistol.

"You always ride so heavily armed?"

"Well Mister Tillman, I'll tell you; out here a man can never be too careful. You just never know when you're liable to run into a snake."

"Kinda late in the year for snakes."

"Same thing my uncle Floyd use to say, buried him too. Yes sir; snake got him right through the heart."

"You don't say. Must have been a heck of a snake."

"Were for a fact. You might say he was forty-five caliber size," Pauly grins over at Matt. "Yes sir, he was a big snake."

The men ride on in silence, rarely speaking, as their attention is riveting on the surrounding country where a man can conceal himself. Watching Pauly, Matt knows the man is not out here about the fence. Climbing a short rise, a perfect place for a man to conceal himself, Matt notices a small dust cloud of a rider retreating away from them in a hurry. Riding hard to the crest, they are just in time to get a glimpse of a man horseback, disappearing into the far cedars.

"Someone you know?" Matt nods towards the dust trail.

"Maybe, Mister Tillman, maybe."

"Wylie Palette?"

"A little too far to tell for sure," Pauly shrugs.

"What's his game?"

"Let's just say he doesn't plan on sharing."

"Miss Gorman?"

"Maybe so."

"He saw me at the ranch?"

"For a fact," Pauly grins. "Kinda upset his plans for breakfast."

"It appears I'm in your debt, and the name's Matt." Matt extends his hand.

"I'm ashamed of standing by doing nothing after Palette killed Mister Gorman, but I'm no gunman and I've been with this outfit almost twenty years, long before the Gorman's took over." Pauly removes his hat, wiping his forehead. "I'm getting long in the tooth, Matt, and I would kinda hate to go to slinging hash for another outfit."

"You don't have to explain to me Cody."

"Well, just wanted you to know, Vickie sets a score by Palette."

"I don't understand it. Palette killed her man, yet she lets him come calling."

"Well that's where we're both lost, 'cause I don't understand it either."

"I'd figure she would hate the man."

"Me too."

"Is she scared of him?"

"Don't act like it." Pauly rubs his chin. "But, I ain't a genius when it comes to women, and that's a pure fact."

"He come here often?"

"No, maybe once every week or two. Look here Matt, I don't like Palette, but the man's already killed over her, and he's pure poison with a pistol. No, I aim to do my job and keep my nose out of Wylie Palette's business."

The two men ride on at a slow lope, each deep in thought. Matt knows Pauly is no coward, but the foreman was not a gun hand either. Miss Gorman's relation with Palette is her own business. Still he wonders, why would she let the man anywhere near her. Stopping at the pass, Matt quickly shows Pauly where he wants the fence.

"I owe you Cody. Thanks." Matt nods, kicking the gelding on toward the Elkhorn home range. Pulling up, he turns the roan back to where the big man sits his horse. "You ever get in the mood, there's always a job for you at the Elkhorn."

"I'll remember that Matt, and I appreciate it."

"We'll see you tomorrow."

Chapter 7

Five horses stand hipshot inside the falling down excuse for a corral. The rough cut house is not much better. Years and neglect took its toll on what was, at one time, a nice little homestead. Smoke drifts lazily from the rusty stovepipe protruding from a paneless window. Three men sit playing cards around a rickety table. A fourth sits off by himself, his wide deep blue eyes taking in everything, missing nothing. A cigar clamped tightly in the corner of the man's slash of a mouth, curls smoke upwards toward the ceiling. A dark beard covers his face, a cruel face, shadowed by the dark corded hat of an army officer of the union forces.

The cardplayers were unkempt, in need of both a haircut and shave. The blue-eyed one, by himself, is different. He sits ramrod straight, his clothes immaculate, the beard trimmed neatly. An air of authority emanates from him. Even the sleeveless left arm seems to make him more formidable.

A fourth man pushes the wooden door open, making the hinges groan with the effort. Walking straight to the big man, he salutes smartly and waits as the man pours himself another cup of coffee.

"He's coming up the road, General."

"Thank you Sergeant, now we can get to it."

"Yes sir."

"Is Johnson still on lookout?"

"Yes Sir."

"Send one of the others to relieve him and get Red in here as soon as he arrives."

"Yes Sir." With a stiff salute, the man retreats from the cabin, taking one of the cardplayers with him.

A horse comes at a quick trot, to the cabin and boot steps sound on the rickety porch. A tall red headed man enters and approaches. "Howdy General." The man has a lock of red hair protruding from under his slouch hat.

Irritated at the man's lack of discipline and complete disregard for authority, the big man nods, sipping his coffee. "Red, you been gone three days. What took you so long?" He sits the tin cup down and stares at the red headed one.

"Big country, took some time asking, and a lot of riding."

"Elk Springs is a small town."

"It is that, General," the man fidgets. "But, it took some doing. People get suspicious when you start asking questions soon as you hit town."

"I guess enough whiskey loosened their tongues?"

"It helped."

"Well?"

"He's here and got a ranch called the Elkhorn, north of here. His name is Tillman."

"You're sure?"

"I'm sure, big man, six two, two hundred twenty pounds, and sandy brown hair."

The General pulls the cigar from his mouth and studies it quietly as if looking at the past. "Sandy hair, I could swear he was black headed. I must be thinking of the black that rode beside him that day. Who knows, in the heat of battle."

"His ranch house is due north of here, about ten miles."

"What about the black man?"

"Here sir, people were eager to talk about him, his size and all."

"Good, good, figured he'd go back south after the war or get himself killed."

"Yes, sir."

"Funny, we we're fighting to get them coloreds free and they still fought for the south." The General studies the man as if he can see through him.

"Yes sir." Red fidgets under the scrutiny.

"The stallion, did you see him?"

"No sir, but he's there. People of Elk Springs described him to me. Blood bay thoroughbred, heavy muscled, with a star in his forehead."

"You know where he's at?"

"Yes Sir, well, not exactly; seems this Tillman's ranch is split, some in the lowlands, some up high. They took the stallion up to the higher mountains and got 'em some mares up there. Shouldn't be too hard to locate"

"You figured the best way to get him?"

"I've got some men waiting in town now. One used to work for the older Tillman, years ago. He knows the layout, and for a fee, he'll take us right to him." Red wants to sit, but no one ever sits down in the presence of the General.

"I don't want anything to happen to the horse, nothing."

"Yes Sir, General."

"You take that horse and Tillman's riders will follow you right here." The General puffs on the cigar. "Leave him a good trail to follow, don't lose him."

"What about Tillman himself?"

"Get the horse. I'll be waiting word from you and we'll be ready with a reception party for the men following, then Red, we'll see to Mister Tillman."

"I've got an idea for that too, General."

"Tell me."

"In two weeks there will be a dance in town; a fall dance. They say Tillman and his Missus never misses one."

"And?"

"We'll be waiting at a place they call the Elkhorn Divide. Perfect ambush site. That's where we'll get Mister Tillman, if he don't come with his men after the horse."

"How many ride for the Elkhorn?"

"Maybe ten, but we'll narrow that down some when I get the horse."

"And this dance, you sure it's in two weeks?"

"Yes Sir, General, two weeks."

"Well, I've waited this long two more weeks won't matter."

"Yes Sir."

"Go back to town and wait. Time it just right, so we can take out Mister Tillman before he realizes what happened to the horse and his men on the upper ranch." The General leans back in his chair and smiles, sending a chill up Red's back. He met few men in his time that actually scared him, but this General is one of them. The man has a menacing arrogance surrounding him, a look Red cannot understand.

"I'll be needing some cash."

The General pulls out several gold coins and places them on the table. As Red reaches for it, the right hand of the man snakes out and takes his wrist in a powerful grip, almost making him cry out. "Don't you dare get drunk and bungle this raid or I'll kill you personally, do you understand me completely?"

"You got my word, General." Red shudders slightly under the man's scowl, stumbling as he backs from the house.

"I've got you now, you rebel scum." The huge hand smashes down on the table, making the cardplayers jump. The big man walks to the dirty window, and feeling of his empty sleeve in front of him, he grins harshly. "Yes my rebel friend, I've got you now!"

It was four days since Matt's visit to the Gorman Ranch. The big house was finished. Sam stands with his hands crossed, smiling proudly. Out of nothing but raw materials and a few tools, he built a log house surrounded with porches and two fireplaces, one on each end. This is a home to make a man proud.

Matt smiles and shakes the man's hand. Yes, indeed, it is a magnificent undertaking and a beautiful beginning, for the Elkhorn Horse Ranch. Only one thing is missing, he could almost visualize her standing in the doorway.

"I'll get started on some tables and such, come first light."

"Sam, you are a true artist with a saw and a hammer, thank you."

"You're welcome."

Matt passes through the heavy oak door and into the large room that will be his office and general headquarters for the ranch. The pitch of the roof is steeper than most log cabins, but this can hardly be called a cabin. The high cathedral ceilings were crossed with huge clean stripped logs. Several deer racks, an elk, and one set of longhorn horns, huge at the base, spanning seven feet or more, hang from the rafters. Matt muses, must have been one of them old mossy horns his uncle brought up from Texas. Yes, this is a masterpiece of work. He will give Sam a bonus, befitting the great job he accomplished. The ranch is turning into something he is already proud of.

Matt ambles through the house, his spurs ringing on the smooth rock flooring. Stepping outside, he walks to where the bunkhouse for the men is laid out. A damp chill in the air brings a promise of the deep snow soon to follow. Tomorrow they will start work on the smaller bunkhouse, but in the meantime, the men can pitch their bedrolls in the big house.

When the heavy snows come, it will cover the ground, putting a stop to all work except riding herd on the horses and cattle, and putting out hay. Being from the south, Matt does not know what to expect here in the high country, but Jim Cloud and Tin Cup tell him to figure on the worst and maybe a little more. Looking at the barn Matt hopes he laid in enough hay for the winter. Hay will always keep over for another year and you just never know how severe these winters can be in the high country.

April rings the cowbell for dinner and the Elkhorn crew drifts over for their supper, when Tin Cup spots a rider coming from the direction of the lake. Everyone turns, as the sound of a gunshot comes from the rider. They watch the man, whipping his hard running horse, riding hell-bent for leather, jumping gullies, riding like the old devil is in hot pursuit of him. Something is wrong but for the life of him, Matt cannot figure out what it could possibly be.

"Something has sure set fire to his britches." Tin Cup spit a stream of tobacco across the yard.

"It's Chink." Matt can hear the man hollering but he is still too far to make out.

"Seen a turpentined cat run like that once, quite a sight," Tin Cup squints.

"Maybe he's just hungry," Sam offers.

"It better be more than hunger causing him to run one of my horses that way." Matt steps toward the oncoming rider.

Pulling the blowing gelding to a sliding stop almost on top of Tin Cup, Chink throws himself from the saddle and turns toward Matt.

"Dang it Chink, what's the matter?" Matt swears.

"Trouble boss, it's the stallion."

"The stallion!" Matt stiffens at the words. "What about the stallion?"

"He's gone; him and two or three of your best mares."

"Gone?"

"Yes Sir, I looked the herd over good. Him and them two mares you were so proud of are gone. Maybe one or two others, I didn't take time to tally the whole bunch."

"Where's Cloud?"

"He's trying to pick up tracks. Told me to tell you to come running and bring rifles and grub," Chink answers. "I'm sorry Boss, we've been watching the horses like you said."

Matt whirls toward the corrals, his long legs churning up the dirt as he runs.

Tin Cup runs up beside him, gasping for breath as Matt swings the gate open and reaches for his bridle. Seeing Tin Cup grab up his bridle, Matt shakes his head at the old rider.

"You ain't going."

"Uh huh, and you ain't bossing this drive."

"Tin Cup!" Matt swings a loop over the roan's neck. "I said."

"I heard you." The old man catches his paint and starts saddling up, ignoring Matt. "I ain't too dang old to hold up my part of this outfit."

Hob comes out of the dim gloom of evening, producing a gunnysack of grub and two rifles. "Reckon I ain't going, Masta?"

"Not this time. I need you to watch after things." Matt turns to Hob. "Keep a close eye out this may be more than a horse raid."

"I'll watch."

Five minutes later, Matt and Tin Cup are headed toward the lake at an easy lope. As late as it is, there was no hurry. Cloud will be somewhere ahead, waiting for them. Matt hopes the horses just wandered off by themselves, but he doubts the stallion would leave his band of mares. The air promises of cold weather to come soon and maybe bring snow with it. Matt tied their heavy overcoats onto his saddle. They will probably need them.

Passing the west end of the lake, they slow their horses to a walk. Somewhere ahead, Cloud will intercept them or have a fire going so they can locate him. An hour passes as they keep their horses traveling slowly to the west toward the pass and Arapaho country. The moon is full and the trail is easy to follow. Only the shadows of the tall pines cast darkness on the trail. Suddenly, Matt's sharp eyes pick up the outline of a rider and a horse standing in the trail ahead. Cocking the Henry, he walks the gelding slowly forward uncertain if this is Cloud or one of the horse thieves.

"It's me Matt, don't get nervous." Cloud speaks from the dark.

"Good to see you Jim; find anything?"

"Yea, four horses, all wearing shoes headed to the west."

"Arapahos?"

"Don't think so, unless they stole the horses they are riding and that ain't too likely. No, it's whites." Cloud rolls a cigarette. "Yellow Bonnet gave you his word and no other Arapaho will break it."

"Are you sure?"

"It's whites; took the stud about daylight this morning I figure."

"Where you figure they're headed?" Matt looks off, into the darkening woods.

"That's what has me stumped, they started off toward Arapaho country. No white man stealing horses would dare enter Indian land, not if they want to keep their hair or the horses they took."

Tin Cup spit a stream and eases off the Sharps, cradled in his arm. "We might as well make camp for the night and pick 'em up come daybreak. We ain't gonna do no tracking tonight in this gloom."

"That's my figuring." Cloud turns his gelding into some trees and starts unsaddling.

Only a small fire lights the gloom as the three men sit around it drinking coffee. Tin Cup watches Matt's face as he stares into the flickering firelight. Only a mask shows, but it is enough to make the old man shiver. Never has he seen death on a man's face as when he looks at Matt. Tomorrow, or the next, there will be some horse thieves mighty sorry if he does not miss his guess, providing of course the snows hold off and don't cover their tracks. But, as the old man looks across at Matt, he thought, snow ain't gonna help them fellers any either.

Daylight comes cold and damp as Cloud takes to the trail. Matt thought Cloud reminds him of a hunting dog on a hot track. No longer is he half-white, the Indian in him came out and his sharp eyes miss nothing. Noon finds them skirting a small ravine, the track suddenly turns due south toward the Gorman Ranch or Elk Springs. Cloud is surprised. He did not figure on them turning back toward town or any settled parts of the country.

Breathing the horses after a hard pull from the canyon, Cloud strikes a sulphur to his cigarette and turns to where Matt sits. "Appreciate you bringing this sheepskin coat, Matt, sure feels good this morning."

"How far ahead are they?"

"Six, eight hours maybe, we're gaining on them."

"Where do you think they're heading?"

"Hard to tell, right now. If I don't miss my guess they'll turn east and bypass the Gorman spread and town. Everyone knows that stallion and I doubt if they want to be spotted. I'm surprised they even took this route."

"Can we cut across and make up a little time?"

"It'd be a gamble Boss, if we guess wrong we're liable to lose them," Cloud frowns. "Most likely they've got a hideout somewhere. They think they can lay up awhile and let things cool down."

"You're the boss on this one, Jim."

"Let's ride then."

Late afternoon finds Cloud's prediction to be true. The trail turns back to the east a few miles from the Gorman headquarters. It also brought the riders up short as they ride up on the stiffening bodies of two of the mares. Their saddle horses smelled something a ways back and were acting up, but the riders figured it for a bear or mountain cat.

Tin Cup swears as their horses spook at the blood smell coming from the mares. "I'll be, they killed them, those sorry skunks."

Cloud dismounts and studies the ground around the mares. "Their feet are worn down bad. They were too sore footed. They still haven't hardened up from the drive to the ranch."

"But why did they kill 'em?" Tin Cup looks down at the horses. "My guess is, they didn't want Matt to get them back, so they cut their throats." Cloud studies the mares closely. "Boss, I don't think these are ordinary horse thieves."

"What kind of a low snake would do a thing like that?" Tin Cup is dumbstruck.

"Dead men!" Matt's face is as hard as flint. "Let's ride."

"This could be a long trail Matt, let's swing by the Gorman place and pick up some fresh horses."

"We'll lose time."

"We'll make it up. They'll have to pass through the roughs east of here and we'll pick their trail up there."

Kicking their tired horses into a lope, toward the Gorman Ranch, Matt looks back at the dead mares. He hates to detour but he knows Cloud is right. They will gain on the horse stealing scum with fresh horses under them.

Riding into the ranch, Matt quickly explains to Pauly what is happening, and short minutes later, they leave the ranch on the best horses the Gorman foreman has. Pauly offers to bring men and come along, but Matt refuses. Pauly knows the look on the man's face. The look of a man that wants to do his own killing. Nodding, he waves, as the three men ride on.

Cloud was right. The tracks of the riders lay plain in the soft sand that is the beginning of the roughs, a rock-strewn trail leading into some of the roughest country in the mountains. Cloud takes the lead and pushes his horse hard down the rough trail. The trail is plain to read in the sandy soil. Six horses passed, four wearing shoes. The tracks disappear as the ground becomes rockier, but the Arapaho can see where the horses overturned rocks in their passing. Night finds the trackers closing the gap, but darkness stops the pursuit.

"We can't follow them at night Matt it's too dangerous," Cloud explains, as he pulls up at a small stream.

"You reckon they'll try an ambush?"

"They know we're following, yep, I figure somewhere ahead they'll be waiting. They have to, we've been steadily gaining on them for two days and their horses are worn out. Yes Sir, they'll make a stand somewhere tomorrow or the next day. Don't matter though, if the snow holds off, we've got 'em." Cloud nods. "We've got 'em as sure as I'm sitting here."

Cloud is in the saddle at daybreak but tracking at a slower pace. He checks out every rise and turn of the rough ground before riding into view. Matt is fretting, if anything happens to the stallion. Chomping at the bit, he rides up beside Cloud. "We've got to catch up."

"We will. If they are going to kill the stallion, we can't stop them, but we don't have to get ourselves dead, too." Slowly they ride out of the roughs and back into a lower valley, covered with aspens and cedars. "Your brother's land," Tin Cup speaks up from the rear. "Runs about two miles that direction and about twenty that a way." The old man points with his chin.

"How much further to the main ranch?"

"Ten mile or so, I reckon."

"They'll pass way to the south of the ranch house." Cloud points to a tall peak, "there's where they'll hit us."

"You seem awful sure. How do you know?"

"I'm injun, remember?" Cloud laughs. "The trail splits ahead. That's the best place for them to waylay us."

The hair on Matt's neck stands up as they start across the narrow valley, but Cloud does not seem to worry. The beginning of the uphill climb, toward the tall peak, is at least two miles. Somewhere ahead, the horse thieves will make their stand. The smart thing to do will be to get out of the country as fast as they can, but for some reason, the riders ahead are in no hurry, and that worries Jim Cloud. They are trying to lure their pursuers on, but for what reason.

Matt knows Cloud is right, somewhere ahead, the thieves wait. This is more than plain horse stealing. The two dead mares were killed purposely, to keep them coming on, straight into a trap maybe. Whatever it is, Matt is anxious to catch up. After seeing the dead mares, rage took hold of him. Maybe it was the pent up anger and frustration over Jessie, but Matt does not want to admit to it. Ahead is his quarry and the sooner they pay for killing the mares, the better.

Cloud pulls his sorrel to a stop at the mouth of a canyon, where the trail split. Dismounting, he hands Tin Cup the reins and pulls his rifle from the boot. His dark eyes scan the far timber and his nose smells the air. The tracks of the men and horses lead off to the right branch of the canyon.

"Give me twenty minutes and then come on slow, real slow."

Turning, Cloud takes the left branch, the opposite trail the thieves took and disappears around a bend.

"You know these trails, Tin Cup?" Matt says to the old cowboy.

"I know them. They come together again about a mile further on. There's a good place, where they meet, to ambush a critter foolish enough to follow them."

Twenty minutes pass and Matt kicks his gelding forward, taking the lead. The tracks are plain on the carpeted trail, where the leaves and small limbs are disturbed. Matt studies each turn carefully, before moving into the open. If the shooting starts, the horse thieves will be close, as the thick trees do not allow a man to see too far ahead.

Cloud is waiting for them as they come to where the two trails combine. "Something spooked them, they were waiting behind those pines, but they pulled out."

"Let's ride, they can't be far ahead." Matt kicks his horse up the narrow trail. The men are close ahead and he is anxious to catch up to them.

Again the trail dips into a valley where a small stream rushes downhill, its icy cold water spraying against their horse's legs, as they watered. Matt studies the small valley, feeling the peaceful serenity of the surrounding mountains and letting the calm quiet of the place settle on him. It is difficult to believe that here, in this beautiful land, they are on the trail of horse thieves.

The heavy boom of a rifle breaks the stillness, as Matt falls from his saddle, hitting the cold water with a splash. Dragging himself behind a near tree, he feels the breath of a bullet as it tears a heel from his boot. Again a bullet rips the ground, close to the tree he is trying to conceal himself behind.

Tin Cup fires several rounds toward the sound of the gunfire, then rushes to Matt's side, his big Sharps grasped tightly in his hand. "You hit, lad?"

"Caught one in the side." Matt lies back on the leaves, as Tin Cup unbuttons his heavy sheepskin coat. Blood flows freely from a deep gash in Matt's side.

"Bad tear, but only hide deep; no muscle or vitals. Gonna be sore as the dickens for a while though and you're liable to lose a lot of blood, if'n I can't get it to stop."

Matt feels the penetrating cold and dampness as Tin Cup pulls away his shirt to wrap the wound.

"Let it go. We got other fish to fry."

"You keep bleeding out like you're doing and we'll be frying your fish, now hush and be still. Cloud's up there, he thinks there's just one left behind to slow us down, and no one man can handle that injun in the woods."

Several minutes later, a gurgling sound, then a scream comes from a hundred feet up the trail as Cloud walks into view, wiping his skinning knife on his chaps. Matt watches him replace the knife in its sheath and breaks into a trot back to them. Even dressed in the garb of a working cowhand there is no mistaking Jim Cloud for what he is. You can take an Indian's hand and lead him down the white man's trail, but they are still Indian and you do not want one for an enemy.

"He laid back to slow us down a bit," Cloud grins and hunkers down beside Matt. "You hurt bad?"

"I can ride."

"Not yet; we'll wait a spell." Cloud looks at Tin Cup. "Old man, your shooting was a little off, so why don't you take a few practice shots while I rest a little."

"My shootin' off, the devil you say. Why, you young...." Then the old cowhand grins. "I got it. You want them to think their man still got us pinned."

"Sound does carry a long way in these mountains," Cloud grins.

The powerful recoil of the heavy Sharps rifle sounds and resounds, up and down the valley. Tin Cup reloads and let's go, again. Cloud responds with the lighter Henry of the outlaw.

"Matt, can you stay here and keep up the noise while we ease after them?" Cloud starts gathering his rifle and coat.

"Tin Cup will stay; I'm going," Matt said. Cloud starts to protest. "That's it, let's go."

"It's your funeral." Cloud added the word "Boss" as Matt shoots him a cold look.

The blood clots and the heavy bandage, Tin Cup applied, stopped the bleeding, but the ache in his side is giving Matt fits with each stride the horse makes. Dark is almost on them when Cloud reins in hard. From out of the gloom, a small flicker of light shows itself across the canyon.

"There they are, Matt. They made their second mistake. Now we got 'em," Cloud whispers, stepping lightly to the ground.

"What was their first mistake?"

"Shucks, the dang fools stole your horses."

Cloud knows the noise of the gunfire, Tin Cup was making, had the thieves fooled into thinking their rider still had his quarry pinned down. As it grew darker, Tin Cup slowed down on his firing, but you can barely hear the occasional boom of the Sharps, even from where they sit their horses. Sound carries a long way in these mountains at night, especially when there is no wind.

"We'll let them relax then I'll move in."

"There's still three of them down there. We'll move in."

"Think you can make it?"

"I'll make it."

Every step Matt takes sends sharp stabbing pain through his side. Several times, Cloud stops, on one pretense or another, to let Matt rest. Even in the dark, Cloud can see the wound reopened and blood spread all the way down to Matt's boots. Still, Cloud cannot get the wounded man to stay behind.

The camp of the thieves are lying beside a stream of water. Thinking they were safe, no guard was posted. It is close to six miles back, where they left their man. The gunfire still echoes dimly, across the canyons, and there is no way riders can cross the canyons in the dark, even if they got past the man. Lying lazily in their bedrolls, around the warm fire, Red lights a cigar and laughs to himself. The General will pay well for the stallion. The mares, he would have liked to keep, but it did not bother him to kill them. There is no way he was letting Tillman have them back. No, Mister Tillman's men will follow him to the ends of the earth now, and with a mad mind, they might just get a little careless.

Matt and Cloud step into the dim light of the fire. The sound of Cloud cocking his rifle, bring the men fully awake. Matt shoots the first man as he grabs for the pistol laying beside his bedroll. The two others climb slowly to their feet, hands raised. Matt's bullet struck the first man through the stomach. Moaning, the man rolls from side to side, on the ground.

Matt steps beside the man, looking down at him. "Why'd you men kill my mares, instead of just turning them loose?" Only the man moaning on the ground, makes a sound. Matt pulls his pistol and shoots the man through the leg. Screaming, the man rolls almost into the fire.

One of the other men gasps in disbelief. "What kind of man would deliberately shoot another that was already lying disabled, on the ground?"

"I'll ask you one more time." Matt points the pistol at the other leg.

"You go to…" He never finishes, as Matt's shot took him between the eyes.

Turning his cold eyes, on the other two men, Matt's eyes blaze hotter than the fire. The sound of the pistol being cocked, sounds like a cannon. Both men look into the eyes of death and they know it.

"Who are you, Mister?" The one with bright red hair asks.

"Matt Tillman."

"You're not Matt Tillman, he's bigger, heavier than you are, light hair."

Matt looks to where Cloud stands impassive. "What do you know of this Tillman?"

"Nothing; seen him and his wife once or twice in Elk Springs, is all," the red headed man answers, bitterly.

"My brother is who you saw." Matt steps closer to the man. "Did you men have anything to do with the trouble my brother's wife had on her way to town a while back?"

"Wouldn't know anything about that."

"You wouldn't or you're not telling?"

"We wouldn't and that's the truth," Red glares at Matt. "So there's two of you?"

"Yea, two of us, now why did you kill my mares?" The pistol rises slowly toward the men.

The second of the men, raises his hands, pleadingly, toward Matt. "Don't shoot mister please, I'll tell you."

"Shut up, you yeller cur!" The red haired man cuffs the second, just before Matt's shot knocks him backward across the fire. Neither Matt nor Cloud bothers to remove the body, as the flames engulf Red's clothes.

"Now mister, you've got one second to talk." The coldness in Matt's voice left no doubt, he means business. "Talk or so help me, I'll burn you alive."

"I'll talk; just promise you won't shoot me. I don't want to die," the man pleads. "The General told us to steal the stallion and bring him the horse. He didn't say anything about the mares; that was Red's idea." The man nods at the red head who hit him. "He wanted the mares for bait."

"Why'd you kill the mares?"

"Red figured ya'll would get mad enough and blunder right into our trap." The man was so terrified, he soiled his pants, and Matt knew he wasn't lying.

"Why did he want us dead?"

"The General wants your men dead; not you. We didn't figure you'd come yourself."

"You were with him, now who is this General?"

"Don't know, a man we're hired out to and calls himself a General. That's what Red told us. That's all I know."

"Where's he at?"

"Somewhere north of here, we were supposed to lure you to him; Red knew where." The man is trembling so hard his entire body is shaking.

"What else?"

"That's all I know, except he's got several riders with him. Red says they are like an army unit or something. You can tell, even Red was scared of the man."

"That's all you know?"

"Yes sir, I swear, that's all."

"Then I don't reckon we'll need your company anymore."

"You said you wouldn't shoot me."

"I'll keep my word and I won't shoot you because I aim to hang you."

Tin Cup rides in, two hours past sunup. Looking around the clearing, he dismounts and walks to Matt, still wrapped in his bedroll. The old eyes take in the two dead men and the one hanging from a limb swinging gently in the light morning breeze. He missed out on something. He can see the sick look on Cloud's face. Whatever it was, maybe it was better he wasn't here.

"How's he doing?" Tin Cup asks, as Cloud hands him a hot cup of coffee.

"Lost a lot of blood but he'll make it." Cloud swallows hard and looks to where Matt lies. "I didn't believe it but I do now."

"Believe what?"

"His brother said he was a mean one. Take my word for it, he is." Cloud nods at the dead bodies and then looks back at Tin Cup.

"He done all this?" Tin Cup motions with his cup.

"Yep, there's one man I wouldn't want on my back trail, no siree bob. He's colder than a banker's heart and twice as hard."

Tin Cup walks over to the dead men and peers down at them. Squatting, he pushes back his hat and swears. "What do you know? You know who this is Cloud?"

Cloud stands and walks to where Tin Cup stood up. "I'll be, it's old Dan Wheeler. I just didn't take a close look."

"Yep that be him. Came with us up from Texas, twenty year ago." Tin

Cup shakes his head. "One of our best hands."

"Why would he be helping horse thieves?"

"Can't say. Maybe needin' money. Old Dan was a crusty old goat." Tin Cup straightens up and takes a look at the one called Red.

"Well, I'll give him one thing, he had grit up to the end. Told the Boss where he could go, before Matt shot him." Cloud comments.

"That'd be Dan, not much sense but loaded with sand," Tin Cup spit. "Most of them Texas boys were like that. Fight a grizzly bear if he thought he was being insulted, and some would do it just to be fighting."

"We better make tracks and get Matt to Doctor Wallace."

"What about these men?"

"Don't 'spect they need doctoring." Cloud spits a stream of tobacco at the dead mans forehead.

"You're right but kinda hate to leave old Dan uncovered though," Tin Cup looks back at the dead man. "You run with a bad bunch, you get what's coming to you."

"I'll wrap the stallion's front feet, he's pretty tender. You catch up the other horses and we'll pull out."

Tin Cup takes one last look at the dead men and starts gathering horses. Matt is weak and needs help getting on his horse. Cloud mounts behind him.

Matt cusses, "I can stay in the saddle."

Cloud only nods and heads the horse toward Elk Springs.

Chapter 8

The town of Elk Springs comes to life as Cloud and Tin Cup leads the horses down the main street, such as it was. Cloud is holding Matt in front of him. Kate Howard stands in front of the store, sweeping the board walkway. Recognizing Matt and seeing his side covered in dried blood, she hurries into the street, stopping next to Cloud's horse.

"Is he alive?" She grabs onto Matt's leg.

"Barely, we'll take him to Doc's house."

"No, bring him into the store, I'll send someone for the doctor."

Cloud and one of the town men carry Matt upstairs, above the store to Kate's room, and lay him on her bed. Kate pushes Cloud out of the way and starts removing his boots and coat. Reaching down, she unbuckles his gun belt. Sliding the belt under the unconscious man, she starts to unbutton his shirt and pants.

"You want me to do that, Miss Kate?"

"No Jim, just hurry the doctor."

"I'll get him right away." Cloud rushes, embarrassed, from the room.

Kate has Matt undressed by the time Cloud returns with Doctor Wallace. Bailey and Abigail try to come into the room with the doctor but Kate ushers them back out, into the hall.

Seeing no use for him to wait, Cloud walks to help Tin Cup unsaddle and feed the horses. Tin Cup finishes with the last one and is closing the corral gate when Cloud comes into the livery. "How's he doing?"

"Doc's up there with him now. Did you put the stallion in a stall out of sight?"

"He's in the barn. When do you plan on moving him back to the ranch?"

"Don't know he's pretty sore on the front end. We need to get some shoes on him so he can travel and then we'll see what Matt wants to do." Cloud looks around carefully. "Anybody see the stallion when you brought him in here?"

"Several town folk watched me bring the horses in here but I doubt they recognized the stallion, very few have ever seen him anyway."

"Well, I better stay close to the stable and make sure he doesn't up and disappear again." Cloud places his bedroll and saddle in the barn where he can be near the stallion's stall.

"I don't think that will be a problem, when word gets out about what happened to the last bunch that stole him." Tin Cup spit tobacco and rubs his chin clean. "No Sir, I don't think you'll have anyone else wanting to try their luck with the Elkhorn."

"What about this General?"

"Yea, reckon you're right, I clean forgot about him."

"Go get you some grub and keep your eyes out for anybody from the Gorman spread. They can send word back to the ranch," Cloud instructs Tin Cup.

Cloud rolls into his bedroll as Tin Cup starts back toward town. It's been a long ride to town, having to hold Matt in the saddle, and Cloud is dead tired. Taking one last glance at the stallion, he closes his eyes.

Just as Tin Cup steps on the boardwalk in front of the store, he notices Tom Ward of the Gorman Ranch, exiting the saloon. Crossing the street, he walks to where the rider is tightening his cinch strap. Ward is an amiable youngster and a top hand. Tin Cup knows he can trust the rider.

"Howdy, Tom, are ya headed home?"

"Morning Tin Cup, you old reprobate. Yep, picked up some sewing needles for Miss Gorman. 'Spect she'll be looking for me, so I best be getting them home." Ward waves the small package at Tin Cup and grins.

"Need a favor from you."

Ward stops what he is doing and turns his attention fully on Tin Cup. He can tell the old cowman is serious for once, when he does not even bother to banter with him.

"All you have to do is ask, old friend."

"I need someone to ride out to the Elkhorn and tell Hob to come a runnin'." Tin Cup went on to tell Ward what transpired and that Matt had been shot.

"He's the Black."

"That's him and they don't get much blacker."

"Alright, I'll drop off the needles and head right out there."

"Tom, tell him to come quick, but tell him to have everyone else stay close to the ranch and on their guard."

"You expecting trouble?"

"We already had trouble, but there could be more coming, don't know yet." Tin Cup eyes the saloon hungrily but he knows he needs to be sober. This General and his men can come into town any time and with Matt laid up, anything can happen.

"It's hard to believe Tillman really killed them all by himself, even old Dan Wheeler?" Ward looks to Tin Cup.

"Well, if I was you, I'd believe it."

Shaking his head, Ward mounts and rides out of town in a hard lope. Tin Cup goes over to the store and climbs the stairs, almost bumping into Abigail as he enters the room. Matt is pale but sleeping peacefully. The new bandages show above the turned down sheet covering him.

"Doc Wallace just left," Kate announces as he enters.

"What's the verdict?"

"He's weak from loss of blood and it's going to take several days for him to get his strength back." Kate looks toward the bed. "But he's going to be fine."

"I'll have him moved over to the hotel if…." Tin Cup does not get to finish.

"You'll do no such thing. He's staying right here." Kate sticks her chin out.

"Yes ma'am." The old puncher knows there is no use arguing.

The sun starts to show itself through the window, when Matt wakes and looks around the feminine room, his face whiter than the sheet that covers him. Trying to sit up, makes his head spin, almost causing him to pass out, putting an excruciating pain in his side. Lying back on the pillow, Matt feels the bandages that wrap around his waist and the clean, long underwear bottoms, he was wearing long handles that he knows are not his.

Turning, he sees the figure of Kate, staring out the window. His eyes stare at the woman's back as if he never saw her before. Twice or maybe three times, they met, yet until now, he hardly spoke to her. He was always on the defensive towards her. Why, he does not know. For some unknown reason, he felt threatened by her.

Settling back, on his pillow, he clears his throat. "Where am I, Miss Howard?"

"Well, I see you are awake." She turns and walks to the bed. "You are in Elk Springs."

"Where in Elk Springs?"

"My bedroom."

"Your..." Matt stammers, turning red. "Yes."

"Who undressed me?"

"I have brothers." Kate wants to laugh at Matt's embarrassment. She can see the red color running across his face.

"Yes, Miss Howard, you do, but I don't happen to be one of them." Matt looks around the room for Tin Cup or Cloud.

"Really, Mister Tillman, I...."

Matt cuts her off. "Miss Howard, I'm deeply in your debt and I thank you, now if you would get me my clothes." Matt starts to rise then settles back on the bed. He is just too weak to move.

"Mister Tillman, you are in no shape to go anywhere and you are definitely in no shape to undress yourself." Kate folds her arms. "I don't really think you are in any condition to argue the point right now."

Matt feels of his head and nods. "Yes ma'am, I believe you, dang thing feels like it's coming off."

Kate smiles. "That's better. You've lost a lot of blood and Doc Wallace says it'll take a few days for you to get back on your feet."

"How long have I been here?"

"Two days."

"Reckon he's right." Matt nods. "I'll try to stay out of your way."

"The only place you're going to stay is in that bed, besides you have to be well by Saturday week," she smiles down at him.

"Why Saturday week?"

"You've forgotten already?"

"Forgotten what?"

"Last night you asked me to the fall dance."

Matt looks at her, shock showing on his face.

"I did what?"

"You, Sir, asked me to go to the fall dance with you and I accepted."

"I don't remember." Matt shakes his head.

"Do you wish to withdraw your invitation? After all you were feeling poorly." She smiles, her white teeth sparkling even in the dimness of the room. Matt takes in her broad forehead and widespread eyes that bore into a man, unabashed when she looks at him. Her face is encased in long auburn locks. He has to admit, she was a thing of beauty. Until now, he really did not perceive just how beautiful she really is.

"No, a gentleman never takes back an invitation to a lady. Saturday night it is."

"Good, now I'll get you some broth, doctor's orders."

"Miss Howard." Matt watches as she turns back to him gracefully. "Were you going to starve me into submission?"

"My name is Kate and if that what it took, yes, I think I would have." She laughs, her voice soft and rich. "Would you have given up easily?"

"Yes ma'am, I believe I would have." Matt smiles. "Would you send Jim Cloud up here?"

"You are not going to try and get up?"

"No ma'am, but I do need to talk with him."

A short while later, Matt hears the sound of Cloud's boots clanking on the stairs. The jingle bobs, hanging from his spurs, make a ringing noise as he walks. Cloud knocks and enters to find Matt awake.

"Pull up a chair."

"How are you feeling this morning?" Cloud takes in Matt's haggard appearance. "Bailey came to the barn and said you asked for me to come up."

"Weak and sore and yes, we need to talk." Matt tries to rise up on his pillows.

"Imagine so, the wound wasn't bad, just a nasty tear but with all that riding you lost a lot of blood."

"That's what the Doc told Miss Howard. Where's Tin Cup?"

"I've got him watching the stallion."

"Good. Something is funny about this whole horse stealing deal and this man they call the General; can't figure it." Matt rubs his chin. "But, until we do figure out what's going on, we need to be very alert."

Cloud nods. "One thing for sure, they weren't the smartest bunch of horse thieves I ever had dealings with."

"Jim, I want you to send for Hob right away."

"It's already took care of, what else?"

"Watch for strangers. Look for anything odd or out of place. This wasn't just horse stealing. I just feel there's got to be more to it."

"I'll keep my nose to the ground."

"What about the stallion, is he out of sight?"

"Tin Cups got him in a stall at the livery barn, but you can't keep much a secret in this town." Cloud grins. "Nosiest bunch of people I ever met."

"Good, have Tin Cup stay with him until Hob gets here."

Cloud stands up and looks down at Matt. "We'll take care of things, you just get back on your feet. I'll be back after dark."

Cloud passes Kate on the stairs as she's bringing Matt a tray of soup and hot coffee, laced with honey.

Easing him up on his pillows she starts to feed him.

"Miss Howard, Kate, I can feed myself." Matt protests.

"Yes, you can, but not tonight."

"You are a strong willed woman."

She smiles. "People have said that."

Matt wakes with a start, as the first rays of sunlight cross his face. Sensing someone in the room with him, he peers into the dimness of the morning. A figure stirs, as the mattress under Matt moves.

"It's just me, Masta Matt."

"Hob, is that you?"

"Yassa."

"Good to see you. You made good time."

"Yas suh, picked me up a fresh horse at Miss Gorman's Ranch. She's a nice lady, said to tell you to hurry and get well."

"Yes, she is."

"Met Miss Howard downstairs. She told me to come up here and wait for you to wake up. She's a real nice lady too."

"Hobnail, they are all nice ladies." Matt shakes his head and grins, knowing exactly what Hob is getting at.

"Pretty, too."

"Hob!"

"Yas Suh."

"We may have problems."

"What problems? Jim Cloud said you got the horses back, ceptin' them two good mares, he said the stallion is fine."

"We did that."

"Then what, Masta Matt?" Hob looks over toward Matt.

Matt went over the events of the last few days and the recovering of the stallion. The part about the General perks Hob's attention. He studies Matt's face intently as he finishes his story and settles back in bed.

"The stallion got himself stolen, and a General puttin' them up to it." Hob muses thoughtfully to himself.

"The General with the horse and money, could it be the same man?" Matt studies carefully. "I thought we killed him at Malvern Crossing."

"I seen him fall, but lead was flying so fast and hot that day I didn't look at him no more, just kept shootin' till they were all dead or runnin'."

"Hob, if this is the same General, how could he have followed us this far from the east and the war?"

"I don't know, he sure 'nuff looked dead to me, but if he wasn't kilt maybe he did follow us out here."

"How could he know who we were or where we went?"

"We left wounded men that day. Maybe they wrote letters and this General found them. I don't know but anything's possible."

"The red headed one was positive I wasn't Tillman and," Matt stops and looks off, "he described Cage to me."

"He described Masta Cage?"

"Hob, something's going on and I don't know what it is, so be on the lookout at the ranch. Keep the men close until I get back." Matt studies the dark face. "Send word to Cage. Have him keep a close watch. Make sure he understands to be careful until we find out what's going on; make him understand."

"Yes, Sir."

"I want you to get the stallion and mare and head home right now," Matt looks up at Hob. "And you take care of yourself."

"But, Masta Matt, you ain't able to fend for yourself."

"I'll keep Jim Cloud here and you take Tin Cup with you."

"Yassir."

"Fort up until I get back. Keep the stallion corralled and keep the hands close."

"I'll tend to things." Hob stands up and slowly turns to the door. Walking back to the bed, "Masta Matt, maybe Jim Cloud could go back to the ranch and I could wait here."

"Hob," Matt looks hard at the big man then grins, "you've got April and the boys, I'll be along directly."

"Yassa, we'll be lookin' fer you."

Kate comes into the room after Hob leaves and places some new clothes on the bed. Walking to the window she looks out, as Tin Cup and Hob ride out of town, leading the mare and stallion. "You know your friend didn't want to leave you."

"I know."

"You two been friends long?"

"We had the same mother." Matt watches her face to see her reaction. When none came he continued. "Hob's mother nursed me after my Ma died at childbirth."

She walks to the bed and picks up the new clothes. "Now, Mister Tillman, we'll slip these on you and you'll be able to get up when you feel stronger."

"I'll do it, Kate." Matt reaches for the clothes.

Smiling mischievously, she walks to the door and turns. "Well, if you need help."

"I won't." Matt heard her laughing all the way downstairs then grins himself. He found out, she was quite a woman and one with a sense of humor.

The General is in a fit of rage. His lookout, Fen Blalock, posted in Elk Springs, just rides in with the word. Tillman's riders are in town. One wounded man stayed in town, the others rode back to the Elkhorn. Worse, the lookout reports, Red, all of his men, and the stallion, dead. Blalock failed to recognize one of the horses being led by Hob out of town as the stallion, he reported as dead. He had never seen the horse and Hob was careful leaving town to keep the stallion hemmed between the other horses.

"Are you sure the horse is dead?"

"That's what the Elkhorn rider told in the saloon. Said Red and the boys killed all the horses after they became too sore footed to keep up. Fellow named Cloud did the talking, looks like he's half injun."

The General's face is livid red at the words. "What else?" He growls.

"Said, they killed three of the horse thieves and hung the fourth. The way this feller told it, the wounded man in town did most of the killing." Blalock watches the General's face. "Never laid eyes on him, shot up pretty bad I reckon. This Cloud feller said the wounds were bad and the man couldn't get out of bed by himself."

"What's his name?"

"Fellow didn't say, just that he was an Elkhorn rider," Blalock replies. "I listened to him talk in the saloon and then hurried back here with the news. Figured you'd want to hear it right away so I didn't wait to hear more."

"Then nothing was said about us?"

"Nothing, they just think it was horse thieves."

"Why'd the fool kill that stallion? He was one of a kind. There will never be another like him. I took him from a southern plantation, outside Vicksburg. You might say it was a government requisition," the General sneers. "But, we still have business there, Mister Tillman and my money."

"Yes sir, General." Blalock is spooked. The General looks crazed to him with his eyes bloodred and his face puffed out."

"Go back to town. Find out exactly where this wounded man is, and bring word the day before the dance." The General paces toward the door then turns and walks back. "Is Payne still in town?"

"Yes Sir, General, he's keeping a watch on the Elkhorn rider," Blalock answers nervously.

"You have your orders," the General said, dismissing him.

Sergeant Walls stands beside the General and watches Blalock ride off toward Elk Springs. "The stallion dead, Sir, it's hard to believe."

"Red was an idiot." The cigar curls smoke as the man peers out the window. "If he hadn't killed the horse, we might have recovered him. It's too late now but Mister Tillman will pay, I'll grant you that. He'll pay and I'll have my revenge."

"Yes sir and your money. Are we going to wait like we planned?"

"The money be hanged. I want Tillman. We will wait Sergeant but with one slight change." Puffing hard on the cigar, the big man repeats himself. "One slight change."

"And what will that be, Sir?"

"You will take Private Long into Elk Springs the night of the dance and take care of this gentleman that killed Red and our men. At the same time, I will tend to Mister Tillman at the place Red called the Divide."

The Sergeant grins. "Yes Sir, it'll be my pleasure. I just wish that black was there." Rubbing his scared face he looks at the General. "I owe him."

"They owe both of us. Our luck was bad the day we happened to run accidentally into that reb patrol. All we was wanting to do was quit the army and head west. Yes, Sergeant, we had everything and we lost it all. Now, it's Mister Tillman's turn."

Matt stands in front of the store talking to Kate and Howard Bailey. It was five days since Cloud brought him into town covered in blood. Still weak, he remains in bed or sitting in a chair upstairs as long as he can stand it. Kate hovers over him like a sitting hen. Nevertheless, sore side and all, he is determined to get back to the ranch. The General is always on his mind and he is worried about the Elkhorn. Did the man actually exist? Would he make another try for the stallion?

Seeing Cloud approaching with the horses, Kate looks worriedly at Matt. "Are you sure you can ride that far?"

"I'll make it."

"At least take a buckboard."

"The bumping, over those rough roads, would be worse." Matt reaches out his hand to Bailey then to Kate. "Thanks, both of you, for everything."

Ignoring his outstretched hand Kate stands on her tiptoes and kisses him. "You owe me at least one," she laughs, as he looks around blushing.

"Yes Ma'am, I expect I do, and a lot more, thank you."

"Well, you know where I live."

"I'll see you Saturday night."

"Promise?"

"Guarantee it. I'll be there."

Cloud leads the horses up to the store and crowds Matt's gelding close to the porch. Hanging his gun belt around the horn he nods at Cloud. "Sides still a little sore to strap it on."

"I imagine," Cloud grins.

Easing onto the gelding, Matt tips his hat to Kate and starts down the street at a walk, unaware of being watched closely by two men standing in the saloon's doorway. Matt and Cloud reach the edge of town when one of the men mounts and follows slowly behind them.

"I guess that's the way you treat a dangerous man," Abigail teases, coming from the store. "Kissing him in front of the whole town."

"What?" Kate is paying little attention to her sister as she is engrossed in watching the man following Matt. Could he be one of the General's men Matt was worried about? Fear clutches at her, as she looks to where Matt and Cloud disappear from sight and the rider still following them. "Bailey, take that horse and go bring Matt back." She nods towards a black gelding tied, to the hitch rail.

"But Sis, that's Luke Thomas' horse."

"I'll fix it, go!"

Bailey lit a shuck out of town, catching Matt and Cloud before they had ridden far. "Sis said she wants you to come back to town."

He hollers, reining the black in next to Matt's roan gelding. "What does she want?"

"Said for you to come back and that's all I know."

Shrugging, Matt turns back to Elk Springs. The rider, Bailey passed in her hurry to catch Matt, is nowhere to be seen.

Riding up to the store, Matt starts to dismount when Kate stops him. Quickly explaining why she had sent Bailey after them, Kate touches Matt's leg. She waves, as they turn back, toward the Elkhorn.

Cloud easily picks up the fresh tracks of the lone horseman but the tracks suddenly turn off into the trees heading east.

Matt studies the tracks awhile and looks over at Cloud. "Follow him a little ways, see where he's heading then catch up."

"Yes, Sir."

"Jim, watch your back side."

"I'll catch up to you, just ride slow and take care of that side." Cloud turns his horse onto the small trail heading due east.

Matt covers nearly five miles and is on the Gorman range when Cloud catches up. "Something funny alright, when he figured out he was being followed he started getting shy about leaving tracks."

"How shy?"

"Turned off, into the brush. He sure didn't want to be followed." Cloud rolls himself a smoke and offers Matt the makings.

Shaking his head, Matt kicks the roan. "Let's head on in."

"I can find him and bring him in."

Matt studies a minute, then, shakes his head. "No, it's not a job for one man. If he is the General's man, that outfit could be anywhere."

Matt and Cloud only stop long enough, at the Gorman spread, to say their hello's and thank Miss Gorman and Pauly for lending them the fresh horses. Matt is weaker than he thought and wants to get on to the ranch. Supper and a bed are going to look mighty good by the time they ride into the Elkhorn.

Shrugging deeper into his sheepskin lined coat, he pulls his hat lower and hunkers down in his saddle. The north wind is picking up and it's turning colder. Matt thinks of the warm room above the store and of Kate then a smile comes to his face. She's quite a woman.

"It'll snow before morning." Cloud blows out a cloud of smoke. "I'm surprised it's held off this long. We're way past due, for a ripsnorter."

"How do you know?"

"I can smell it," Cloud said, matter of factly. "Is your side hurting bad?"

"Well, I'll be glad to get off this horse." Snow or not, it is getting colder with each mile they travel. Matt can feel the cold penetrating into his boots. The easy swaying of the horse makes Matt doze off, as he is not aware of their surroundings, until Cloud shakes his shoulder. Looking around at the corrals, he blinks in surprise. With Cloud's help, he eases slowly from the saddle onto the frozen ground.

"You go on in, I'll unsaddle."

"This time, I'll take you up on it." Matt turns unsteadily toward the smaller cabin when he feels a strong pair of hands take hold of him. "Hob, is that you?"

"Yassa, Masta Matt."

"Just plain Matt! I swear Hob, you've got to be the most stubborn varmint I ever knew and lately I've been running into a lot of them."

"I can't hold you a light to go by and you knows it." Hob laughs as he pushes his way into the warmth of the small cabin.

April and the boys, quickly surround Matt as Hob eases him into one of the new kitchen chairs. Matt looks at the smaller table that replaced the longer one that sat in the cabin.

As Matt eats, Hob fills him in on the new bunkhouse and the work that was finished, while he was away. Hob made the trip to the lower Elkhorn to warn Cage about the General, and to be on the lookout for any strange riders. Cage promised to keep a sharp eye out and come to the ranch to talk with Matt as soon as he returns to the Elkhorn.

Cloud knocks on the cabin door and steps inside, putting Matt's saddlebags on the floor. He just set the gear down, when May Bell throws herself into his arms causing Cloud considerable embarrassment. However, by his smile, anyone can tell he is a happy man.

"Has Cage had any problems?"

"No Suh, says everything be quiet down there."

"That it?"

"Except I seen Miss Jessie and the boy." Hob laughs. "He be a handful, just like you, and he look like you too.

Matt looks down at his coffee cup, "Is she happy?"

"Yassuh, she seems to be."

"Well, I guess I'll ease down to the bunkhouse and see the men." Matt stands stiffly and puts on his hat. As Cloud and Hob start to follow him he waves them back to their chairs and opens the door. "Goodnight, thanks for the supper, April."

Matt rolls and lights a cigarette as he stands, looking off into the darkness. The wind whips across his face but he seems not to notice. For the first time, his stomach does not ache, when he thinks of her. He smiles and he is actually thankful that she found happiness. His thoughts turn to Kate, standing framed against the window. Saturday night seems a long time away.

A light snow starts coming down as he walks toward the bunkhouse. Turning his collar up, to ward off the chilling wind, he makes his way, silently, toward the light. Inside, the men are gathered around a small table where they have a poker game going in full swing. Matchsticks are piled up high in front of Sam, and his smile is as big.

Entering, Matt shakes hands and answer questions as the Elkhorn men usher him into the room, as they are genuinely overjoyed to see him back.

His eyes roam the room as everyone settles back to their game of cards. Bunks, double tiered line both walls, enough to sleep twenty riders. Several chairs line the walls and surround the long table that once occupied the smaller cabin. Pegs were drilled into the upright cedar posts that surround the wall with hats, clothes, chaps, and gun belts, everything hanging orderly from them. A smaller room was built into the east side of the bunkhouse that holds the cookstove and several cabinets. Matt is amazed, Sam piped water into the small kitchen from a spring out back.

Rollie, acting as cook, grins as he pulls a cork from the pipe, letting water flow into the cistern. "Sam's fixed us up with all the comforts, Boss."

"I see."

"Wait until you see the big house."

"Sam, you're a wonder." Matt is amazed that so much was accomplished in such a short time. "This is some of the finest work I've ever seen and it was done so quickly. I can't believe you did it all."

"I had help and lots of it Matt." Sam walks to the kitchen. "The boys worked every night while you were away."

Matt looks around the room at the beaming faces. "Thank you, all of you, a man couldn't ask for a better crew."

"What's next Boss?" Sam asks."

"First, a couple days off!" The men let out with a rebel yell. "Then we'll start on some corrals."

"Snow and a hard freeze is coming, Boss," Chink speaks up from the table. "Don't figure we've got more than a day or two."

"We'll cut and snake the timber down this winter, buck 'em into rails and be ready come warm up."

"Sounds good," Chink agrees.

"You boys have got yourselves a bonus coming, and a couple days off to spend it." Matt lights a cigarette from the coal oil light. "See Hob in the morning and he'll pay you and let you go in pairs to town." Matt neglects to tell the men Hob couldn't count money but he wants them to get used to taking orders from him. He will count the money out and let Hob give it to them so they will never know. Hob is a partner in the Elkhorn and one of the few men Matt trusts completely. He has to take it easy as white men still do not like the idea of blacks giving orders.

The men whoop with joy. It's been awhile since they went to town and with money in their pockets to spend.

"Remember, we still have horses and cattle to feed when ya'll get back to the ranch."

Chapter 9

Two days rest and good food works wonders on Matt's constitution. His strength is returning. Even his side quit throbbing with every twist and turn.

He's watching Sam, Rollie, and Hob splitting cedar poles for the new corral when he notices several riders coming from the lake. Steam blows from their horse's nostrils and clods of fresh snow fly from their hooves, as they lope toward the ranch buildings. Too far to recognize the riders, Matt alerts Hob and the men. He retreats to the big house to buckle on his gun belt. Stepping stiffly back out on the porch, he gazes toward the approaching horses and recognizes the large frame of Cage leading the men.

Walking toward the corrals, away from April and the boys, Matt waits. Pulling his horse in easy, on the slick ground, Cage gazes around the ranch grounds, taking in the new house and bunkhouse. "You have been busy."

"My men have." Matt stares easily, at his brother. "You're a long ways from home. What brings you here?"

"Come to check on you and see what this is all about."

"Alright, come into the house." He doesn't miss the frown on Palette's face, as he turns toward the new ranch house.

Matt pours Cage a cup of coffee, as the older Tillman walks admiringly through the big rooms. Motioning for Cage to sit down, Matt finds a chair across from him.

"You have done a magnificent bit of work here, brother."

"Sam Basset did most of it. He's quite a carpenter." Matt didn't miss the word brother, as Cage spoke to him.

"Yes, he is." Cage agrees. "Maybe you'll lend him to me. I can sure use him for a spell. My place could use some upkeep. Uncle Matt wasn't much on house repair."

"We'll see. Now, why have you come here? What's on your mind?"

"Hob came to the ranch. He told me you had been shot and your horses stolen. He gave us the warning about this General, so when I heard you were home, I came to see if you needed anything and if you knew anything else." Cage sips on his coffee.

"No, to both questions, but I thank you for coming." Matt refills the coffee cups as he looks across at Cage. "I won't apologize Cage but in time maybe we can become brothers again, but it'll take a little time."

"We're still brothers, brother, but you take all the time you need."

Hob eases into the room and looks closely at the two brothers, sitting at the table. No animosity exists between them, instead there is a peaceful calm over the room and it almost seems like old times, before the war.

"Hob, you ready to come work for me yet?" Cage smiles. "Matt's probably working you too hard."

"I would Masta Cage but who would look after Masta Matt?" Hob grins. "You knows he be needin' a baby-sitter."

Cage laughs aloud, making the walls resound with his voice. "You've got a point there."

Matt smiles as he said, "Many times I've started to run him off, but he happens to be married to the best biscuit maker in the south."

"Where are April and the boys?" Cage questions Hob. "I'd like to see them before I leave."

Hob smiles. "She be at the cabin fixin' dinner. You and your men stay and eat with us and you can visit with them." Matt fixes Hob with a hard stare, which Cage does not miss.

"Not this time, maybe next, wouldn't want to overstay my welcome."

"No, you'll stay and you're welcome." Matt speaks up. "April would be furious at me if you left without having dinner and seeing her."

"Alright Matt, I would like that."

Cage's men ate in the bunkhouse while Cage and Matt eat dinner at the cabin. The small talk takes them back to the times of their youth, in the Deep South. The boys stare, bug eyed, as Hob tells them of the pranks the brothers did in their youth. April frowns from where she sits. Such talk might put ideas in the youngster's heads and they are getting wild enough already.

Bidding April and Hob good-bye, Cage looks down at Matt from his horse and smiles. "Thank you, brother, for the dinner." Turning his gelding, he starts to ride away then turns back. "Matt, you come see the boy anytime you've a mind to and you'll be welcome."

Matt watches as Cage rides toward home.

Only Palette stays, riding over to where Matt and Hob are standing. "You stay away from the Gorman spread."

"Says who?" Matt looks coldly at the man.

"Me."

"I'll take it under consideration."

"You do that, Mister Tillman." Palette wheels his horse and follows the others, his back ramrod straight.

"Someday, I'll have to kill that man." Matt looks at Hob and spits.

"Yassuh, you will."

Hob and Matt watch, as Palette catches up with the others, and the riders disappear into the cedars and pines at the lake. Somehow, his brother's visit helped bring them back a little closer as a family. Jessie made her choice. She was lost to him now, somehow he resolved himself to losing her and she seems to be out of his system for good. No, he can never forget her but the thought of her walking or dancing with Cage will no longer bring a rush of jealous rage upon him. No, this way is best for her and for the boy.

Matt's thoughts drift to the boy. Cage is his father and a good man. Matt always admired him, as he had no other man. He'd make the boy a better father than he would have. Yes, things are working out and in time, he will forget.

Smiling, he thinks of Kate. He is eager for Saturday to come, for he will get to see her. He did not realize it until now but he wants to see her. He can still smell her perfume as he pictures her in his mind. Her beautiful smile, poise, and grace, plus her strength, yes, she is quite a woman.

Walking, to where the men are splitting rails for the new corrals, Matt picks up some wedges and a splitting maul and selects him a cedar log to start on. Yes, they say time works wonders, he will find out.

Sam eyed him dubiously. "Boss, you sure you are up to swinging an axe?"

"We'll see." Matt nods. "Need to start earning my keep around here."

Sam leans on his double bitted axe and looks longingly, toward the mountains. "Bet old Chink and Rollie are snookered already."

Matt sinks the axe into a log. "Wouldn't doubt it a bit."

It is almost midnight, as Rollie stands bellied up to the oaken bar in the saloon, and Sam was right, he was snookered, loaded to the gills. Fen Blalock, the General's lookout in town, eases up beside him. Bill Payne, the other lookout, followed the Elkhorn riders out a few days earlier to see where they went but did not come back yet. Blalock told the General he was still in town. Well, he was when Blalock rode to inform the General of what he learned. Glancing sideways at the newcomer, Rollie's eyes barely focus on the full bottle of whiskey the man sits down on the bar.

"Evening cowboy, how about a drink?" Rollie eyed the bottle greedily. No one ever accused him of being a cowboy before, but for a free drink, this newcomer can call him anything he wants. Rollie starts to speak but his words slur or his tongue is swollen. Nodding his head groggily, he finally manages to get out a yes answer.

"You ride for the Elkhorn Ranch?" Rollie nods. "Best outfit around."

"That's what I've been hearing. Also heard you practically built it yourself." Blalock was laying it on thick.

"I did my fair share." The drunk man acknowledges.

Blalock fills the empty glasses and studies Rollie. "Thought I might try to land a job with your outfit. Heard Cage Tillman is a good man to work for."

"Wouldn't know about that."

"You wouldn't?" Blalock sets his drink back down, curious.

"I thought you worked for Tillman and the Elkhorn Ranch."

"I do work for the Elkhorn." Rollie's words become more slurred. "But, I work for Matt Tillman."

"Matt Tillman, who's he?"

"Cage Tillman's brother."

"Brother?" Blalock tries to remember the things he heard from the General's talks. "Was this Matt Tillman the one in the war?"

"Yep, good soldier too, he was a Colonel, so I've been told."

"Use to have a black man with him, didn't he?"

"That'll be old Hob." Rollie sways, leaning heavily on the bar for support. "He's still with us out at the ranch."

Blalock rubs his jaw and looks into the bar mirror. Red was wrong; dead wrong. "Was that Matt Tillman who left town a few days ago and the man who killed the horse thieves?"

"Yep, one and the same. Hung some, shot some, and got the stallion back." "The stallions alive?" Blalock is astounded. "You don't say. Bay, thoroughbred looking horse, wasn't he?"

Rollie turns drunkenly toward the man. "Say, you sure ask a lot of questions."

"Forget it, here's the bottle. Enjoy yourself friend."

"Well thank you. Come out to the Elkhorn and I'll put in a good word for you. Blalock is already halfway to the door when Rollie realizes he is alone. Looking at the bottle he grins and pulls it to him.

Blalock looks at the timepiece on the wall, before he steps through the doors and out onto the boardwalk, into the cold north wind. He does not relish a long cold ride in the middle of the night but he has no choice. Tomorrow is Saturday and the General has to know he is after the wrong man.

Flipping his cigarette into the street, he walks towards the livery. The cabin is a good four, probably five hour, hard ride in the dark. He knows he will have to leave now to arrive before the General pulls out to ambush Tillman. The rancher doesn't matter to Blalock, but money does. He knows the General will pay well for this information.

Rousting the hostler from his bunk, Blalock buttons on his chaps and overcoat, while the man is saddling his horse. Wrapping a wool scarf around his hat, to keep the wind from blowing it off, he pulls on his heavy, wool lined gloves.

"Man you're crazy going out on a night like this."

"I won't be gone long," Blalock lies. "Sides, I'm dressed for it."

"Better not go at all. We got us a bad storm coming." The hostler tries to argue him out of going. "You ain't dressed near warm enough."

"I'll be back." Blalock mounts and waits for the man to swing the double doors open. "If I put anything else on, this old hoss couldn't tote me."

Shaking his head, he yells, as Blalock disappears into the wind. "Good luck, you'll need it, you dang fool."

The stable man was right. Blalock hardly left town when the snow starts coming in swirls. The gelding ducks his head and walks into the blowing snow and icy wind. Blalock considers turning back for town but the thinks of the General's money and it keeps him heading north, into the wind. The cold grips his arms and legs until he can hardly feel them.

Two hours pass and the snow is coming down harder. The trail he is following is obliterated with snow, and new to the country, Blalock is unsure of the trail. Pulling the horse to a halt he tries to blow into his gloves, to bring feeling back into his hands. He's cold and with the wrong turn he will be lost. Death is only one mistake away. He is not prepared to spend the night outside in this blizzard.

"We can't travel in this mess hoss. I hope you can get us back to town." Blalock mumbles, giving the horse his head, hoping the gelding will head back to the livery for some feed.

Three hours later and almost dawn, Blalock staggers, half frozen into the livery. The horse brought him straight back to town and a warm stall.

"Well, you said you wouldn't be long." The hostler is surprised to see the man and horse. "I'll take care of the horse; you get to the stove."

"Man it's cold out there." Blalock's teeth chatter as he speaks. "You were right. I should have listened to you."

"Yep, but it'll blow over before long and then it'll just be cold." The hostler looks at Blalock. "You're lucky that horse brought you home."

"Reckon I was at that."

"Anyhoo, folks will still be able to come in for the dance." The hostler grins.

"Travel in this mess, just for a dance?" Blalock looks dubious.

The hostler turns the gelding into a stall and walks to the potbellied stove. "Not just a dance, it's the biggest shindig we have all year. I'll guarantee a little cold won't stop them from coming."

"I've been outside and I wouldn't ride ten feet, for ten dances." Blalock spit.

"Maybe not, but you rode five hours last night for something."

Blalock tries to grin. "You're right partner. Some people are pretty foolish."

"You gonna be here for the dance?"

"No, hate to admit it but I've got some more riding to do."

"You're joking? In this mess?" The hostler laughs.

"Feller at the saloon last night told me I can land a job at the Elkhorn Ranch." Blalock isn't exactly lying, maybe stretching the truth a bit. "I need to work. Some money will sure come in handy."

"Doubt they'll be hiring this time of year."

"Well, won't hurt to ride out and see. You said it was gonna clear up."

"It is, but I don't see why you want to go to all that trouble when there's no need."

"What do you mean?"

"Shucks mister, they'll all be in here this afternoon for the dance, all the ranchers. They wouldn't miss this hoedown for nothing."

"Feller said they weren't coming." Blalock lies again.

"That right?"

"How far is it to this place they call the Elkhorn Divide?"

"About seven miles due north, can't miss it as the road splits. Take the right road to the ranch, the left just turns into a cattle trail mostly."

"Seven miles."

The hostler nods. "Yes sir, just about to the inch."

Blalock looks over at his horse. "He okay after that ride last night?"

"Fine, he's a stout horse."

"Well, feed him heavy, I'll grab some breakfast and be back."

The hostler shakes his head. "You're sure a glutton for punishment. I'll have him ready whenever you are."

Seven miles, Blalock thought, as he tramps through the drifts of snow covering the board sidewalk. It didn't snow much but the wind left it piled in places, while in other spots the ground is bare.

It is coming daylight. The ride last night tired him but he has no choice. He must get word to the General or saddle up and ride south to a warmer and healthier climate. No, the money is here and he wants it, he earned it. Pushing inside the small, noisy café, Blalock finds an empty table and sits down. Letting his eyes rove over the room, he notices the Elkhorn rider from last night, sitting with another man. The man was probably too drunk to remember him, as neither of the men look his way. Blalock eats his breakfast and downs the hot coffee in silence, all the while dreading the long, cold ride north.

Hob harnesses and hitches the team to the lighter wagon as soon as breakfast is finished. Extra blankets and a basket of food are piled into the wagon atop the ample buffalo robes that cover the floor. April and May Bell bring hot pies to the wagon and place them carefully beside the blankets.

"You and April better change your minds. They say it's a real party," Matt says to Hob, as he cinches up his saddle.

"No Sir, better not, the youngest boy is coming down with the croop. We best keep him home this time."

"Alright, we'll be back tomorrow, barring we don't get snowed in."

"You take your time and spend some time with Miss Howard," Hob grins. "She sure is a nice lady."

"Hob, I swear." Matt shakes his head.

Jim Cloud and May Bell emerge from the cabin with the last of the pies. Cloud was apprehensive about taking May Bell into town, but Matt finally convinces him to go. The country is young yet, and an Indian, even a half

Indian with a white woman, will not sit well with the town's people. Matt convinces Cloud that May Bell can pass as half Arapaho with her dark hair and complexion. Cloud is still shaking his head no, when May Bell comes out of the backroom in one of April's new dresses that Matt bought in town. The happy smile on her face did the trick, but he is still worrying.

"Hope we don't cause a commotion."

"We're going in to have a good time, now get in." Matt motions at the wagon. "I'll take care of any commotions."

Cloud and May Bell climb onto the seat, and wrap up in a buffalo robe, against the cold wind. Tin Cup, Sam, and Lonnie Hall come out of the bunkhouse, all duded up in their Sunday best. All but Tin Cup, climb into the bed of the wagon. After weeks on the ranch and, as Tin Cup put it, dry as a sun-baked fish out of water, they are ready for town and the dance. Wrapping themselves in buffalo robes, they whoop and holler for Tin Cup to climb in.

"Not on ya'lls life. I ain't about to be jarred all the way to town." Tin Cup leads his paint gelding from the corral already saddled. The others laugh as the old cowboy climbs into the saddle and rests the Sharps rifle across his lap.

"Old man, you're gonna freeze solid by the time we reach town, and me and old Sam will have to do all the dancing and drinking," Lonnie cackles. "But, don't fret, I'll take care of the women and drinking stuff for you. Besides you're a mite too old for such doings."

Tin Cup glares, his eyebrows bobbing up and down. "Why you young whippersnapper!" The rest trailed off, into the blowing wind.

Matt stands alongside his gelding and looks at Hob and April. "Can I bring you anything from town?"

From the cabin door he hears Isaac holler. "Candy."

"Candy it is, for you and your brother." Matt grins. "April, what can I bring you? How about a new dress or bonnet?"

"Have a good time for me, like we use to do back home." She smiles remembering. "You deserve a good time Matthew."

"Then you do remember the dances we use to have?" Matt smiles. She was the only one that ever called him Mathew, since Hob's mother passed.

"Yassa Mister Matthew, I do, and I remember you out dancin' everyone." April laughs.

"We had some high old times when Pa was alive, didn't we?"

"Yassa, we sure 'nuff did."

Matt mounts and starts after the wagon. "I'll see ya'll tomorrow." He throws back at her, over his shoulder. His mind wanders back to Virginia and the barn dances they use to attend. Yes, those were good times.

Vickie Gorman, has hot coffee waiting for the Elkhorn partygoers, as they pull into the ranch. Her team of high stepping grays, are hitched to a fringed top surrey.

Matt half expects to see Wylie Palette waiting with her but then remembers Palette will ride into town with Cage and Jessie.

Cody, Pauly, and several ranch hands lead their horses from the barn. Matt can smell the lilac water on them from where he stands. He wrinkles his nose, thinking they must have bathed in the stuff as strong as the smell is.

Gulping the hot coffee, as fast as they can, everyone hands the cups back to Vickie quickly, so they can get on into town. Looking at Matt questioningly, she frowns when he stays mounted and then speaks sharply to Pauly. Tying his horse to the surrey, the foreman climbs in and takes the lines. Vickie shoots one last glance at Matt, and climbs into the surrey.

Tin Cup takes his place in the lead as the gray team pulls the surrey toward town at a good clip.

The wind blows hard all the way, but the sky is clear as they enter town about midafternoon. Elk Springs is crowded with wagons and saddle horses. Matt figures everyone in the country is in attendance. Kate said nothing will stop the dance, outside of a blizzard, and it had better be a big one.

Pulling the teams up to the livery, Matt looks at the full corrals and wonders if there is any room left for their horses.

"I'll check." Tin Cup hands his reins to Matt and walks into the stable.

Dismounting, Matt walks over to Cloud and May Bell sitting perched on the wagon seat. "Just to be safe, May Bell, maybe you better stick to talking Arapaho this time while we're in town."

"I like that idea." Cloud seems relieved.

Tin Cup returns, motioning Matt and Pauly inside. "Hostler's got a covered corral out back."

"That'll work." Both men agree.

"Twenty-five bucks for the night," Tin Cup winces, as he looks at Matt's face. "It's for the whole corral."

"I don't want to buy it, I just want to rent the dang thing for the night."

"Feeds extra too, Matt."

"Crap." Matt shakes his head looking back at the expectant faces, waiting in the wagon. "We'll take it, but you tell him no more horses in with ours."

"Yes, Sir." Tin Cup heads back to the livery, while Matt and the rest start unsaddling the horses. Turning them into the large corral, the riders watch, as the horses lay their ears back and kick a little, establishing their pecking order.

"Funny thing, ain't it Boss?" Cloud watches the horses bluffing one another.

"What's that Jim?"

"Horses are kinda like people. They know who they can whip and who they can't, and they leave alone, the one they're not sure of."

"You're right about that." Matt agrees. "Never knew a man to jump on another feller, he wasn't sure he couldn't get the best of."

Matt looks up, to see Tin Cup motioning him into the barn. "What now, more money?" He wonders aloud. Walking into the livery and out of the wind, Matt sees Tin Cup and the skinny, beanpole of a hostler, deep in conversation.

The inside of the barn is larger than it looks from the outside. Stalls run the length of each wall with another set running down the middle. From every stall, a horse sticks his head out. At the prices he quoted Tin Cup, the man is making a killing.

"Tell Mister Tillman what you just told me."

"You Matt Tillman?"

"That's me."

"Had never met you yet. I know your brother well." The skinny hostler looks Matt over closely, from head to foot.

Tin Cup frowns at the man and spits a stream of tobacco juice at his feet. "Tell him."

"I'm getting to it. Hold your horses." The hostler clears his throat. "All I said was, I told a fella named Blalock if he'd wait awhile, you'd be in town for the dance. Instead, like a dang fool, he was hardheaded and started out for the Divide this morning."

"Who's this Blalock?"

"Stranger, been hanging around town for a few days."

"What'd he want with me?"

"Somebody over at the saloon last night, said you'd give him a riding job, if he came to the Divide." The hostler shakes his head. "Fool started out last night, but come back this morning, almost froze to death."

"Why the Divide? Why not the ranch?"

"Couldn't answer that, but he was sure a glutton for punishment, just to land a job with you boys. I tried to warn him, Mister Tillman."

"Thanks. He should have taken your advice." Matt motions for Tin Cup and they walk outside, out of the man's hearing. Matt calls Jim Cloud over to where they were standing and relates what the hostler said.

"This Blalock must have been talking to Rollie and Chink." Tin Cup looks at Matt.

"Maybe."

"You reckon he was just a cowboy looking for a job?" Cloud rubs his hands against the cold.

"Could be, but would you ride out on a day like this to get a job?" Matt questions himself as much as the other two men.

Tin Cup grins. "Shucks, we rode all the way in for a dance, didn't we? Feller might have been broke and needing work bad."

"Matt, he's just one man. Hob's got Chink and Rollie with him at the ranch." Jim Cloud reasons. "You know Hob, ain't nobody gonna sneak in on him."

"Why did he ask directions to the Divide?"

"If you'll remember, that's the way you came in first." Tin Cup reminds Matt.

Finally Matt is argued out of heading back to the ranch, to check on things. Matt knows Cloud is right. Hob can take care of himself. Agreeing to stay for the dance, Matt shakes his head, as Tin Cup lets out with a yell and takes off for the saloon.

"Moves pretty good for a man his age, don't he?" Cloud laughs, helping May Bell down from the wagon.

Matt nods in agreement and watches as the old man disappears through the doors. Handing May Bell her bundled up new dress, he walks over to where Pauly and Vickie are standing. All the Gorman hands are hot on the heels of Tin Cup. The lure of the saloon beckoning them on.

Pauly grins, as Vickie watches her riders disappear into the saloon. "Beats me, how whiskey and cards can turn a man into a raving lunatic," she frowns.

"Yes ma'am," the foreman agrees.

"Well, Mister Tillman." Vickie looks at Matt. "Save me a dance."

"Miss Gorman." Matt tips his hat and watches the slow grin on Pauly's face spread as Vickie Gorman turns and walks toward the hotel, her shoulders squared and her head held high. Matt can tell she isn't exactly happy with him.

Matt gathers Cloud and May Bell, and ushers them down the street to Kate's store. As he enters the store, he watches as Kate walks toward him smiling.

"So, you did make it, Mister Tillman?"

"Thought it was Matt?" He grins. "And I told you I would."

"A gentleman's word, Matt?" She stops in front of him, putting out her hands. "It's good to see you. How is your side?"

"My side's fine. I don't know about the gentleman thing." He takes her hands in his and holds them for the longest.

"Do I get lots and lots of dances tonight?" She laughs.

"As many as you want, but I reckon there will be several wanting to dance with such a beautiful lady." Matt smiles, completely taken with her charm and wonderful smile.

Seeing May Bell, Kate looks curiously at Matt, asking Cloud to introduce her to the bashful girl. Taking her by the hand she leads her toward the stairs. Looking back down at Matt and Jim she smiles. "You two make yourself at home, us women have things to do."

"She knows," Cloud whispers, as soon as Kate was out of hearing.

Matt smiles. "Sure she does but she won't say anything."

The General has his men hiding, behind the boulders, where the Elkhorn Divide, split the ranches. Little does he know he is after the wrong Tillman. Red fed him the wrong information and Bill Payne did not learn anything different when he followed Matt and Jim Cloud from town. The big man has his riders concealed perfectly. He did not become a General by accident. He is an expert at deploying men for battle and his men are ready. The wagons and riders will not have a chance. Lighting a cigar, he leans back against a slab of rock and smiles. Cold and harsh, his eyes glitter like a madman. Something snapped in him. The stallion was dead and now even the money means nothing. Only killing Tillman, getting his revenge, means something to him.

"Private Thomas."

"Yes, Sir."

"I want Tillman alive if possible."

"And the rest, Sir?" The Private rode with the General all through the war. Following the General's orders to the letter is automatic to him. He learned long ago never to question the man.

"Kill them!"

"Sir, what about the woman?"

The General does not answer. Only his cold eyes answer his question as they look back at him through the morning chill. Nodding, he turns back to the men and passes the word. Tillman is not to be killed.

Blalock rode at a fast trot toward the place called the Elkhorn Divide. It's cold but at least the snow held off. The gelding is moving easily over the frozen ground. The caulks on his shoes, hold to the icy ground, preventing him from slipping. The horse is surefooted and as tough an animal as Blalock has ever owned. Cold as it is, he does not want the horse to heat up, causing him to sweat.

Blalock figures, he should almost be where the trail splits. The place the hostler calls the Divide. The wind is still blowing hard, sending its cold icy blast across the mountain. Pulling the horse in hard, he listens. Was that a gunshot? The wind in his ears, makes it almost impossible to tell if he actually heard a shot and from what direction it came. Kicking the gelding into a lope he tops a slow rise and pulls the horse to a stop. The reverberating sound of gunfire, lifts up to him, from the valley below. He is too late. Below in the valley, he can see men moving into view from where they were concealed from the oncoming Elkhorn riders.

Suddenly a man springs from behind the wagon, his pistol blazing. Blalock watches as two of the General's men go down, under a hail of bullets. The man then crumples and falls against the wagon. Blalock watches as they drag another unconscious man from the back of the wagon. Kicking the gelding forward, he arrives, as they finish hanging the man from a tree.

Rifles swing his way, lowering as they recognize him. The body of a woman slumps across the wagon seat, blood covering her face and calico dress. Her dark blue eyes gaze at him but they no longer see anything. Turning, he looks at the body swinging gently in the wind, blood soaks the man's shirt. He knows it was Cage Tillman. He had been scalped.

It is a useless, needless killing. Blalock is not a saint by any means, but shooting a woman makes him sick. The General is crazy. He has to be, to kill this way. Looking to where the man stands, he can see the satisfaction in his eyes, the face of insanity.

The General walks to where Blalock sits his horse. "You got here a little late Mister Blalock, missed all the fun." Then, he turns his attention on one of his men. "Private Thomas, I believe I gave orders for Mister Tillman to be spared."

"Yes, Sir, you did Sir, but he wouldn't surrender."

"No matter, I got him." The General looks to where Cage's body swings at the end of the rope.

"Yea, I got here too late General, too late to prevent a senseless killing."

"What's that supposed to mean? We got Tillman."

Blalock looks at the hanging man. "Yes Sir, you got Tillman alright. The wrong Tillman. That's Cage Tillman."

"What?" The General is at Blalock's horse in two strides, staring up at the man. "Dismount mister, I don't look up to a man when I speak to him."

"Yes, Sir." Blalock dismounts.

"Now, what do you mean, we got the wrong man?" The General points at Cage Tillman. "He admitted he was Tillman, but he was too far gone and stubborn to admit anything else."

"Figures, he's the brother to the one you're after, Matt Tillman."

"Matt Tillman!" The big man growls then steps closer to Blalock. "There were two of them?"

Blalock takes a step backward. The look in the big man's eyes, worry him. It's the look of a crazy man and crazy people always scared him. "Red was wrong about everything, wrong brother, wrong ranch, and even the stallion is still alive."

"What?" The General's eyes light up. "Are you sure?"

"I'm positive."

"Where is my horse?"

"I don't know for sure. I didn't want to ask too many questions, but he's alive, and so is the black man that you were asking about." Blalock shrugs. "I figure they're on the upper Elkhorn Ranch, west of here. Leastways, that's the way the hostler in town explained it to me."

For the first time Blalock notices the boy sitting alone beside a small pine tree. His face is tear stained from crying, but for now, he is quiet. He is surprised this madman didn't kill the boy too.

"Well now, this is interesting Mister Blalock, why did you wait so long to report?"

"Started out last night General, but the storm got so bad I had to turn back." Blalock studies the cigar protruding from the man's mouth.

"No matter, this will just bring the real Mister Tillman faster. Plus, I've another idea."

Blalock is curious. "What's that General?" He secretly hopes the new scheme does not involve him.

The big man walks behind the wagon and motions for Blalock to follow.

A small blood soaked man is propped up against the front wheel. "Him, he's still alive. Even shot to pieces, he stood up and killed two of my men then passed out, he's a tough one, a good soldier."

Blalock is amazed at the General, bragging on a man he just ambushed and probably killed. Wouldn't be surprised if the crazy devil comes out with a medal and pins the dang thing on the man.

Kneeling beside the man, Blalock leans over. "What's your name cowboy?"

The General laughs when the wounded man spits at Blalock. "I told you, he's a tough one."

Standing, Blalock turns to the General. "What's your plan, Sir?"

"I'm sending word by this gentleman," the General nods down at the wounded man, "and, to the right Mister Tillman this time, that I've got the boy, his nephew I reckon. I want my horse and money, or the boy, well, we don't have to be crude do we? I think Mister Tillman knows what I'll do."

"That ought to bring him." Blalock agrees. "Did this Tillman tell you anything?"

"Yes he did." The General laughs. "Told me where I could go. They raise them Tillmans tough around these parts."

"Sir, this man is in no shape to ride back to town."

"You'll drive him in Mister Blalock. Sergeant Walls and Private Long are already in town, left this morning. They're going to take care of the man that killed Red and our boys. He's supposed to be in town."

"That man, General, is Matt Tillman."

"Is he still in Elk Springs?"

Blalock shrugs. "Probably, everyone in the county is supposed to come in for the dance tonight."

"Haul this man in and dump him at this dance. If he is still able to talk, he'll tell Tillman what I want him to know. Bring Sergeant Walls back with you and tell him I said to leave Tillman alone, he's mine."

"Yes Sir, where do I meet you?"

Taking the wounded man by the hair the General pulls his head back, where he can look him in the face. "You stay alive, you hear me?"

"I'll stay alive." The words are barely audible but Blalock can hear the threat in them.

"Tell this Matt Tillman, I'll give him the boy when I get my property back."

Motioning at two men, the General steps back as they load the wounded man in the wagon and cover him with blankets. Before closing the end gate Blalock steps close to the man. "What's your name mister, in case you don't make it?"

The blue eyes roll upward and look at Blalock. "I'll make it, but just so you know who killed you, the name is Wylie Palette."

"I'll say one thing for you feller, you're salty as an old ridge back coon," the General laughs.

"What about the woman, General?" Blalock looks to where the woman is still lying on the seat.

"Toss her on the ground."

Blalock hears the man in the back moan, the word "no" coming from his lips. He figures the woman and the wounded man are probably kin, but no matter, they will both be dead by morning. Watching as the woman is laid out on the ground, under the man hanging from the tree, Blalock shakes his head. They could at least cover her with a blanket, but he was not about to argue with this lunatic.

The sooner he sheds this bunch the better he is going to like it. The whole blasted bunch is crazy and bloodthirsty to boot. He wonders if the war made them that way. If so, he was glad he missed it.

"Where should we meet you, Sir?"

"At the cabin, where we'll lead Mister Tillman into our trap," the big man laughs.

"I'm broke General, what about my money?"

Reaching into his pocket, the general pulls out a small sack of coins and tosses them to Blalock.

"Your forty pieces of silver, Sir," The General laughs again.

Blalock cannot figure out the man. He's always talking in riddles, forty pieces of silver, now what did that mean. He knows the General is highly educated, some military school back east, but he also knows the man is mad. Even so, he still has the cunning of a lobo wolf. Shivering slightly, under his heavy wool coat, Blalock ties his horse to the rear of the wagon, moving up front and climbs up to the seat. Placing a blanket over the already frozen blood of the woman, he looks once to where she lies and then clucks to the team.

Motioning a rider to him, the General nods at the wagon. "Follow our friend Mister Blalock and see that he finds his way to town then get back to the cabin quick."

"Yes, Sir and if he doesn't?"

"Then Private Payne, you have my permission to kill him."

Matt and Cloud sit by the store's potbellied stove and smoke while the women are in the kitchen putting the finishing touches on the food they are preparing for the dance. Cloud is nervous. Dancing is for whites and he feels out of place. May Bell will keep quiet but when she speaks, she will only speak in Arapaho, but he still feels uneasy. She doesn't look Indian to him but then he doesn't look half-white either. Matt only laughs at his nervousness and tells him not to worry. Looking at the clock, he reaches for his coat. It is almost five o'clock. The dance will begin at six.

The sun is already starting to cast dark shadows across the street, when Kate comes out of the kitchen, dressed for the dance. Matt's eyes cannot leave her. Abigail and May Bell are beside Kate and all three are dressed, their hair done up and beautiful, but Kate alone holds his eyes. Her beauty takes his breath.

Slipping close to him, Kate whispers in his ear. "May Bell's beautiful and no more Arapaho than I am."

"How did you know?"

"Well, for one thing, she told me," Kate laughs.

"You mean she speaks English?" Matt acts dumbfounded and smiles.

Slipping the sheepskin over the new, blue cotton shirt, he purchased only this afternoon at the store, Matt hurriedly turns toward the door. "Guess I'll bed down the horses right quick."

Cloud reaches to get his coat." I'll take care of the horses, Boss."

Matt motions him back, glancing over at Kate. "You stay with May Bell." Matt steps down off the porch, into the street, when he sees two men step from the saloon and start toward him. Being new here, most men in town are strangers to him, but these two catch his eye. Unbuttoning his coat, Matt watches as they separate in front of him. Hardly twenty feet separate them when they halt and pull their coats open. Matt can see the Cavalry holsters, strapped to the men's sides.

The clothes they wear are mismatched now, but Matt knows, at one time, they were union soldiers, probably some of this unknown General's men. The taller of the men grins wickedly at Matt, as he seems to recognize him.

"You remember me, Reb?" The taller man with the Sergeant stripes asks. "Do you remember this?" He points at the scar on his face.

Matt studies the blond headed man closely. "No, can't say that I do."

"Well Sir, I remember you and your black. The black in particular. You remember Malvern Crossing don't you?" The tall man takes another step forward. "You Johnnie Rebs shot us up pretty bad."

"I remember Malvern Crossing Sergeant, but that was a long time ago." Matt knows the man is going to draw. He can feel it.

The tall man spit. "Not long enough. Your black put this scar on my face and the General lost an arm. I had no idea it was you, the General sent me in here to kill. I didn't know you were a Tillman but I remember your ugly face."

"That was war."

"I'm gonna kill you, Reb, for the war and for our men you killed a few days back." The men go for their pistols.

"Horse thieves, not men." Matt watches, as pistols appear in the men's hands feels the snap of his coat, as a bullet tears through it. Bringing his own pistol into play, he empties it into the men, firing the gun until it snaps on an empty chamber. The roar of the gunshots is deafening, as the sound reverberates up and down the street, causing horses to tear loose and run off.

Matt starts reloading his weapon and watches, as men from the saloon start crowding around the two dead men. Walking over to the bodies, Matt studies both faces, then looks up at the gathered men. He tries to remember the man, but Malvern Crossing was a long time ago and many a man died that day, on both sides, blue and grey.

Looking up at the curious bystanders, he sees Tin Cup and his men in the crowd. Pauly walks over to where he stands and looks down at the dead men. Not a word is spoken, as Matt again, turns his attention on the gathered men.

"You men saw it. They came after me."

Several nod. "I seen it, Mister Tillman, and I've never seen anyone faster. Even Bill Hickok couldn't pull with you," an older man adds.

Turning from the crowd, Matt hesitates as he becomes aware of Kate watching from the store's porch. Her face is waxen, her hands clutched tightly to her chest. Matt walks over to where Kate, Cloud, and May Bell are waiting. He stares at her distraught face then turns and starts for the corrals. Cloud takes May Bell by the arm and ushers her back inside, stopping Abigail and Bailey as they exit the store.

Kate follows Matt down the street, until they are away from everyone. "Matt, wait." She catches him by the arm.

"I'm sorry Kate, I ruined your evening."

Shaking her head, she steps closer to him. "Matt Tillman you didn't ruin anything. Don't you realize, I was afraid for you, not those men. It just scared me when they started shooting at you."

"You saw it all?"

"I was following you outside when it started."

Matt smiles and looks down into her strong face. "I should have known, but I thought you were upset with me."

"A woman supports her man, Matt, right or wrong, she stands by him." She hooks her arm into his. "And we're still going to the dance, if you're my man?"

"Are you sure?"

"I'm sure, that is, if you feel like going."

Matt grins then bends down and kisses her. "I'm your man, Miss Howard. Let's check the horses and then we'll go."

The band opens the dance with the Tennessee Waltz and several couples are dancing, when Matt and Kate, along with Cloud and May Bell, enter the big hall. Matt figures all eyes will turn on him, but it was May Bell and Cloud who took everyone's attention.

Kate did May Bell's hair up and the new red dress fit her snugly, showing off her hourglass figure. Only the moccasins on her feet separate her clothes from any white woman at the dance. Abigail smiles brightly, as she walks with Cloud and May Bell to a bench along the wall. Matt has to grin. Cloud's face is redder than normal. He is completely out of place, but for the first time in years, Matt himself is finally at peace.

Pauly is swirling Vickie Gorman, when they pass Matt and Kate, but he cannot miss the look she gives him. Bowing slightly to Vickie, he extends his hand to Kate and steps onto the dance floor with her. Everyone watches Matt curiously as he dances, but not one person mentions the fight. They make the perfect couple, and people smile as they dance by. Both are tall and slender and they dance gracefully together.

Abigail can hardly catch her breath, as the single men of town, and cowboys from the outlying ranches, keep her continually on the dance floor. Matt, after considerable talking and coaxing, manages to get Cloud and May Bell onto the dance floor. May Bell walks like an Indian and talks Arapaho, so everyone assumes she is Indian, without any questions asked. Many of the men shake hands with Cloud congratulating him on his upcoming wedding, which takes him by surprise, since he didn't know he was getting married. He cannot figure who started the marriage rumor.

Walking up to Matt, later in the evening, with a confused look on his face, Cloud is about to ask who told them he was getting married, when a commotion at the door stops him. Several women scream and the dancers part. Wylie Palette stands propped against the doorframe, his clothes covered in blood. Only by the fiery eyes, looking at them, can they tell he is alive. The ride in, from the Divide, seem to help Palette. The cold air clotted the bleeding and cleared his head from the shock of the bullets.

Matt and Cloud rush to his side and ease him to the floor. Doctor Wallace follows Matt and Cloud, but as he nears Palette, the wounded man waves him back.

Vickie Gorman kneels and places his head in her lap. "Wylie." Tears run down her face as she wipes the blood from his cheek. "What have they done to you?"

"Don't cry, Sis. I've been shot worse, maybe not as many times but these aren't where they count." He smiles up at her.

"Sis?" Matt mutters.

Vickie looks up at Matt, sadly. "Yes Mister Tillman, Wylie is my brother."

"I didn't know," Matt said quietly. He wanted to ask, why Palette killed his own sister's husband.

"Sis, before the Doctor goes to work, I need a minute with Mister Tillman." Palette waves Matt closer to him and takes him by the sleeve, pulling him even closer. "Tillman," he waits to catch air into his lungs. "Tillman, I have never liked you but I want you to steady yourself now. I've got bad news, real bad news."

Matt lowers his head. "I'm listening."

"They ambushed us at the Divide. Everyone's dead, except the boy. They let me live to bring you a message." Palette takes a shallow breath then starts again. "He wants his money and horse."

"The one they call the General?"

"He's crazy Tillman!"

"Cage and Jessie?"

"I'm sorry, I tried to protect them. I'm sorry, we didn't have a chance. They were on us so quick." Palette looks directly into Matt's eyes. "You kill every one of them murdering back shooters."

A muffled cry comes from Matt, as he turns blindly toward the door. Cloud and Kate follow at a distance, hesitant to get too near the distraught man. Turning into the corrals, Matt builds a loop and ropes his gelding. Saddling the horse, he turns to where Kate is waiting.

Taking Kate gently by the arms, he pulls her to him and holds her for a few seconds. "Find Tin Cup. Tell him to ride to the ranch and get Hob. Have them meet me at the Divide with provisions for several days. Tell them to have the men stay close to the ranch. Tell Lonnie to bring the wagon out to the Divide as fast as he can."

"Be careful Matt." She holds on to him, not wanting to let go. "Come back to me."

Cloud is saddling his horse when the hostler runs into the livery. "There's a body in the wagon; one of the Elkhorn riders."

"I'd appreciate it, if you would take care of it."

"Yes sir, Mister Tillman."

Several of the men from town walk up as Matt and Cloud mount. "We'll ride with you."

"I thank you, but this is Elkhorn business. These are bad men and you men have families to look after."

"Yes Sir." The men drop their heads. Most are good men, but Matt is right, they all have families.

"You have family too, Matt." Kate whispers.

"I know Kate, and some of them lay out at the Divide. I'll be back."

"I'll be waiting for you."

Chapter 10

The wind stopped blowing as Matt and Cloud make their way toward the north. Snow is starting to fall again. The further they travel from town, the harder the snow comes down. Matt pulls up on the rise, looking down at the Divide. He hesitates for several minutes before kicking the gelding forward. Cloud knows Matt dreads seeing what lies ahead, for he had seen his own family killed by Crow Warriors when he was small. Shaking his head, Cloud sadly follows him down into the small valley. He can already see the dead bodies lying about on the ground, their frozen bodies distorted where they had fallen.

Matt steps slowly from the saddle and walks to where his brother still hangs from a tree, his body stiff, not moving now as there is no wind. Kneeling beside Jessie's frozen body, he wipes the snow from her face gingerly. Cloud, hearing him cry out, watches as Matt drops his head, his shoulders shaking in grief. Laying his hand on Matt's shoulder, he can feel the tremors racking his body.

Only time can heal the grief and despair a man feels after seeing his loved ones massacred, lying uncovered and cold. Standing, he walks off and rolls a smoke. Some things, a man needs to endure by himself, alone. There is nothing a friend can say at a time like this and nothing he can do.

Cloud looks at Matt once more and turns, making his way back across the small clearing, looking for any sign left that was not covered with snow.

Hoof prints of four riders show plainly, where the snow did not fall yet on the trail heading east. Cloud turns back to the bodies and examines each of the dead men lying about. Two of the men are complete strangers. They must have been the General's men. Palette must have killed them before he went down. He did not like Wylie Palette, but he has to admit, the man was a fighter. Like him or not, you have to admire he was a brave man.

The wagon clatters, coming down the road from the rise, its trace chains rattling noisily, breaking the stillness of the valley.

Matt calls to Cloud and motions him over. "Help me with Cage. I don't want Lonnie to see him this way." Matt wraps Cage's hat tightly around his head, but not before Cloud saw he had been scalped. He holds the frozen body as Matt cut the hemp rope that held him. Why would white men scalp another white man? Lowering the body to the ground next to Jessie, Matt unrolls a blanket and covers them both. Standing back, he waits for the wagon. Cloud rolls a smoke and hands it to him.

"Found some tracks, Matt. Four men heading east."

"Any ranches in that direction?"

"An old farm place is all. Nobody's lived there for years."

"We'll wait on Hob then we'll ride that way."

"The snows gonna work against us," Cloud inhales on his cigarette then blows smoke to the wind, "but, if they are headed to the farmhouse, there's only one trail leading there through the mountains."

Matt flips his butt into the snow. "I've got a lifetime and I aim to find every one of them. They can't travel far enough or fast enough to get away."

Cloud looks away. He knows, from the look on Matt's face, that he will never give up the chase. "At least we know which direction they headed."

"And I know at least one of the men I'm after," Matt adds.

The bodies were wrapped in blankets and laid out in the back of the wagon. Lonnie is uncomfortable. He does not know what to say to Matt. What does a man say at a time like this? It has always been unspoken, but the men all heard rumors about Jessie and Matt. An hour later, Hob, Tin Cup, and Rollie ride into view. Two packhorses are being led. Hob had come prepared for a long trail. The bodies were loaded, but Hob knows by the look on Matt's face, what awaits him in the wagon.

Matt meets them, as they dismount and pull Hob off where they can be alone for a moment. Cloud watches as Matt converses in private with the big black man. Walking to the wagon, Hob lifts the blanket from Cage and Jessie. "I'm sorry Mister Cage. I should have been here with you and

Miss Jessie." Tears rolled down the big man's face.

Matt gives him several minutes, then walks over and takes the blanket from his trembling hand. Taking Hob's arm, he has to pull him away from the wagon. The others wait, not knowing exactly what to do, except give the two men time to grieve.

Tin Cup approaches Matt. "We've gotta go son, before the snow covers everything." When no response comes, he touches Matt on the arm. "I'm sorry Matt, but if we're gonna track these varmints, we need to go now."

Matt composes himself then nods slowly and turns toward the wagon. "Rollie, you and Lonnie take the wagon on to the Elkhorn. I'm sure my brother left men there to take care of the stock. Have Lonnie ride to town for the undertaker and the preacher. See that they are laid out properly and words read over them. If we're not back in time, go ahead and have their services. Have him stop in at the store and tell Miss Howard what has happened."

"I'll take care of it, Matt." Rollie steps up on the wagon. "I'm sorry as I can be."

Cloud leads out warily. He saw how the General laid his trap for the Elkhorn men. The man is smart and knows his business. They'll have to be cautious and take their time. Somewhere ahead, an ambush is being set for them, the same kind of ambush Cage Tillman and the Elkhorn riders rode into. The three riders following catch up in their own thoughts, paying little attention to their surroundings, their grief putting them almost into a trance. Cloud will have to be their eyes until they come out of it.

The snow is coming down harder, covering all signs of the riders ahead. Occasionally, Cloud can make out a slight indentation of a horse's hoof but he knows he will soon be following a cold trail. Pulling his horse to a stop, he reaches in his pocket for the makings. Striking a sulphur, Cloud inhales and blows out the smoke, as Matt pulls alongside him. Offering Matt his cigarette, Cloud shrugs when Matt shakes his head.

"No thanks, I'm okay. Snow sure is coming down harder."

"I'm not tracking them anymore Boss, snow's covered the trail." Cloud blows out a stream of smoke. "I'm still on their trail though."

"Where are we headed?"

"Got me a hunch; I think it's the old farmhouse I told you about." Cloud nods down the trail then looks up at the mountains, covered in a blanket of snow.

"How far to it?"

Cloud flips his cigarette and looks over at Matt. "I figure its due east, about eight or ten miles."

"Well, it's worth a try, we've nothing to lose."

"Got me another hunch, Matt."

"What's that?"

"He'll be waiting there. He's wanting us to come in." Cloud slaps snow from his overcoat and hat. "He's crafty and completely bloodthirsty. He'll be waiting alright."

"I want him to wait."

"You didn't bring the horse."

"No." Matt looks across at Cloud. "I'm not here to trade and neither is he. There's only one way this is going to end for one of us, maybe both."

"He'll kill the boy."

"Maybe, but I don't think so, not until I'm finished. He needs the boy for bait to lure me in. No, this so called General will keep him alive."

"It's a big gamble but I guess we've got no other choice," Cloud shrugs.

"Let's not keep him waiting then."

The trail is narrow that Cloud follows, winding its way through the heavy timbered mountains. Snow completely covers everything and Cloud can only follow the slight indention of the trail as it heads due south. He knows where it will lead, as the mountain passes are familiar to him. He has ridden this way before, hunting wild horses and cattle. The farmhouse is ahead, maybe five more miles. Only the crunching of the horse's hooves on the snow breaks the stillness. It's cold, as steam blows from the horse's nostrils, and not a man makes a sound. They are too numb and miserable to make conversation. The deep cold penetrates even the heavy sheepskin coats they wear, and ice hangs from the horse's manes and muzzles. Except for a grey fox watching them pass, they see nothing since leaving the Divide.

Pulling into a sheltered overhang, Cloud dismounts and waits for Matt to ride up.

"What'd you stop for?"

"Gonna have some coffee and hardtack and warm a little."

"We need to be pushing on."

"Matt, we're almost there. I want some coffee and something to eat before I get killed and I want the horses to rest a spell."

Matt looks to where Tin Cup and Hob sit their horses in silence. "Alright Jim, build a fire. We'll warm a little."

The fire is small. Cloud starts it with dry squaw branches that give out only a little smoke. Matt stands off to one side, as the others gather around the pitiful blaze, trying to absorb some of its heat. Cloud walks over to Matt and pushes a hot cup of coffee into his hand, and rolls a smoke.

"Matt, I know what the girl meant to you." Cloud pushes back his hat.

"Careful, Cloud!" Matt does not want to talk about Jessie. Everything is just too fresh in his mind and on his conscience.

Cloud knows he is on dangerous ground, as he continues. "She was a fine lady but she's dead."

Matt whirls, slinging his coffee.

Cloud continues. "You've still got the boy."

"Shut up, Jim!"

"No Boss, you're gonna listen. You have to listen. This General is smart and he's waiting up ahead and you're only thinking about getting to him." Cloud flips his cigarette butt. "We've got to be ready and not ride headlong into a trap."

"Anything else?"

"Getting yourself and us killed is not going to bring her or your brother back."

Matt swings, knocking Cloud backward into the snow. Rolling over, Cloud retrieves his hat and stands up slowly. "I know you're hurting but don't try that again."

Matt slowly straightens, the tenseness going out of his face. He needs to hit at something, anything. Cloud knows it and takes no offense. Maybe he will start thinking straight now. He watches as Matt drops his head and retrieves the coffee cup. Looking up at Cloud, he nods as all the frustration is now gone from his haggard face.

"I'm sorry, Jim."

Cloud grins and rubs his chin.

"You hit hard."

"Do you remember what I told you, when we were after the horse thieves that stole the stallion?"

"No, guess I don't recollect."

"I said then, it is your party."

"Yes, Sir."

"I'm telling you the same now. You're leading this manhunt. All I want is my boy and the General, swinging from a rope." Matt rubs his eyes. "I'm just too wrought up right now to think straight."

Nodding, Cloud walks back to the fire where Tin Cup pours him another cup of coffee. Hob looks to where Matt is standing and, then drops his eyes back to the fire. Sometimes, hitting out at something helps relieve the grief a man carries. It is as hard for Hob as well. Cage and Jessie had been like family to him. No, they were family. He knew them all his life and he loved them as much as Matt or April. It tears at him for them to die as they did, and then their bodies left out on the frozen ground all alone.

The cabin is near. Matt and the others wait, while Cloud slips forward to get a closer look. Easing quietly back to where they are waiting, Cloud quickly fills them in on the situation. "They're in there alright. Horses are in the corral and smoke's coming from the cabin." Cloud takes a cup of coffee from Hob.

"Did you see the boy?" Matt asks.

"Didn't see anybody, but I couldn't get too close in the daylight."

"Why did he stop?" Tin Cup speaks up. "Surely he knows we're following."

"He knows." Cloud answers. "But, he's human, and it's cold. I don't know but I do know they're over there in that farmhouse."

Matt pulls his hat off and wipes his brow. "He'll figure us to come in after dark."

"Maybe," Cloud squats beside the small fire and reaches out his hands for the warmth. "I don't like it. He doesn't even have a guard posted."

"Careless of him, I'd say," Matt speaks up. "We'll go in as soon as it gets dark and accommodate the man."

"What about the boy, Mista Matt?"

"I'm going in first." Matt looks at Hob. "Soon as I get the boy I'll signal and ya'll come a shooting."

"Sounds good, except for one thing." Cloud blows into his hands. "I'll get the boy. I know the layout of the place."

"He's my boy."

"I'm better at sneaking Boss, you're better at shooting," Cloud grins. "I'll get your boy before they wake up, I give you my word."

"Alright Jim, I told you it's your party."

The snow is still coming down hard when Cloud leads the small party to the farmhouse. A lamp glows from the front window. Its beacon of warmth almost seems to be calling to the cold men surrounding the house.

Matt senses something is wrong. No General would ever be so careless, as to neglect putting out sentries at night. In the army, it didn't matter what the weather was doing, sentries were always posted. "Watch yourself, Jim."

Matt places his hand on Cloud's arm as he starts toward the house. "There's something funny about this set up."

"You smell it too."

"It's too quiet." Nodding, Cloud moves off, into the darkness toward the old barn and corrals. Kneeling in the snow, alongside the corral poles, his dark eyes strain to see in the shadows. Something is not right. The corral gate was thrown wide open. The horses are gone and not a thing stirs. The crafty old fox fooled him and pulled out; or did he.

Pulling back beside the barn, he waits. The General is slick as a peeled onion. He might be lying up, waiting for some dang fool half breed to show himself. Well, it is too cold to camp out here all night; a man can freeze.

Rising, he makes his way to the rear of the house, peering through the dirty window. Nothing, empty as a dry well, except for the lamp placed conveniently in the window. Cloud knows the lamp would betray anyone trying to enter the house through the front door.

Suddenly, a shot rings out in the dark then several more. He can feel the bullets buzzing around him like a hornet's nest. Diving behind the woodpile, alongside the house, Cloud feels a hot sear along his arm as he lands. Feeling the tear in his coat, he knows a bullet barely scratched his arm. Several bullets slam harmlessly into the logs.

Quickly, as it began, the firing subsides. Cloud knows Matt and the boys never fired a shot. They cannot fire blindly, not knowing where he was positioned. Backing away quietly, from the cabin, Cloud finds Matt and Hob concealed in a stand of pine trees in front of the house. From the woods, to the rear of the barn, they hear horses retreating to the east.

"They're pulling out," Tin Cup announces, slipping into the trees. "Rode right by me, but I couldn't shoot. I didn't know which horse the boy was on."

"You done right," Matt nods his head.

"Let's get after them skunks," Tin Cup cusses.

"No!" Cloud looks at the men. "He's got us and knows it. We can't shoot in the dark as long as he has the boy. We'll have to wait until daylight, so we can tell what we're shooting at."

"He'll get away." Tin Cup argues.

Matt stands up. "No he won't, we'll wait until morning, like Jim says and then go after him. He won't get away."

"Snow's gonna cover his tracks. I say we go now." Tin Cup is mad and he's persistent. His jaw is set as he looks around at the others.

Matt starts for the horses. "Let's put the animals in the corral and feed them. Quit arguing and get us some warm grub Tin Cup."

"Alright, you're the boss. I'll start you boys some coffee and sourdough."

Matt and Cloud, unsaddle, while Hob stands watch. One surprise today is enough and there will be no more. Pouring oats from the packsaddle into a wooden trough, Matt looks over at Cloud. "The old man is right; snow is going to cover his tracks."

"True enough," Cloud agrees, "but, this General isn't about to lose us. He wants the money, horse, and your hide. He doesn't know you didn't bring anything to this party, but yourself. No, he won't dare lose us."

"Where do you think he'll head now?"

"That, I don't know, but I'll guarantee, he'll leave us some kind of a trail." Cloud swings his saddle over a stall gate.

Walking to where Hob stands, leaning against the barn, Matt rolls a cigarette, handing Hob the makings, "I'll go eat then relieve you."

"Yassa," Hob answers sadly. "We'es got to get that little boy back, no matter if that General kills us all. I never knew this could happen to Mister Cage and Miss Jessie, never. I wouldn't have taken the horse and money."

"We'll get him before this is over. We'll get him, I promise you."

"Yassa, I hopes you be right."

Cloud can smell the hot coffee and biscuits as soon as he steps into the dark house. The lamp was extinguished and the only light illuminating the room is coming from the stove and a small candle.

Stamping the snow from his boots, Matt removes his heavy sheepskin and tosses it across an empty chair. Pulling another chair to the table, he sits down across from Cloud and Tin Cup. Noticing Cloud's torn coat Matt nods at it, "You hit?"

"Just a scratch."

"Let me see it."

The slight wound is barely noticeable, like Cloud said, but Matt has him remove his coat so he can wrap it.

"Thanks Boss," Cloud responds gratefully.

Matt walks to the stove and pours himself a scalding cup of coffee. "What'll he do now?"

"He'll let us follow along, until we get careless and then our Mister General will hit us again. This time, he'll do it in the daylight, when he can see better and shoot straighter. I think he'll get tired of playing games with us pretty soon."

"How do you know?" Matt asks.

"This General is ruthless and shrewd. He knows his business." Cloud shrugs. "What would you do?"

Matt studies his coffee. "Same thing, I guess."

Downing a quick meal of biscuits and warmed up beef, Matt puts his coat back on and walks out to where Hob is standing watch. The snow is still coming down in large soft flakes settling over the farmstead in a silent blanket. Nothing moves, not a sound comes from the darkness, only the horse's teeth grind as they eat. Sending Hob to the house, Matt stands watch from the barn. Inside he cannot stand still. He keeps pacing back and forth, across the dirt floor of the barn, to ward off the cold and the anxiety he feels. He's eager to trail the General, and wishes morning would hurry, so he can once more be on the move. He does not want anything to happen to the boy.

He trusts Cloud's judgment in believing the General wants the horse and money. He will leave some kind of trail for them to follow, of that he is sure. Somewhere down the trail, he and his men will be waiting. When and where, is the question.

Matt catches a glimpse of movement, from the corner of his eye. Turning his head slowly, he scans the grounds around the old house carefully. In the shadows of the dim light coming from the front window of the house, he watches, as a coyote sniffs cautiously, along the front wall of the house.

A smart and wily animal, Coyotes normally stay away from humans, but this one is hungry. He was pulled in by the smell of the beef Tin Cup cooks on the stove. Coyotes are always aware of everything around them and they are seldom seen by man. Matt smiles, as the coyote does not detect him in the barn watching him. He knows if a coyote does not detect him, then no man lurking out in the dark will be able to. Matt watches, as the coyote walks back and forth by the door, finally withdrawing into the shadows, out of sight.

Two hours passed slowly. Matt keeps stamping his feet to warm them until Cloud exits the house, making his way to the barn. If Matt did not seen him leave the doorway, he would never have known Cloud is near him. So silently, the man approaches his hiding place.

"Over here, Jim," Matt whispers softly.

"Seen anything?" Cloud walks closer when Matt whispers his name.

"Just a coyote, snooping around."

"Yea, I saw his tracks when I opened the door."

Matt is amazed Cloud is so observant. Most men would walk right over the tracks, without looking down. "It's cold out here Jim. Reckon we need to keep a man on guard?"

"Yes Sir, I do. This General is one cagey character. I don't trust him. He could be coming in right now. I'm gonna sleep with one eye open, until we put out his lights or until he puts ours out, whichever comes first." Clouds voice is cold.

"Alright, I'll have Hob relieve you in two hours." Matt starts to turn toward the house then stops. "Jim, what are the boy's chances, out in the cold?"

"Cold won't bother him that much, youngsters are hotter natured than we are." Cloud hesitates. "It's the General; we don't know what he will do."

"Well, we know he's capable of cold blooded murder. I figure he's capable of doing almost anything."

"We'll start first light Matt. I promise you this, I'll catch up to this bunch and we'll get the boy back," Cloud swears. "We'll get him."

"I've got to, Jim. He's all I have left of her."

"Go warm up and don't worry."

Daylight creeps over the mountains when Cloud leads them from the homestead. Tin Cup warmed them up with biscuits and hot coffee before they climbed into their cold saddles. Following the only trail, leading south from the homestead, it is as Tin Cup predicted, the tracks of the General are obliterated by fresh snow. The old cowboy is not about to let Cloud forget his predictions either.

"I told the young whippersnapper, I told him." Matt can hear Tin Cup mumbling behind him.

Several small trails, mostly deer and varmint, join the main track they follow, but Cloud pays them little attention. He knows the General will not change direction and take a chance of losing his pursuers. Sure enough, Cloud finds a freshly broken limb hanging from a small pine tree. Dismounting, he brushes snow back carefully from it and feels the ground. A grunt of satisfaction comes from his mouth, as he looks back at Matt and nods. He can feel the slight indentation of a horseshoe under the snow.

Mounting, Cloud kicks his horse and continues to follow the trail south. All morning his sharp eyes study the trail, missing nothing.

Two hours past noon, Cloud pulls his gelding in and dismounts. Another broken branch lays across the trail, blocking their way. Snow covers most of it, but Cloud can see where the trail turns.

Pushing his hat back to expose his thick dark hair, he feels around in the snow then turns to where Matt sits. Pointing, he shakes his head in disbelief. "He turned west, straight back towards the Elkhorn and Arapaho lands."

Matt dismounts and studies the small trail leading off into the trees. "Where do you think he's heading, Jim?"

"Could be anywhere, but for now, he's heading straight back toward the ranch." Cloud shakes his head. "I told you, someone is leading this bunch that knows this country."

"Who?"

"That, my friend, I don't know." Cloud stands in the deep snow looking up at Matt. "But, whoever he is, he's a local."

"Why do you think that?"

"Not too many people know these trails. Hardly anybody uses them, since the Indians and the Mountain Men are gone. Your Uncle Matt didn't tolerate trespassers and we're sitting dead in the middle of Elkhorn Range."

Looking around, Matt has to admire the beauty of these mountains. The trees are covered with snow, and the ground was blanketed, but the quiet peacefulness of the mountains speaks to him. For as far as the eye can see, only small valleys and mountains dot the landscape.

Matt looks back to where Tin Cup and Hob sit their horses, watching Cloud snoop around the trail. He wishes secretly, Hob would take up smoking or chewing, anything to break the solemn stare of his forlorn face. He knows the man is feeling guilty, thinking he brought the General and his men down on Cage by taking the money. No amount of talking will change his mind once it is set. Matt knows Hob will have to work it out himself.

Cloud gathers the reins to his horse and looks at Matt. "Yep, he's headed west. This trail will lead to a large valley, about four miles further on."

Matt nods. "Then what?"

"That, Mister Tillman, is where he'll spring his trap, if I'm not mistaken." Cloud mounts and spins his horse to face the others.

Matt looks down the trail. It's already starting on its downward course, leading off the mountain, down into the next valley.

"Are you positive?" He asks.

"Positive, no," Cloud blows smoke into the air, "but we're catching up and soon his tracks will start showing up. He needs to set his trap before that happens."

"You don't think he'll ride on in to Elk Springs?"

Cloud shakes his head. "Don't think so, he knows people heard about the killings and will question any newcomers in town. No, he'll swing wide of town and make for wilder country, which is Arapaho land."

"Could he be riding for the ranch?" Matt looks worriedly at Cloud. "We have all of our good fighting men here."

"No, I don't think he intends to go there. He's got what he wants following him. They just happen to turn west toward the ranch is all."

"Well, let's go see." Matt takes one last look at the trail, then follows Cloud.

"You boys stay spread out, a good distance apart." Cloud grins. "No sense all of us getting ourselves ventilated."

Chapter 11

The afternoon wears on, as the trackers plod slowly to the west, careful that no trap is laid for them. Sundown is almost upon them, when Cloud first starts seeing horse tracks ahead of them on the trail. The snow quit falling at a little past daybreak, so Cloud figures the General and his men are still four to five hours ahead, if he isn't lying waiting to spring his ambush.

Cloud dismounts and waits for Matt to ride closer. "This General is cagey and he's patient."

Matt studies the tracks. "You got any suggestions?"

Cloud shrugs. "Like I said; whoever is leading him, knows this neck of the woods real good. Our friend the General is having him pick out a perfect place to wait for us. Ahead, about four miles, is another good spot for him to take us."

"I'm listening."

"I say let's rest the horses and get us a good supper. Let our General stew, and maybe freeze a little tonight and then we'll go get him in the morning."

"And the boy?"

"He'll be alright."

Matt nods, turning to Tin Cup and Hob. "Ya'll light, we're staying here for a spell." With the side of his boot, Matt starts scraping snow away, down to hard ground, big enough for them to build a campfire.

Hob and Cloud unsaddle and grain the horses, while Matt and Tin Cup start supper. Tin Cup keeps adding snow to the fire smoked coffeepot, until enough melts to fill it. Coffee grounds are added and the men sit leaning back on their saddles to wait for it to boil.

Warming his hands over the small blaze, Matt finally loosens them enough to roll a cigarette and light it. Wincing a little, as he straightens up, he notices Cloud, watching him intently from across the fire.

"How's the side, Matt?"

"It's holding together, a little touchy tonight."

"In the morning I want to try something." Cloud looks across at Matt.

"Go ahead, I'm listening."

"Up ahead, about a mile or maybe a little more, the trail splits. Both end in the valley ahead; one is just a little steeper, but it'll get you there an hour or so faster," Cloud hesitates, swallowing some coffee.

"Okay."

"They'll probably take the easier trail off the mountain. That is, if I'm right and they have a man with them, that knows this country and I'm sure they do. Anyway, I'm taking the upper trail tonight and with a little luck, I'll come in behind them come first light."

"Then what?" Matt rolls another cigarette.

"They'll be watching their back trail for you. Just maybe, with a little luck, I can slip in and get the boy away from them before they know I'm there."

Matt strikes a sulphur and studies the small flame before he answers, "Might just work at that."

Cloud adds, "We've got to get the boy away from them. As long as they have him, we can't come to grips with that bunch and this may be our only chance."

"Alright Jim, when are you pulling out?"

"Reckon about midnight."

"You watch your backside, you hear me." Matt smiles, which is a rarity but he smiled. "And Jim, I want to thank you for everything."

"You boys wait until daybreak and then come on slow because somewhere up ahead the General will be waiting for you, I can feel it."

"We'll be careful, you can bank on it."

"Matt, I want you to know, I'll get the boy back. If there's any chance at all, I'll bring him out of this."

"I know you will." Matt nods. "Do you want to take Hob with you?"

"Not this time. This is a one-man job. If they're waiting for you up ahead, I figure you'll be needing his help, more than I will."

"Alright then, get some sleep and I'll wake you at midnight and Jim, good luck to you."

"Same to you, boys."

Matt has Cloud's horse saddled and ready at midnight then wakes him. Watching, as Jim swallows a hot cup of coffee and smokes a quick cigarette, he nods at everyone, then mounts, and disappears into the night.

Matt sits silently, for a while, looking into the flames and then rolls into his bedroll with his Henry rifle cradled across his lap. Looking at the moon that came from behind a large cloud, he wishes it was all over. He's suddenly tired of all the fighting and killing. Seems he has been at war all his life. A coyote gives a long mournful yelp, reminding Matt of just how lonely he feels. Maybe tomorrow it will all be over. Looking over at Hob, he wonders what the big man is thinking.

Morning finds Matt leading, with Tin Cup and Hob following at intervals. It's possible, their quarry can be waiting close by. Matt figures like Cloud, the General will lay his trap in the valley ahead. Here on the trail, the men are too strung out to get them all, but when they enter the flat valley, the men ahead will figure they will bunch up and make a better target.

Matt holds the roan to a slow walk, letting his eyes look over every possible hiding place, for the ambush he knows is coming. The General's tracks are plain in the deep snow with four horses ahead of them. No extra pack animals are in the bunch. Matt knows, all the provisions the General has, must be tied to their saddle horses, so it cannot be much. Looking back, he sees the sharp eyes of Tin Cup and Hob staring back at him through the heavy steam of their horse's nostrils. They are alert and it will be hard to surprise them.

The trail is starting to flatten out, the first sign they are entering the lower ground of the valley. Suddenly, out of the quietness of the valley ahead, gunfire erupts, making the horses flick their ears forward. Several shots, echo back, where they wait. Finally, the sound of running horses, going deeper into the valley and away from them, can be heard. Kicking their horses into motion, Matt hurries toward the valley floor. Cloud is in trouble; it has to be him the General pursues.

The flat meadow is eerily quiet, no gunfire, and no running horses, nothing. Matt pulls up and studies the tracks in the snow. Riding slowly forward, he finds where the General made camp and he discovers the body of one of the men. From the signs, Cloud managed to slip in on him and put a knife into his ribs, before the man even knew he was anywhere near. Small footprints show where the boy stood and apparently was picked up by Cloud and carried back to his horse that was tied to a pine tree.

He did not know how the General was alerted, but by the blood spots covering Cloud's tracks, Matt knows he was hit. How bad he cannot tell, but Cloud was able to make his escape. Fear grips his insides. Could the bullet have hit the boy? Unlikely, he reasons Cloud would have been holding the boy in front, to protect him.

Hob walks up beside Matt, careful not to disturb the tracks. "He get the boy away?"

Nodding, Matt stands up. "He got him away but he's wounded. Can't tell how bad but he's dripping blood."

Tin Cup spit. "Then there's nothing to keep us from going after this bunch anymore, if the boy's safe."

Matt leads out, following the General and his men. The odds are getting better. The General only has two or three men left. Tin Cup wants to move faster but Matt holds him back. Halfway across the valley, Matt finds where Cloud's tracks veer away, toward the mountain cliffs, while the General and his men continue straight down the valley. Turning to follow Cloud's trail, Matt pulls his horse in as Tin Cup balks.

"We've got the scallywag Matt, dang it, let's git." Tin Cup is waving the big Sharps' rifle and pointing it down the valley.

"No," Matt's voice is forceful. "We'll see to Jim and the boy then we'll go after him. I've got a life time to catch him."

Nodding, Tin Cup falls back in line and follows.

The lone horse tracks ahead of them, zigzag across the flat bottom, like a loose horse would, that isn't being ridden. Cloud must be hurt worse than Matt figured, as he wasn't reining the horse at all. Kicking his horse into a hard trot, Matt hurries forward and pulls up, to look back at Tin Cup.

"Why would the General go straight down the valley instead of following Jim's trail?" Matt looks straight at Tin Cup. "He knows he needs the boy, to get me to follow him."

The old man's eyes suddenly light up. "That's it, this trail comes out into the next valley, and Jim will ride right into the General's lap, that is, if this General runs his horses to death to head him off."

"Let's ride." Matt kicks the roan into a hard lope, following Cloud's trail. He has to reach Jim and the boy before they enter the next valley. In places, the horses have to lunge to get through the deep drifts, but Matt must hurry. He has no way of knowing how far ahead Cloud and the boy are.

The trail straightens, as the horse starts climbing upwards, out of the valley. The path is merely a deer and cow trail, winding narrowly toward the top of the mountain. It will follow a hogback ridge a ways and start back down into the next valley. All the trails in these mountains crisscross much the same. Several times, Matt can tell where Cloud's horse stopped and bit off bark from a pine or aspen tree. Topping out over a rock ledge, Matt spies the horse ground tied, standing beside a group of cedar trees. Easing around the cedars, Matt stops short as he comes face to face with the muzzle of Cloud's wavering rifle.

"It's us Jim, don't shoot." Matt rushes to the man's side. The boy is bundled up beside Cloud, staring, as the three men all kneel around them.

Picking the boy up, Matt hands him to Hob, turning back to Jim. Pulling his coat back he examines the high shoulder wound.

"Howdy, Boss. It's sure good to see you," Cloud grins. "Wouldn't have a spare smoke, would you?"

"Looks like you forgot to duck."

Tin Cup hands Jim a lit cigarette then leans forward. "Well, what do you know, you injuns bleed the same color as whites."

Cloud grins. "You old rascal, never figured I'd be glad to see your ugly mug. I could sure use a cup of that stuff you call coffee."

Tin Cup nods. "Coming right up, keep your pants on."

Matt examines the wound carefully, placing some dry bandages on it to stem the flow of blood, until Tin Cup gets some water heated to clean the wound.

"Looks like it went clean through, without touching the bone." Matt pats Cloud's arm. "I figure you'll live to have a hundred kids."

"One like that boy will do." Cloud nods, to where Hob is holding the boy. "He's got more sand than I do. How is he?"

"Well, don't know for sure. Looks like he's scared half to death of Hob, but other than being cold and hungry, he looks fine," Tin Cup laughs.

"You know what he told me, when the bullets were screeching around our heads?" Cloud laughs. "Said to me, mister, you better run faster."

Matt looks to where the boy is eating a cold biscuit. "Yea, his mother had spunk."

"So did his pappy," Hob speaks up.

"Tin Cup, make yourself helpful and fix up Jim's shoulder as best you can." Tin Cup waits until the coffee and water is boiling, then walks to where Cloud rests on a dry bed, Matt laid out for him.

"Which you want first, the coffee or the doctoring?"

"Both, I have to be in pain, to drink your coffee, you old goat."

"Why you young pup, I'm the best sawbones in these mountains." Tin Cup hands him a steaming cup of coffee.

"Yea, and the only one, too."

Matt sips on his coffee and watches as Tin Cup works on Cloud. Not a word or moan comes from the injured man, as his shoulder is cleaned and wrapped. Matt was shot and he knows first hand, how painful it could be, but he heard Indians could withstand pain and not make a sound.

"Tell me what happened, Jim," Matt asks, when Tin Cup finishes with his doctoring and steps back.

"After I left you, I got lucky and found the General's camp. Dang fool didn't even try to hide it. Well anyway, I waited until sunup, figuring they would all be asleep. Then I slipped in and found the boy and their night guard." Cloud pats his knife. "Old Betsy here took care of him, but as I was slipping out of there, someone got me in the back."

"That's when all the shooting started?"

"That's when it broke loose. I don't see how they missed us. They were trying their best, I'll give them that."

Matt squats down. "How many men does he have left?"

"Three, besides himself, is all I counted."

Matt rolls a fresh cigarette and places it between Cloud's lips. "Can you ride?"

"If I don't, I'm liable to lay here and get lazy."

Walking over, to where Hob is feeding the boy some cold beef and hot coffee, Matt kneels down and looks into the boy's face. "How are you Michael?"

The little eyes only look back at him saying nothing, just staring.

Hob pulls him closer and wraps a big arm around the boy. "He's had a rough time Masta Matt."

"Yea." Matt stands up. "I reckon he has."

"What are we gonna do Matt?" Tin Cup asks, as Matt walks back to where Cloud is lying.

"You boys head back. Tin Cup, you'll take Jim on in to Elk Springs, to the doctor and Hob will take the boy back to the ranch."

"You're the boss. I guess you'll be going on after them skunks?"

Matt nods, "I'm going on."

"Then, good luck to you." Tin Cup reaches out his hand.

"Hob will ride with you as far as the Divide to make sure you don't have any trouble. If the boy is alright and doesn't need a doctor, he'll split off and go on to the ranch."

"I can't leave you here alone."

"Hob, I want you to take the boy home to a warm fire and food. That's all that matters to me." Matt stares hard at the big man.

"Yassa; what's you gonna do?"

"I've got business down the mountain."

Tin Cup empties his coffee cup and looks at Matt. "There's four of them, boy."

"You just get Jim to the doctor, and the boy too, if you think he needs one."

"I'll get them there."

"One more thing. While I'm gone, Hob will run the upper ranch, and when Jim's able, he'll run the lower ranch. You're a witness to it, Tin Cup."

"Yes Sir."

"And you, you old mossy horn, will have the run of both places, as long as you want. No work, just plenty of good smoking tobacco and grub." Matt grins.

"What about whiskey?"

"And whiskey, in moderation of course."

"What's that word mean? Something bad I bet."

"Means a quart, a day, you idiot," Cloud laughs.

"When you get well, Jim Cloud, me and you got a date behind the smokehouse," Tin Cup grins. "A quart a day, not bad, not bad."

Gathering their horses and blankets, Matt helps Hob lift Cloud into the saddle. Handing the boy up to Hob, Matt steps back and looks up at the boy and then at Hob.

"You takes care of yourself, Mathew." Hob extends his hand. He never calls Matt by his given name unless it is something serious and he is worried.

"I'll be back."

Hob can see something in Matt's eyes, something that, even in the thick of battle, with bullets flying everywhere, he has never seen. Matt slaps Hob's horse on the rump, then watches, as the riders make their way slowly down the slick trail, back toward the Elkhorn Divide. Hob turns and waves once then rounds a stand of cedars and disappears. Matt flips his cigarette into the cold snow and looks toward the west, his face as cold as the mountains themselves.

"Now Mister General Sir, it's my turn," he mutters as he mounts the roan and starts over the mountain, after his quarry.

An hour later Matt reaches the first valley, exactly as Cloud and Tin Cup said he would. Riding slowly along the tree lined valley, he finds the rocks where they told Matt to wait. The General and his men will come into sight three to four hundred yards further along the valley, coming down to wait for Cloud and the boy to ride into their trap.

As Tin Cup rode out earlier, he stopped, handing Matt the Sharps Rifle and a bag of shells. "She'll shoot a mile and give you change, just hold her steady."

Matt can see the valley and the trail where he expects the General to come from. Dismounting, he stands the Sharps and Henry, both against a rock. Tying the roan behind a rock ledge, out of the way of a stray bullet, he returns to the rifles and waits. Tin Cup figured the General would be another two hours reaching this valley across the easier trail. Figuring the time, he spent with Cloud and then crossing the mountain, Matt guesses the General will be along any time, if in fact this is where he intended to ambush Cloud.

Matt watches the valley and the mountain trail, coming down into it, nervously. Rolling himself another smoke, he looks up at the sun. "What is taking them so long? Did they turn back toward the east? Will they run into Hob and the rest if they did?" Matt is nervous, undecided whether to wait or ride back after Hob. If the General decides to turn back, Matt knows he can never catch up to the men in time to help. No, he will wait here, as Hob is no greenhorn. He knows the General and his men are somewhere in these mountains. He will be on the lookout for him and his men.

Toward the far end of the valley, Matt's eyes snap. He hears what sounds like an iron horseshoe, hitting on a rock. Again, the sound carries to him. Matt flips his cigarette into the snow and picks up the Sharps. They're coming down off the mountain. Matt can see the tops of their hats as they pass through a small growth of new pines and cedars. Setting two extra cartridges on the rock in easy reach, Matt sights the rifle on the far trail and waits.

Four men come into sight on the mountain trail that intersects the valley, working their way cautiously, down the slippery path. Matt's cold eyes, study each man carefully. He has no qualms, as he picks the target he wants. This time, the General is riding into a trap.

The first man to bottom out, on the valley floor, has to be the local Cloud spoke of, the man who knows this country. He isn't the man Matt wants out of the way first. He needs this man to lead the General. Matt watches as the four men dismount and pull their saddles back into place on their horse's back. They slid forward, coming down the mountain. The big man in black, has to be the General. Matt cannot remember the man from the running fight at Malvern Crossing, as it was too fast for a man to look at faces. How the man in town remembered Matt's face was a mystery, but he somehow remembered.

Matt watches as the men pull their cinches tight. He carefully, settles the rifle sights on the man who is last in line. Setting the hair-trigger, Matt slowly squeezes, feeling the recoil of the huge gun. Looking through the smoke, he sees the man down and the rest of the men hurrying into their saddles. Several rifle rounds fall harmlessly in front of the rock, where Matt stands.

Shrugging, Matt watches the men race toward the end of the valley. He reloads, and stands the big rifle back beside the Henry. There is no way they can get behind him, unless they cross the mountain and come in from the east end of the valley. That would take too long and now the General lost his advantage. He will have to travel fast and hard to stay ahead of the far shooting Sharps, in a country as wild and rough as can be.

The hunt changes now. The General is the hunted and no longer the hunter, and he knows it. He should remember the sound the Sharps made from the war and he will know he's outgunned. He can never get close enough to the man behind him to exchange gunfire. He will have to ride out of these mountains to escape death or set an ambush.

Mounting the roan, Matt replaces the Henry in its scabbard. Crossing the valley floor, toward the dead man, he scans the end of the flat meadow as far as he can see. Reining in, he looks down at the man. He's old and grey, reminding him of Tin Cup or the older horse thief. The big rifle did its work well. The whole front of the man's chest was blown away. Oh well, Matt shrugs, "One more to pay for her death." The cold eyes looking down, show no mercy, there will be plenty more dead men to follow this one to his maker.

Now there are only three, the General and two men. Matt knees the roan and starts him along the trail heading due west. Matt does not know the country, but all he has to do is follow the General until he gets another man into his sights. There is no hurry and Matt lets the roan pick his way slowly across the snow-covered trail. He can tell where the General pulled in his horses and let them blow from their long hard run across the valley floor. The roan is tired. He came a long way on very little feed and no roughage at all. Soon, Matt will have to let him graze on some of the rough mountain grass that sticks up from the snow. He figures the General's horses to be in worse shape than his.

The air is crisp and cold but Matt hardly feels it. As long as the snow holds off, the trail will be easy to follow and he does not have to hurry. Matt knows he is not the tracker Jim Cloud is, but following tracks in the snow isn't tracking. If it starts to snow, he could lose the General in these rugged mountains. He also figures the General to be low on food. He will have to hunt or starve, either way it's to Matt's advantage. He intends to hang the man and he is in no hurry to do it.

Matt glimpses the riders ahead, as they clear the summit of a long trail up the mountain. This is where he'll have to be careful, as he makes his way up the rocky trail. If the General and his men are waiting up there, they can easily shoot down at him as he makes the climb. Matt studies the surrounding woods and mountainside. There's no way around, only straight up. Patting the roan on the neck, he clucks to him and starts up. It will take almost an hour to top out, over this mountain to see what lies ahead.

The roan is struggling. The trail is steep, so he steps easily to the ground and leads the horse up the rocky trail. Looking up, he wonders if the General is waiting at the top.

Chapter 12

As Matt leads the roan slowly up the mountain trail, he scans the top for any sign of the General. He knows this narrow trail, which gives little cover, is the perfect place for an ambush. There is no other choice, he has to follow it, as it is the only trail to the summit. Strapping the Henry Rifle across his back, he clutches the Sharps, tightly in his hand. He doesn't want to lose the rifles, should the General and his men fire down at him and spook the roan.

The trail is almost impossible to climb without slipping and sliding. Watching his footing, and for the men above him, at the same time, is impossible. Finally, nearing the crest he drops the horse's reins and eases cautiously to the top. Crouching, he peers over the last knoll and is surprised to find it vacant. The General, for some reason, passed up a good chance of getting him.

Matt shakes his head. Did the general lose his nerve and be in full retreat? He doubts it, a union officer running from one pursuer. Must be related to General McClellan, Matt thought, remembering the union General who always thought Bobby Lee had more men than he actually had.

Kicking the snow from his boots, Matt mounts and starts the roan down the first incline. Not a thing moves as far as the eye can see. This side of the mountain is much heavier timbered than the other side was. Trees line both sides of the trail. Matt can see the General's tracks as they descend downward. Three horses are ahead of him.

He is still curious, why did the man not take a shot at him as he ascended the other side?

Suddenly, the hairs on Matt's neck stand up. Flinging himself sideways from the roan, he lands in the snow and rolls behind a small boulder, hardly large enough to conceal him, as shots ring out from the tree line below. The roan rears sideways, falling on his side, as several rounds of lead hit him, making a smacking sound. Silence comes once more across the mountains, as Matt cusses himself for a dang fool. Only a tenderfoot would ride into the General's trap. Trying to get a glimpse downhill, he jerks back, as bullets whine off the boulder, causing rock fragments to spray everywhere.

Matt swears, as they have him pinned down. He will have to wait until dark to move. As the man said, the fortune of war has reversed again. Now the General has the advantage over him. His only consolation is, they cannot come up after him, but he cannot move either. Matt looks over at the roan. He hates losing a good horse, just one more thing to chalk up against the General.

The sun starts to fade when Matt hears the sound of retreating riders, scrambling down the steep trail. He waits, fearing another ruse. Now, he knows what Cloud meant, this General is cagey. As dark falls, Matt stands up stiffly, and moves to the roan. Rifling his saddlebags, he mentally tallies what he can carry and what will have to be left behind.

Discarding his Cavalry boots for a pair of moccasins Hob shoved into his bags, he grabs extra ammunition and what little food he can carry. He wraps a blanket across his shoulders and starts downhill.

Without a horse, it is going to be a long walk. Walk or not, the men that killed Cage and Jessie are going to pay even if he has to crawl all the way to Arapaho country. Traveling through the night, Matt stops only occasionally to catch his breath on the uphill slopes. He doubts the General will risk his horses on these steep trails in the dark, so he pushes on. With a little luck maybe he can get within rifle shot of them by daylight.

The moccasins are more comfortable to walk in, but they are already soaked through and his feet were half frozen. Matt knows he will have to stop soon, build a fire, and dry out. The last thing he needs is frostbitten toes if he is going to continue the chase. Bottoming out on a small shelf, Matt sniffs the air. He swears he can smell wood smoke. Did he close in on them during the night while they are resting warm and comfortable around their campfire?

Cautiously, he advances to the edge of the shelf and looks downward toward another one of the small valleys that dot the mountains. Below him, he can see the smoke of their breakfast fire. He eases over the sharp cliff and works his way downward, staying away from the trail. The General will not expect him to come through the woods. Matt doubts if the man expects him to follow at all without a horse.

Trying to get within range of the camp, he curses silently as he is brought up short by a sheer drop of fifteen feet or more. Looking around, he can see no way down, unless he retreats the way he came and detours to the north. Lying behind a downed log, he peers down at the activity in the camp. The men are saddling their horses and preparing to break camp.

A downhill shot at this range is tricky, and it is hard to guess an accurate distance. Resting the Sharps over the log, he sights in on one of the men and waits as he pulls his cinch tight. Slowly tightening the trigger, Matt feels the slap of the stock against his shoulder and hears the roar of the Sharps. Matt cusses, as he did not anticipate the man bending down just as he pulled the trigger. The bullet misses its intended victim, striking the man's horse instead. The animal falls like a pole axed steer, as the big fifty-four caliber shell, hits him dead behind the shoulder.

Matt is amazed when the other two riders take off, down the trail at a dead run, abandoning the man with the dead horse. Rolling himself a smoke, Matt waits. The man throws himself behind the horse. Lying prone in the snow, it's only a matter of time before the cold will make him move. Matt cannot believe the General turned tail and ran off on one of his own, but he saw it happen more than once in the war.

Reloading the Sharps, Matt sights a little below the line of the horse's back and squeezes off another round. This time, his shot went high, hitting a full foot above the horse's back. Reloading, he takes aim a little lower and is about to pull the trigger when the man sprang up from the ground and starts toward the nearest tree. Aiming low, Matt fired again. The man turned a flip in midair with his legs knocked out from under him.

Matt watches, as the man writhes in pain as his bloodstains the snow red. Standing slowly, Matt flips his cigarette away and gathers the Henry and the blanket containing what little food he has left. Taking his time, he works his way slowly down to the abandoned camp and wounded man. Coming out of the woods, he studies the place closely, before stepping into view.

The big caliber of the Sharps did its job. The man bled out before Matt could get to him. The dead man is another of the General's ex-soldiers. Matt can tell from what is left of the union uniform that he was a soldier. Looking down, the way the other two men rode, Matt knows the only ones left are the General and the local that knows this country. Searching the camp for anything the men might have left in their haste to depart, Matt finds only a little food in the dead man's saddlebags. Something better than food, catches his attention. A clean pair of wool socks is in the bottom of the bags. A soldier marches on his feet mostly, and they know to keep a dry pair of socks handy. Building up the dying embers of the fire, Matt removes his wet moccasins and socks, propping them up next to the fire to dry. Slipping on the dry wool socks, Matt leans back next to the fire and rolls a cigarette. Things are definitely looking up.

The General is up ahead, time is on Matt's side. He wants the man to know he is following, and he's in no hurry to catch up. Let him sweat. Swallowing some hardtack and hot coffee, Matt rolls up next to the fire and sleeps lightly. The moccasins will dry and he will be on the General's trail soon. Two hours passed and the moccasins were dry to Matt's satisfaction. Slipping them on, he shoulders his supplies and starts slogging his way down the trail, walking in the General's tracks. The fear of ambush does not worry him so much anymore. The General has only one man left. It's not bad odds if you have the big Sharps rifle on your side. Now they will leave the mountains as fast as their horses can carry them.

Dark comes and Matt did not seen any sign of the men but their tracks are plain to follow in the unbroken snow. Matt can tell their horses are almost done in. Signs show where one went to its knees, then recovered. If the men do not rest the horses soon they will be afoot themselves. Matt stops under the overhang of a large cedar tree. Pulling the branches back that hang to the ground, he breaks dry squaw wood and quickly gets a fire going.

Pulling out the battered coffeepot, Matt shakes his head, muttering to himself, "Pack something like that, just so you can enjoy your coffee. I must be getting soft in the head." The branches of the cedar make a perfect place to hold up for the night. The small fire will be almost impossible to see and the tight snow covered branches will hold the heat. Matt rolls out his blanket and sits back against the trunk. The sap, sticking to his coat, is ignored; only the hot coffee and his newly rolled cigarette matter.

Matt wonders where the General is and how far he is ahead? The moon should come up full tonight. It's a good night to travel, but it is going to be cold. Finishing his coffee, Matt rolls up in the heavy blanket, and after throwing a small amount of wood on the fire, he falls asleep. He turns his mind away from Cage and Jessie. He has to because the pain is just too great. In time, maybe it would lessen.

Two hours of sleep is all he allows himself and then he is back on the trail. Coming down the slick mountain trails, he has to use caution and not fall, but out on the valley flats, he can hit a dogtrot to keep warm. He heard Cloud and Tin Cup say a person shouldn't get too hot and sweat in this cold, so as soon as he feels himself beginning to sweat inside his overcoat, he slows down to a walk. The early morning grayness already starts to cast its light over the mountains, and the tracks continue to the west. Matt swears, the General did not stop for the night as he figured he would. His horses have to be exhausted.

Near midmorning, Matt finds where the two men stopped to build a fire. He can see where they emptied their coffeepot onto the snow. The small campfire is beside the trail and it is still smoldering. Gathering some dry limbs, Matt quickly has it going again. Pulling his moccasins off, he props them up with a stick and changes into his dry socks. Matt figures the General to be only a couple of hours ahead. For some reason, the man leading, seems to be stalling. In two different places, Matt saw where he took the longer way across a valley, instead of going straight across.

Matt wonders why he would lead the General astray, unless maybe it is a trick of some kind, to throw him off. With his feet dry once again, Matt strikes out and follows the General's tracks, determined to come upon him before dark. Midafternoon finds him coming down a particularly hazardous trail. Nearing the bottom, he flings himself face down, behind a boulder. Looking around the side of the big rock, he can see a man sitting quietly beside the trail, his horse standing with its head hanging down beside him. The trail took a sharp turn, and Matt did not see the man and horse until he was within a few yards of them.

Fearing a ruse of some kind, Matt slips the Henry from his back, thinking he may need more than one shot if they rush him. Checking the barrel and magazine, he brings the repeater to bear on the man.

"I know you're out there Mister but let me talk to you before you kill me." The man is looking right toward where Matt lies.

"Where's the other man?"

"Left me here and pulled his cowardly freight."

"You could be lying."

"Yea, I could be, but I'm not."

"Stand up and walk this way."

"Can't, horse fell with me and broke my leg," the man curses. "You think I'd be waiting here for you to kill me, like you done them others, if I could run?"

"I'm going to kill you, broke leg or not." Matt sights down the barrel of the Henry.

"I'm not one of these men, please Mister, listen to me," the man pleads. "Why do you think I was stalling the General, so you could catch up. I circled him back from the Divide. I knew you were coming, after you killed Abe Tolbin's horse and we lit out. Did you kill that skunk?"

"I killed him."

"No stars shined the first night, so I could double back, hoping to get loose and head for home," the man said. "Them soldiers sure ain't much on directions."

Matt is already tightening his finger on the Henry's trigger when he hesitates. The man is telling the truth. He has been stalling for the last two days, making it possible for Matt to keep up on foot. Studying the man, as he sits beside the horse, Matt can tell he isn't dressed as the others were. "Talk then and make it short."

"I'm telling you, it's safe, come on in."

"I can hear you plain enough from here."

"My name's Jim Miles. I got me a small spread out of Elk Springs."

"I'm listening." Matt silently pulls back into the surrounding woods while the man talks and then approaches him from the side.

The man's eyes grow wide as Matt appears from behind a tree. The Henry's wide muzzle points straight at his chest, making the man swallow hard. "Take it easy Mister, I ain't done you no wrong."

"You keep that kind of talk up and I'll kill you now."

"I swear to you Mister, I had nothing to do with this."

"You were there when they hung my brother." Matt's face turns stone-cold. "You were there when they shot and killed the woman."

"Yes Sir, I was." The man can see the cold hard eyes looking almost through him and knows he is a dead man. "But, I didn't hurt them none. Shucks, I was chained to a tree."

"You rode with this scum, you were in on it." Matt's voice is accusing and hard, leaving no argument.

"I had to, they came to my place, threatened to kill my wife and little girl if I didn't lead them to the Divide going to the Elkhorn." The man studies Matt, then continues. "They had gotten themselves lost and I knew they would kill my family if I didn't show them the way."

"So you led them straight to my brother and got him killed." The Henry raises ever so slightly, again at the man's chest.

"I didn't know that's what they were going to do, honest Mister." The man can't take his eyes off the Henry. "They were a mean looking bunch and this General is crazy."

"You're lying."

The man looks into the hate filled black eyes and shudders. "Kill me if you want but I'm telling you the truth. I didn't even know your brother was coming into town. Those men said they were heading north, to go buffalo hunting. How was I to know?"

"Do most buffalo hunters force a man to lead them hunting?"

"No Sir, I reckon not, but that's what they told me."

"You finished?" Matt steps in front of the man.

"I'd like to ask one favor."

"Ask." Matt ears back the hammer of the Henry.

"Would you have someone tell my wife what happened to me?"

"If you're telling the truth, I'll let her know."

"I'm a thanking you for that, she'll be worried."

Matt rolls a smoke and tosses the makings to Miles. "This General, is he the only one left of the bunch that came to your place?"

"Depends." Miles tries to roll a cigarette but his hands shake too much. "The one called Blalock, he's the one who took Palette back to town. Did you get him?"

Matt thought back, he did not see anyone when Palette appeared at the dance. Now that he thinks back, in his grief and worry, he didn't even wonder how Palette got back to town. Handing the man his smoking cigarette, Matt takes the makings and rolls another one. "What did this Blalock look like?"

"Stocky man, five ten, brown hair."

"That it?"

"He rode with a hard case called Red. The General sent him after some horse, why I don't know, but Blalock said Red got himself killed west of here."

"I killed him."

"Good." Miles blows smoke and looks at Matt. "Red's the one, sicked this General on your brother."

"Is that how he found me way out here?"

"That's what the men talked about as we made camp that first night after the Divide." Miles shrugs, starting to lose the fear that gripped him. "This General put out some feelers about you and Red mistook your brother for you."

"How far ahead is the General?"

"Not far, maybe two hours or less. His horse is played out, it's not going much further. The dang fool don't know, come here from sick 'em, about these mountains ranges."

"Miles, why did you lead them, after you saw what they did to my brother?" Matt waits for the man to answer before he pulls the trigger.

"Told you, they threatened to kill my family. If I hadn't, they said they would go back to my place and do it. Man, I didn't know they were going to kill your people, I swear."

"Would you have led them if you had of known?" Matt stares hard at the man.

"I reckon I would have, that General is crazy and mean. I would have done whatever he said, to save my family." The man shrugs.

"You cost me my family."

"I'm sorry, I truly am, and if you don't kill me, I'll have that to live with the rest of my days, and Mister, that's a burden to carry."

Matt looks off, down the trail the General took. He's tired of all the killing, but it has to be finished. Is this man lying to save himself or is he telling the truth? "Who's the lady that runs the big ranch north of Elk Springs?"

"You're meaning Vickie Gorman, her husband was killed awhile back in town by Wylie Palette."

"Miles, I'm letting you live but if I find out you're lying to me, I'll be after you if it takes the rest of my life." Matt drops the rifle barrel from the man.

"Thank you Mister Tillman, I just wish I could go with you, I owe this General something myself."

"Right now, Mister Miles, you wouldn't like my company."

Looking at Matt, the man knows he is lucky, getting off with his life. "Yes Sir, I'm no fool and I'll always be indebted to you."

"Think you can make it out of here with that leg?"

"I'll get back, my horse is played out right now but I'll let him rest a couple of days and he'll get me home. My wife and little girl are waiting and I'm all they have."

Matt gathers some straight sticks and cuts leather stripping from Miles' saddle. The break in the man's leg is clean. Pulling it back straight, he binds the leg as tight as he dares. He strips the saddle and blankets from the horse and places everything under a rock overhang for protection from the snow and wind. Matt helps the man over to it.

Matt's feet are dry and he rests and eats a little of his hardtack and coffee before leaving Miles the rest. "I'll leave you what food I have and when I can, I'll send someone looking for you."

"Man couldn't ask for more than that."

"Miles, the General is still out there and he's a mean one, so don't depend too much on that help. You may be on your own getting out of here."

"I'll make it, and I thank you."

"Give me the layout of these mountains and where exactly am I."

"I'll draw it on a piece of hide." Miles pulls out his knife and draws a detailed sketch of the surrounding mountains and valleys. Elk Springs, the Elkhorn Ranch, and the Gorman Place, everything laid out for Matt, almost to the inch.

"I thank you." Matt stakes the horse where he can chew bark and leaves from the surrounding trees and then drags several armloads of dead wood into the overhang. With a nod, he turns west following the General's trail.

"Good luck to you, Mister Tillman. You get that no good," Miles' voice trails off as Matt walks out of sight. Shuddering once uncontrollably, he doesn't envy the General any, for Miles knows hell and brimstone is on his trail. Tillman is the hardest man he ever met and he didn't particularly want to meet up with him again.

It's coming on dark. He needs to close in on the man before it starts to snow again. Hitting a long dogtrot, he follows the broken path of the General. Miles said he didn't believe the General could find his way out of these mountains alone, but Matt knows better. The man didn't become a general in the Union army because of his size.

He will travel through the night as long as he can make out the General's tracks. There is no reason to stop, he has no food or coffee and he needs to get this business finished before he grows weak from hunger. Leaning against a pine tree, he rolls himself a cigarette and catches his breath. Tomorrow, he will find the man. After that he will start on the trail of the one Miles called Blalock. Then, it will be finished.

He didn't think of Kate the last couple of days and he didn't want to. Hate fills his mind and he does not want the thought of her to change his mind. A man has to hate and he has to be cold, to do the things that lay ahead of him, and to survive the snow and bitter temperatures. He wonders if he should have let Miles live, but he is relieved he did. He has enough on his conscious now, to last a lifetime.

From all appearances, the General traveled through the night, keeping to a westerly course, straight toward Arapaho country. The Elkhorn is due north of him now according to Miles. Somewhere ahead, he will cross the road that leads to the Gorman Ranch and Elk Springs, unless he crossed it already during the night.

Daylight comes up slowly, cold, and quiet. Matt studies the landscape but being new to this country, he does not recognize anything. The road has to be either east or west of him. With the heavy snow falling, probably covering the trail, he may have crossed over it not knowingly.

He can turn north and find his way to the ranch to get food and a horse, but then he might lose the General's tracks and that he was not going to do. The General is just as cold and hungry as he is. No, the trail leads west and that's where he will go.

Matt is entering a small valley, when his eyes focus on a dark object, halfway across the flat ground. The sun is shimmering off the snow, making it hard for him to tell what it is. It may be a cow or a buffalo but it's too big for a deer. The General's tracks lead straight toward the still object, lying in the snow. He will have to cross the open meadow without any cover. Matt's stomach is growling from hunger and he's in a hurry. He isn't about to skirt along the woods.

Coming closer, he is surprised to see it's the General's horse, and it hasn't started stiffening up yet. A Cavalry General, who rode his horse to death, Matt can only shake his head in disbelief.

Looking down at the dead horse, Matt pulls his knife and apologizes. "Sorry old man but I'm hungry, and you won't be feeling it anymore." Horsemeat is stringy and tough, but it will fill Matt's stomach, giving him the strength to keep up the chase. Miles said the General was out of food. Blalock was supposed to bring them some back from town but he didn't show at the homestead. Matt places several raw strips in his blanket then shoulders the Henry. He will cook them later. For now, he is intent on the General's tracks that never vary from their westward course.

Matt doubts the man can stay ahead of him for long, as he was unaccustomed to walking and probably not in good shape. It is only a matter of hours now, the cold and snow will stop the man somewhere ahead. Matt just has to be careful and not run into an ambush.

It's late afternoon and the clouds are beginning to spit small snowflakes. To Matt's dismay, the General doesn't appear to be slowing down. Doubling his efforts, Matt falls back into his familiar ground eating dog trot and hurries through the afternoon. The big man has to be close. The snow becomes harder as night falls and Matt still hasn't caught sight of him. What keeps him going?

Darkness closes in around him, and with the heavy snow, tracking is impossible. Matt finds a small overhang and drags in some dead wood for a fire. The fire's little blaze just flares up, when Matt hears a gunshot off to the west. How far, he does not know as the wind picked up, but it has to be the General. Grabbing his bedroll and weapons, Matt runs off in the direction he thinks it came from.

Only minutes pass when another shot sounds from the darkness ahead. This time, Matt can swear it was a pistol that discharged. Hurrying faster, Matt comes to the end of the valley and starts down the descent of the narrow trail. Again, this time much closer, the pistol discharges and then a yell of defiance come from ahead.

Indians! Matt closes in on the fight ahead. The General must have run into the Arapaho. What are they doing so far away from their hunting grounds? Hearing is tricky, but the fight cannot be over a half mile ahead. Slipping cautiously down the trail, Matt ignores his wet feet. If it's Indians, he has to get there before they kill the General. An hour passes and everything ahead is quiet. The fight apparently is over or the combatants are waiting each other out.

Matt eases in cautiously, not knowing exactly where the General or the Indians are. Coming to a deep canyon, Matt looks down at a glowing campfire. Several Indians mill around the fire, their attention on a big man lying in the snow. The General! Matt cusses as he climbs slowly down the rocky canyon, creeping warily, close to the camp.

The General is trussed up with two warriors standing over him. Several other warriors lie about the fire on their buffalo robes. Matt recognizes the two men near the General. Yellow Bonnet is the one he fought with and Fox Tails, May Bell's Indian father.

Stepping into the firelight, where the warriors can see him, Matt raises his hand in greeting, the way he watched Cloud do. Warriors bound from their blankets, brandishing weapons, and advancing upon him. Matt pronounces the words, "Iron Man" and points toward his chest.

Yellow Bonnet steps forward and then Fox Tails approaches, both men are wary. Matt can tell they think he is with the General. Motioning for him to come to the fire, Matt steps over to where the General lies on the ground. Pointing the Sharps at him, Matt pulls the hammer back on the rifle and places it at the man's head.

Fox Tails springs forward and grabs Matt's arm. "This you cannot do, Iron Man."

Matt is shocked, he did not know the man spoke English. "You speak white man tongue?"

"Umh good, Little Flower teach 'em injun good English." Fox Tails grins. "But, white man prisoner of Yellow Bonnet, you no can kill."

"You tell Yellow Bonnet, he owes me a life, now I want this man's life."

Fox Tails speaks quickly to Yellow Bonnet. The man nods and propels Matt toward the fire. Handing him a piece of deer meat, he looks Matt over and sees the sorry state he is in. Looking at Fox Tails, he speaks then nods at Matt.

"Yellow Bonnet asks why you want kill this man, and why you no have horse or food?" Fox Tails asks.

Matt reaches inside his coat and pulls out the fresh-skinned horsemeat, his tobacco, and paper. Rolling three cigarettes, he hands Yellow Bonnet and Fox Tails each one. The men smoke, as the cigarettes burn down to stubs Matt starts his story. The warriors listen respectfully, sometimes their mouths opening in astonishment, especially when Matt tells them about the dead horses. Finishing his long oration, Matt points at the General and looks into Yellow Bonnet's eyes. "That man is mine, I will pay whatever you say for him, but he is mine to kill. It is my blood right to kill him."

Yellow Bonnet can hear the venom in Matt's voice and see the hate in his eyes. He does not need Fox Tails to translate.

Fox Tails nods sadly. "Yes, Iron man, yours is the blood right, this man has done you much wrong. We were on our way to your village to get the wahoos you will give us. The hunting was poor and our villages need meat. We also know of the dead horses and the dead men that killed them. We did not know it was you that killed the men until now. One of our warriors was hunting off our land and watched from hiding when you killed these men. He didn't know you so he said you were a demon. He said you put one in a tree with a rope around his neck. He thinks you are a devil who lives in the mountains, and will not ride into this country with us.

"I am no devil or demon."

"We know now who you are, but he scared us a little also. To shut a man's wind off and kill him does not let the man's spirit walk in the next land."

"I do not want them walking in the next world." Matt slashes his hand down as Fox Tails translates to the gathered warriors. Several back away from him in awe and look toward the General.

"Do you hate this man that much?" Yellow Bonnet asks, speaking in his own language. Matt only stares, when Fox Tails translates to him what Yellow Bonnet asked. Looking over at the General, Matt nods. "How did you capture this man?"

"We came on him at dark and raised our hands in peace. He fired at us and ran away. We chased one arm man and he fire again then we capture." Fox Tails head bobs up and down.

"Yellow Bonnet asks, what will you do with this man?"

"I intend to hang him and then I'm going to skin him."

Fox Tails shakes his head sadly. "This is a bad thing for the Little Iron Man to do. Don't your people want you to bring this bad one into their town?"

"I will pay many guns for this man." Matt raises the Henry and shows it to Yellow Bonnet.

The General tries to rise, only to fall back on the ground, shouting. "He's crazy, I'll pay you more, anything you want, anything!"

"You would not trade guns for the horses, now you trade for this one?" Fox Tails is curious.

"He is mine alone to kill."

Yellow Bonnet looks closely into Matt's eyes, ignoring the General's words. "No guns, no wahoos. You, Iron Man, have given me back my life. The white man is yours, to do as you wish."

"It is good. Go to my village to the east. Tell the black man I said to give you all the blankets and wahoos you need. Tell him all the bad men are dead, except this one and one other. Tell him I will follow the other man tomorrow, and that I am well." Matt stands up and walks toward the General then turns back. "Why is Yellow Bonnet not with Crazy Horse to the north?"

Fox Tails waves his hands. "Too much snow, bad weather. Maybe we go when it warmer."

The warriors watch as Matt boots the man over to a tree. The rawhide rope that binds the man will have to do, as Matt has no rope with him. Laying the tobacco out as payment for the rope, Matt knows the Indians will not touch it again. He looks at them and nods. Untying the man, he stands him up, putting the rope around his neck. The general is still powerful, even with one arm, and he struggles to break free.

Matt knocks him to the ground and removes the General's boots. Pulling his large skinning knife, he makes two slices across the General's ankles hamstringing him. Pulling the screaming man back to his feet, he pulls the rope taut, holding the crippled man upward. The rope cut off the screams as the General can barely breathe.

"Now, General, it's pay-back time, for my brother Cage, his wife Jessie, and the men you killed with them."

"No, no." The words hiss out as the knife slices through his clothing, leaving him naked in the cold air. Blood runs in rivulets down the man's legs as Matt takes his skin off. The General jerks with each slice, finally collapsing as the rope cuts off the air from his lungs. Matt finishes skinning him then buries the knife in the trunk of the tree and walks back to the fire.

The warriors step back in awe. They were used to torturing their enemies, but the crazed look on the Iron Man's face is more than they understand. Maybe he is a demon after all.

"We go now, Iron Man. We will leave you a horse." Fox Tails speaks, as he walks to where the others wait. "We will tell the black man where you are."

Matt never looks up, only staring into the blaze as the warriors ride away. The General sways slowly in the wind, his eyes staring into the unknown.

CHAPTER 13

Matt points the small Indian pony toward the town of Elk Springs. He looks back once more to see the General gently swaying in the cold morning air. Matt feels nothing, no remorse, nor any satisfaction from killing the man. Maybe that will come later. Either way, it does not matter. Now he has only one man to find, Blalock.

He bypasses the Gorman Ranch, not wanting to answer questions. Sitting outside the town of Elk Springs, he waits until dark then skirts the town before slipping silently into the dark livery barn. He remembers Tin Cup and the hostler talking about this man Blalock, but with all the fighting and killing, he completely forgot about the man until Miles spoke of him. Tying the horse to a stall, he finds the liveryman sleeping soundly in his bunk.

Lighting a coal oil lamp, Matt rousts the hostler awake. Rubbing the sleep from his eyes and grumbling from waking up at an odd hour, the man looks up at Matt and recoils backward against his cot in fright.

"It's okay, mister, I'm Matt Tillman."

"Mister Tillman, I thought I was a dead man." The hostler gasps. "What happened to you? Where did all that blood come from?"

"I need supplies and a horse. Also, I want to know about the man named Blalock, the man you mentioned the night of the dance."

"Yes sir." The man stutters, still bug eyed. "Whatever you want, just don't kill me, like you done them others."

"What are you talking about?"

"It's all over town. They found some of the bodies you've been leaving everywhere." The hostler is shaking so bad, he cannot get into his pants.

"I ain't going to harm you, unless you keep stalling me around."

"No sir, Mister Tillman, no sir."

"Did you see this man Blalock after the dance, when Palette came in?"

"Yes sir, he came in right after you all left for the Divide."

"What did he want?"

"A fresh horse and supplies, just like you're a wantin'."

"Where did he go?"

"Said he was headin' south, out of this cold country."

"You believe him?"

"Didn't have any reason not to, seemed like a nice enough fellow." The hostler studies Matt's wild eyes. "Did he help kill your brother?"

"Get me a horse and some grub."

"What about clothes, you look like you just come from a hog killin'."

"You got any here that will fit me?"

"They'll have them at the store."

"No, these will do, just get me the horse, I'll make you out a receipt. Have Cloud or Hob pay you when they come into town."

"Yes Sir, anything else?"

"Just this; you haven't seen me, is that clear?" Matt answers. "Keep the injun pony. I'll be back for him and the Sharps Rifle. If anything happens to it, you'll catch it from Tin Cup."

"I know who it belongs to. I don't want that old heathen down on me. I'll take good care of the blasted thing."

"You just remember that."

"If I haven't seen you how am I gonna get my money?" The hostler bites off a chaw of tobacco and returns it to his pocket. "Oh I see, you mean I'm not to tell Kate at the store. Is that it?"

"That's it. Now I need some money too, if you'll take my marker for it. Folks in the next town may not be so generous."

"Generous, I'd come closer to calling it robbery. Yea, okay, I'll get you some money." The hostler mumbles as he makes his way to his dirty office.

"What's the total?" Matt asks the hostler, as he tightens the cinch on the chunky little bay horse, he brought out.

"Three hundred ought to do it, counting the money I gave you."

Matt quickly scribbles out an IOU to the man and then steps in the saddle. "What's this Blalock look like?"

The hostler quickly gives Matt the same basic description that Miles gave him. "Now in case you ain't sure, just ask that horse you're on."

"What's that supposed to mean?"

"He used to belong to Blalock, best horse in the barn, but he was sure 'nuff wore out by the time Blalock got back to town that night so I swapped him another for it." The hostler grins, relieved to see Matt riding out.

"See Hob, he'll pay you, and thanks." Matt turns the little horse and is almost through the doors when the hostler hollers. Matt pulls up and looks back.

"Forgot to tell you, Wylie Palette left yesterday morning after the same man."

"Wylie Palette? I thought he was shot up, almost dead."

"Nah, most of them holes were just flesh wounds. Old Wylie's tough as iron nails. He's a little on the slow side yet, but he's dead game, and he's after your man Blalock."

Matt turns the bay down the south road, leaving Elk Springs. If his memory serves him well, the next town is just a mud stop in the middle of nowhere, but it does have a store and a saloon. Riding through the night, he comes into the town of Sand Flats, at daybreak. The little gelding is still traveling easy, when Matt stops at the livery stable and dismounts. Pulling the Henry from the saddle scabbard, he has the livery man grain and hay the little gelding and then starts for the store. He removed the heavy blood soaked sheepskin coat before entering town so he would not attract attention.

"I need some clean clothes, boots, shave and a bath, not necessarily in that order." Matt throws a twenty-dollar gold piece on the counter. "Reckon that ought to cover it."

"It'll head that way Mister, bath is through that curtain." The store man points the way. "I'll heat you some water while you're getting a haircut and shave."

"You the barber, too?"

"That's me. You see anybody else around here?" The old man cackles, as he exits the room.

Matt is refreshed. The hot bath and clothes did him wonders. He is surprised when the old store man pulls out a pair of boots that fit him to a tee.

"Feller left them here last year against a bill and never did come back for them." The store man grins. "What else?"

"Tobacco and the makings."

"There you go." The store keep lays the tobacco and paper on the counter. "Say, Mister, I couldn't help but notice, you've misplaced your skinning knife. Just happen to have a real dandy here and it's sharp as a razor and worth the money."

"Let's see it." Matt looks at the knife the store man lay on the counter. "Same fellow leave this too?"

"Now how did you know that?"

"I'm a good guesser, I guess." The store man was right. The knife has a razor's edge and a bone handle. Yes, it was indeed, a dandy. "How much?"

"Five dollars."

"Three."

"Done."

Matt places the knife in his empty knife sheath and lays out three dollars for the man. "Now tell me, did a man ride through here last week named Blalock?"

"Man come through here alright but didn't give his name, most don't, and I sure didn't ask. Another feller came through yesterday, mean lookin' feller, he was feeling kinda poorly."

"You know where they were heading?"

"Feller yesterday asked the same question. South's all I know and that's south my friend," the store man points down the road. "He did ask something about a town south of here called Rio Blanco."

"I'm indebted to you." Matt walks over to the livery. The little bay is indeed a traveling kind of horse. Not quite up to Tin Cup's pinto, but he has a good easy trot and plenty of staying power. Matt is turning over in his mind what the storekeeper said. Rio Blanco is a ways off, maybe two, three days or more, he cannot remember exactly, as he only passed through it once on his way to Elk Springs. What did he tell Cloud, that he has a whole lifetime to track these men? This is a big country. Blalock can change direction at any time; it could take a lifetime.

The road south, over the mountains, is merely a cow path, but it is the only road south. Riding easy, he rests the little bay and lets him graze whenever the opportunity arises when some good grass comes along. Matt has good reason to keep the horse, if it belongs to Blalock, the man might give his hand away and ask something about him, that is, if Matt ever catches up with him.

Matt rides into the town of Meeker, two days later. It's considerably larger than Elk Springs, with several stores lining the street. Matt puts the bay in a livery barn, and hunts down an eating-place for himself. Seating himself at a corner table, he studies the room and the red-checkered tables that fill it. Early yet for the noontime rush, Matt looks out the window and studies the street.

"Can I help you, Sir?" A small, grey haired lady takes his order.

Matt gives her his order and starts in on a hot cup of coffee while he waits. Shoveling the food down, he did not realize how hungry he was for a good meal. As he finishes, and is about to leave, a man wearing a badge enters and sits down at the counter. Walking over, Matt takes a seat beside the town Marshall and orders another cup of coffee. "Mind if I ask you a question or two, Marshall?" Matt notes the cold hard stare that is fixes on him, almost immediately.

"Depends; what's your questions?"

"I'm looking for a man named Blalock; five eight or so, brown hair, stocky build."

"Well now, he a friend of yours?" Matt notices the Marshall's hand resting lightly on his pistol.

"My name's Mathew Tillman. I figure you already heard about the killings around Elk Springs."

"I've heard. I met Cage Tillman a time or two. You his brother?"

"I am and this Blalock is tied in with the murders."

"And you're after him?"

"I'm after him."

"This other feller, Palette; how's he fit into all this?"

Matt sips on his coffee then looks out the door. "He worked for my brother. This Blalock helped shoot Palette and my brother. Palette took it real personal."

"Don't reckon I blame him too much. I'm right sorry to hear about your brother and his Missus. Seemed like real fine people."

"They were the finest I ever knew."

The Marshall nods his head slightly. "From what the barkeep across the street said, this Blalock landed him a job with the Circle Five outfit down by Rio Blanco. Feller named Ferguson owns it. Pretty tough outfit I hear."

"What about Palette?"

"Heard the same thing I did, and headed to Rio Blanco. This Palette, is he a rough customer?"

Matt shrugs. "He took four slugs about a week ago and is in the saddle already. How would you size him up?"

Grinning, the Marshall finishes his coffee. "Tough enough, I would have to say."

Matt sticks out his hand. "Thank you Marshall, hope to see you again."

"Mister Tillman, you watch your back. That Circle Five bunch isn't too fussy about where they shoot you, so I hear."

"How much is the damage, Ma'am." Matt reaches for his money.

"This one is on me." The Marshall pulls money from his pocket.

"Well thank you, Marshall, and the name is Matt."

The hostler tells Matt it is nigh on thirty miles or so to Rio Blanco. Matt pushes the little bay into his fast, running walk, if he can, he wants to overtake Palette before he catches up with Blalock. Somewhere ahead, he and Palette will find Mister Blalock and Matt is not sure Palette is in good enough shape for a gunfight.

Dark is coming quickly, Matt picks out a good location for night camp. He does not know where Blalock or Palette are, so he isn't taking any chances of being surprised during the night.

Watering the bay, he pickets him securely on some tall grass, and rolls into his blankets. Tomorrow will come early and he wants to ride into Rio Blanco by noontime. Rolling a smoke, he looks up at the stars. What will tomorrow bring?

Early morning comes and Matt is up before the crows, with the coffeepot on. Leading the gelding to water, he lets him drink his fill and pours a couple handfuls of corn on the ground. Filling his cup, he sits back and rolls a smoke, wondering if today will end it. He hopes so because he is tired. Flipping his cigarette butt away, Matt saddles the horse and stows his gear. He mounts the little gelding and takes the road to the south.

Rio Blanco is another small town which some call a village. Like most settlements in this country, it is just a wide spot in the road. The main thoroughfare consists of one dusty street spotted with mud holes from the women's laundry tubs, which are mostly occupied by hogs wallowing to their heart's content. Chickens and dogs seem to be the other major occupants of the street.

Matt pulls the gelding up and rolls himself a smoke, studying the ramshackle buildings that line the street. A large beer mug, fades from the sun, adorns a building that Matt figures for the local saloon. The only other building of any size has to be a general store.

Matt shakes his head. No wonder the Circle Five riders were surly, if this is all the entertainment they have to look forward to. Several smaller adobe huts line the streets, Matt figures they are the family structures of the local inhabitants. The wooden buildings are so faded from the sun and for lack of paint they can pass for adobe as well.

"Quite a prosperous enterprise," Matt thinks to himself. Drawing on his cigarette, he studies the little hamlet of paradise. He shakes his head, a man could get rabies just stepping off his horse into this pest hole. The mangy dogs do not look too friendly, the hogs are pretty thin, and even the chickens seem skinny.

Riding over to the local livery, which consists of a few weathered poles thrown together, Matt does not bother to dismount. The place is so nasty. His horse is likely to catch lockjaw or founder before morning.

Matt thinks about Vickie Gorman and her rules about horses using the ground. The manure in the lots is knee high or higher on the bone thin horses. Vickie would sure have her job cut out for herself here. No, the gelding will be better off tied all night to a hitch rail.

Riding back to the store, Matt dismounts and ties the little horse, he dubbed Shorty, to the lone post that graces the store. Even the porch railing looks like it will fall over if a horse sneezes real hard.

Matt's almost afraid to enter the store, he isn't quite sure what he might find inside. Bracing himself, he opens the door and walks in. A potbellied stove is glowing in one corner with a pot of coffee sitting atop it. Walking over to the stove, he pours himself a cup then turns and surveys the room. He is pleasantly surprised as the place is well stocked and clean. One old Mexican man is placing tin goods on a shelf behind the counter. A platter of Tortillas and boiled eggs sit at the end of the counter. Matt walks over and helps himself, rolling some kind of meat and eggs into a tortilla.

The old man taps on the wall and a few minutes later a rotund, greyheaded woman appears. "Yes Sir, can I help you?"

"Yes Ma'am, I need to pay you for the coffee and tortillas I just downed."

"They're on the house stranger." She smiles. "Anything else?"

"Reckon I could use a couple sacks of tobacco and the makings."

"That'll cost you, two bits a sack, paper and sulphur will be a nickel."

"Where will I find the Circle Five spread?"

The rotund lady walks toward the back. "Three miles south and a mile east." She lays the tobacco on the counter. "They having a shindig or free eats out there?"

"Couldn't tell you that," Matt grins.

"Well, there sure as the dickens, something going on out there," she laughs. "Reason I say that, you're the third feller that's been in here the last two days, looking for Ben Ferguson's Circle Five."

"That right. Well, I heard they were hiring." Matt hedges.

"Go over to the saloon and tell that baloney to the Circle Five riders over there." She looks him up and down. "But you watch out for Billy Ferguson. He should be about liquored up enough by now to be on the prod."

"Yes Ma'am."

"I ain't funnin' you Mister; that boy's already killed three men here in the last two years and he ain't turned twenty yet."

"His old man owns the Circle Five, I reckon?"

"His uncle owns it. The boy came to live with Ben when his Pa got himself shot." The woman frowns, "a sorry day for Ben Ferguson when he came."

"Thinks he's bad, huh?"

"He don't think nothin', stranger; he knows. All them fights were fair. He may be a young'un, but he's pure poison with a pistol."

"His uncle approve of all this killing?"

"No, he don't, but Billy Ferguson does what he wants to. I'm warning you, be careful around that little hellion."

"Yes Ma'am, I'll be careful," Matt grins. "Oh, by the way, could you sell me some oats or corn? My horse needs some groceries."

Looking out the window, she laughs. "You call that a horse? Man we got gophers bigger than that. Cost you two bits for corn."

"Yes Ma'am."

"He's kinda short, for a big galoot like you to be riding."

"Yes, but he gets me where I need to go."

"I'll take care of your horse; got me a corral around back." The rotund woman shakes her head.

"Well, I'm thanking you." Matt starts for the door.

"You watch yourself over there, big man," the woman warns him.

Matt pushes through the swinging doors of the saloon and steps into the cool interior. Again, he's surprised at the spacious room, just as the store impressed him. A well-polished bar runs the length of the room, with large mirrors and whiskey bottles and glasses lining the wall under the mirrors. Surveying the room, Matt steps to the bar. Three cowboys play stud poker at the rear table. The rest of the occupants were townsmen, having their afternoon beer. Matt recognizes the young Billy Ferguson right off and the old woman was right, he has a good load of whiskey under his belt. Young, mouthy, and full of himself, Matt has seen his kind in every town in the south.

Matt lays out two dollars in change on the bar, as the barkeep pours him a shot glass of whiskey. Taking twenty cents from the pile, the man goes back to polishing his shot glasses. Matt looks in the mirror and watches the three cowboys at the far table. The old woman was right again, they are a rough looking bunch. Nodding at the barkeep, he pushes two more dimes from the pile and waits until his glass is refilled. "Here's to you barkeep." Matt raises his glass to the man, downing it in one swallow.

"Well now, thank you stranger," the barman nods.

"I'm looking for a friend of mine, supposed to work for the Circle Five Ranch hereabout." Matt watches in the mirror for the effect his words have on the cowboys, playing cards.

"Reckon I can't help you there, Mister." The smile leaves the man's face, his eyes darting toward the cardplayers. "Don't know many of the Circle Five Riders."

"That seems strange. The only saloon in thirty miles, I'd figure you'd know them all." Matt eases the thong from his pistol.

"Sorry."

Matt watches the man's face turn ashen as he retreats down the bar. Looking into the mirror, Matt sees the reason the man retreated. Billy Ferguson is walking toward the bar, a familiar swagger in his step.

Stepping up beside Matt, the young gunman turns. "Who are you looking for, Mister?"

Matt does not like the youngster or his cocky attitude. He is on the prod.

"That any of your business?"

"I'm making it my business."

Matt turns toward the youngster. "In that case, I'm looking for a friend of mine."

"I ride for Circle Five; matter of fact I own it."

"That right? I heard a man named Ben Ferguson owned it, you him?"

"My uncle, but I run the ranch, names Billy Ferguson."

"You're kinda young for such an important position," Matt grins, taunting the youngster. Suddenly, he feels mean.

"I'm old enough to get the job done."

"Well then, Mister Billy Ferguson, I'm looking for a man named Blalock."

"Wouldn't know anybody by that name."

"You probably wouldn't, my friend just hired on yesterday." Matt watches the wild look come into the youngster's eyes. He saw the same look many times during the war. Billy Ferguson is a natural killer and he is working his way up to a killing, he marked Matt for his next victim.

An older puncher steps between them. "Sorry Mister, we don't know your friend."

"Stay out of this Ace," the younger man, growls.

"Billy, you know what your Uncle Ben said."

The backhand slap across the older puncher's face is heard all around the room. The man called Ace flushes, beet red, as his hand drops toward the pistol at his side.

The youngster grins. "Go ahead old man, I'll kill you before you clear leather and you know it for a fact."

"Boy!" Matt takes the young Ferguson's attention away from the older man. "I think you have first call on me."

Two feet separate Matt from the young gunman. Matt grins and hooks both thumbs in his gun belt. He can tell Ferguson does not like the distance between them. His hand waits inches from the cross draw pistol. Matt watches him lick his lips; he doesn't like it. At this close range, neither man can miss.

"It's your play youngster, pull that iron or crawl." Matt is purposely baiting the youngster. He wants to kill him. Matt watches as Ferguson's eyes turn red and madness takes over. As quick as a striking rattler, his hand grabs for the pistol. Matt has to admit, the kid has no fear, but Matt's big hand is faster, grabbing the youngster's hand and crushing his knuckles that curl around the pistol grip. The gun drops to the bar floor and Matt lifts the young gunman onto the bar, dragging him the length of it. Dragging Ferguson outside on the saloon's porch, he finds a chair, pulling the little man's small frame across his lap. Entrapping the youngster's legs with his own, Matt takes his own gun and spanks the youngster, like he would a five year old. Finishing, he pushes the crazed young gunman into the street among the laughing of the local inhabitants.

"I'll kill you for that." Young Ferguson rises to his feet.

"You're lucky, youngster, Mister Tillman is feeling generous toward you today," Wylie Palette speaks up, leaning against the saloon's wall. "I know, he done me the same way once."

Matt looks to where Palette stands and grins. It's good to see a familiar face, even if he didn't particularly like the man. Palette is thin, thinner than he was when he last saw him.

"You alright?" Matt walks to where the man is standing.

"I am now," Palette, grins. "Mister Tillman, it's good to see you."

"Well in that case, Mister Palette, it's good to see you."

"This Mister stuff is a lot of talking, why don't you just call me Wylie."

Matt nods, "alright, you call me Matt."

"You know Matt, we might as well be friends as my sister is gonna need my help now and that'll make us neighbors."

"Okay Wylie, it's a deal, if you'll answer me just one question."

"If I can."

"I know it's none of my business but I've got to know," Matt looks at the man. "Why'd you kill your own sister's husband?"

"I'll speak of it just once; no more."

"I'll never mention it again."

Wylie retreats to a chair, propped against the saloon's wall and sits down. "My exbrother-in-law, Mister Gorman, was a little man; not in size, but he abused Vickie something awful. The last time he laid hands on her; I found him in town and called him on it. He went for his gun and I was forced to kill him."

"Alright, Wylie, it's forgotten." Matt offers Palette the makings.

Palette accepts the tobacco. "Thank you."

"Now I've got a job to finish." Matt watches as Billy Ferguson disappears inside the saloon.

"You talking about Blalock?"

Matt nods. "He's the last."

"Are all the rest dead?"

Matt blows out some smoke into the air. "Dead."

"Then it's finished, I done in Mister Blalock this morning."

"How did you get him at the Circle Five Ranch, all by yourself?"

"Let's just say, the thin boards of an outhouse won't stop a forty-four slug."

Matt grins. "You mean while he wa...?"

"He didn't deserve a fair break."

"You positive he's dead?"

"Reckon they don't come any deader," Wylie smiles. "Sure had a funny look on his face."

Matt nods, turning toward the store. "I'll get my horse and we'll head home, we've got two ranches to run."

"I'm more than ready." Palette walks slowly to where his horse was tied.

"You, big man, turn around!" The challenge comes as Matt starts up the steps to the store. He sees the frightened look of the old woman standing in the doorway. Turning, he watches Billy Ferguson step down from the saloon steps. "It's my turn now to do the spanking."

Waving for Palette to keep back, Matt stares calmly at the livid face of the young gunman. "Let it go, son, I don't want to kill you."

"You've got it to do, big man. No one whips Billy Ferguson and lives to brag about it." The youngster squares himself in the street.

"I didn't whip you, son, I spanked you."

Ferguson sees red. Matt can tell from where he is, the youngster is ready to draw. "I'm gonna kill you for that remark."

"I'm not telling you again, you draw that hog leg and you'll never see tomorrow." Matt's face changes. Palette can almost see the blood lust in his features. Both men are ready to kill and there is no turning back.

Palette watches from where he stands, as the muscles twitch in the young man's face. Not a person moves; the town waits in anticipation. Suddenly, the street becomes deathly quiet. Matt is ready. He knows the moment will come at any minute. Ferguson is fast; Matt senses, rather than sees, when the young gunman reaches for his gun. The roar of the pistols comes first and then fire belches from both men's guns. The people along the street cannot tell who fired first as the reports of the shots were so close.

Matt feels the burn in his side. His gun belches lead and death, as he fires until his hammer comes down on an empty cylinder. Watching Ferguson fall backward into the dust, Matt looks across the dirty street at the crumpled body that now seems so small. Letting the pistol fall to his side, he stands in the street ashamed of himself for killing the youngster. Why didn't he just turn and walk away? Did he turn into a killer, the same as the boy? Did he like to kill?"

Watching the Circle Five riders surrounding the body, he puts a fresh cylinder in his pistol and walks toward them. No one moves, shocked that the young hellion was outdrawn and now was dead. They step back as Matt and Palette approach.

"I didn't want this." Matt's voice is almost a whisper. "You boys in this or is it finished and over with?"

"No Sir, if it hadn't been you, somebody else would have killed him sooner or later, he just pushed too hard." The puncher called Ace shakes his head. "Course, we don't know what his uncle will do."

"Tell Mister Ferguson, Matt Tillman killed the boy and I'm sorry." Matt studies the bloody remains of the young life. "Tell him the kid had sand, plenty of sand."

"I'll tell him."

Matt did not say, he tried to walk away, because he didn't. He was ready to kill Billy Ferguson and he did. Now he wonders if he should have tried harder to avoid a fight or if he really wanted to kill the youngster.

Looking over at Palette, Matt turns toward the store where the old lady and the Mexican man wait. Looking up at her, Matt sees the shock in her face as she looks at him. "You were right Ma'am, he was a bad man."

"Guess you'll be wantin' your horse?" She nods for Matt to follow her around back. "It weren't your fault. That boy had a mean streak in him a yard wide and would have killed more if you hadn't of done him in."

"Is that supposed to make it right?"

"No right or wrong to it, he needed killing, it's as simple as that." The old woman leads the little gelding from the corral.

Matt throws the saddle on and cinches it down, then turns to the woman. "I guess I've killed a lot of men that needed killing, but it's still killing, anyway you add it up."

"Yes, but you've saved a lot of men by killing him," she grins. "Good-bye, Mister Tillman, and if you ever get this way again, stop in. You're always welcome."

Palette walks up beside him. "Let's go home, Matt."

Chapter 14

Elk Springs comes into view late in the afternoon, almost as the sun is going down. They stopped three days earlier in the town of Meeker where a doctor fixed Matt's side. The bullet hit his side almost in the same spot the horse thieves wounded him before. Riding slowly to keep the wound from opening, it takes almost a week to make the ride back to Elk Springs.

Matt speaks very little as they ride and only when Palette asks him a direct question. Palette tries to convince Matt that Ferguson needed killing as much as the General and his men, but to no avail. Shrugging his shoulders, he decides to let it be, no more will be spoken on the subject.

Pulling up, a mile from the outskirts of Elk Springs, Matt sits his horse and studies the road that leads into town. "This is where I leave you, Wylie."

"You ain't riding in with me?"

"No." Matt looks off, toward the mountains. "I need you to do me a favor though. Tell Hob and Cloud to do as I told them, they run the Elkhorn now. Also, have the man at the livery lay me in a supply of things on this list."

"That it?"

"That's it."

"Matt come on home with me." Palette looks over at him. "That boy would have killed you and never thought a thing about it."

"Wylie, I've got some sorting out to do." Matt studies the man. "When I get it done, I'll be along; until I do, I won't be worth living with."

"Alright."

"One more thing, tell Hob to take care of my son."

"I'll do it, first thing tomorrow, if the weather lets me ride over to the Elkhorn."

Matt watches Palette ride on in to town then he finds a place out of the wind and settles down to wait until dark. Rolling a smoke, he leans back against a large oak tree and tries to relax. It is finished and done with. Cage and Jessie's killers are all dead. Why is he unable to ride on to the ranch and try to forget the killings and meanness? He saw killing during the war and even before that. The boy marked him; put a guilty feeling inside him, to where he does not want to see people or even be around them. He has to get away. He has to come to grips with his conscience and the devils that lie inside him.

The snow is coming down hard again as Matt pulls the doors of the livery open and leads the bay in. The hostler is repairing a bridle when he enters. Setting it down, he walks to where Matt is closing the big doors, against the north wind. "Evening Mister Tillman. Palette came through and said you'd be along."

Matt nods and hands the reins of the bay to him. "Feed him good, will you?"

"Yes sir."

"Is that coffee on the stove?"

"Yes sir, help yourself. There's some biscuits and side meat in the warmer."

Matt shrugs out of his overcoat and helps himself to the coffee and grub. Watching, as the hostler unsaddles the bay and puts him in a stall, he feels tired suddenly, as the warmth of the stable hits him. Leaning back in the rope-backed rocking chair, he relaxes for the first time in, what seems like months.

Matt can tell, by the rattling of the shingle roof the wind is picking up. By morning, the storm should blow itself out and he will ride. The bay can use the rest. He was pushed hard with little feed for the last two weeks.

The hostler tosses the saddle over a sawhorse and walks to where Matt sits. "Get plenty to eat?"

"Plenty, thank you." Matt nods.

"Looks like the little horse has seen many a mile, since I saw you last."

Matt ignores the man. "You get your money from Hob?"

"Yes Sir, I did." The hostler looks at Matt curiously. There is something different about him, something he cannot explain, Tillman changed. He seems aloof, colder.

"My supplies?" Matt is crisp, not wanting to engage in conversation.

The stable man nods to a tarp, covering a small pile of supplies Matt ordered. "Right there."

"Any questions?"

"No Sir, Kate asked me if I heard anything. I lied and told her no." The hostler hesitates. "She cares for you, you know?"

Matt ignores him. "You reckon this storm will blow itself out by morning?"

"Maybe, but it'll be back by evening, and soon it'll close the passes and all travel for the winter."

"Wake me up before daylight." Matt starts toward his bedroll.

"Yes Sir. You headed home come morning?"

"Yea, I'm headed home." Matt nods but where home is, he does not know himself.

Morning finds Matt on the trail. He rides the Indian pony that Fox Tails and Yellow Bonnet gave hi. The bay is carrying the supplies that he ordered. He points the horse due west, into Arapaho country, turning his back on the Elkhorn, and Kate.

Palette rides through the cold and snow toward the Elkhorn. Vickie informs him of what was happening while he was away, the funeral and burying of Cage and Jessie. The ranchers from miles around attended their funeral. Cloud recovered from his wound and May Bell drove him out to the lower Elkhorn Ranch. At first, the hands at the ranch resent an Indian taking over. With Tin Cup backing him, he convinces them he is their new boss until Matt returns or the boy grows big enough to take over. She laughs as she tells how Tin Cup laid the big Sharps across his saddle horn and dared any one of them to argue the matter.

Hob returned to the upper Elkhorn with the boy, Michael who takes right up with Isaac and Jacob. April clucks around him like a mother hen, and the boys keep him busy, taking his mind away from the awful things that had befallen him. It was too much for a young boy his age to comprehend. Hob knows he is young and in time, he will forget. Winter comes with a vengeance, promising to be one of the worst locals can remember.

Hob and Sam, make one last trip into Elk Springs with the big wagon a week after he returned with the boy. They stock up on supplies to last them through the winter. Vickie Gorman questions them as they pass through about Matt and Palette. Shaking their heads, they cluck to the team and head on to town. In town, Hob loads up with everything he can think of that they will need for the winter. Several bags of oats and blocks of salt are put in the wagon, with tin goods, flour, and sugar.

When the snows come, a wagon cannot make the trip, only a saddle horse can brave the heavy snows and treacherous trails. Hob wants to be ready. Never before has he had such responsibility, and he does not want to fail Matt. There is no doubt he will return before the winter passes, but Hob does not know how far he will have to pursue Blalock.

Palette rides into the Elkhorn in the early morning as he promised Matt. Dismounting, he looks down the barrel of Tin Cup's Sharps rifle. "Take it easy Tin Cup, we're on the same side from here on in." Palette smiles.

"How do I know you're not lying?"

"We might have had our differences, but have you ever known me to lie?"

Tin Cup lowers the rifle and spits. "No, can't say I have, at that."

"Got some words for Hob and you, from Matt." Palette ties his grey to a corral post. Walking toward the small cabin, Palette notices the big frame of Hob coming from the barn and turns in that direction. Hob recognizes Palette and doesn't trust him anymore than Tin Cup. Palette tells him that he came from Matt and why. Hob listens as Palette tells the story of Blalock, the Ferguson kid, and how it affected Matt.

"Where is he now?" Hob asks.

"That I don't know. I left him outside Elk Springs." Palette tells of Matt ordering supplies for the hostler to have ready.

"You say he was shot?" Tin Cup asks.

Palette nods. "Weren't real bad this time. Lost a little blood but the Doc in Meeker fixed him up."

"Where can I look, what should I do?" Hob's eyes plead for Palette to give him an answer. He has to find Matt.

Palette can see the misery in the black man's eyes. "My advice is to leave him be for now, he'll come in when he gets it all figured out or when time goes by. Right now, he feels real guilty about the Ferguson boy's death."

"It's not just the boy." Hob looks at the ground. "It's about another boy back in Virginia that started all this and about a girl we buried here and a brother." Hob is referring to Matt, Cage, and Jessie. Hob knows it is really about Jessie, the pain and guilt.

"Vickie said they received a good burying." Palette takes off his hat and wipes the brow band, trying to hide the tears in his eyes.

"Come to the house, Mister Palette and we'll talk some." Hob points toward the cabin and waits for Palette to start that way.

Two hours later and full of April's cooking, Palette mounts and turns toward the south. Watching, as the boys wave, he smiles. There is no need to tell Hob to take care of the boy.

Kate stands in the livery and waits for the hostler to answer her question. Wringing his old beat-up hat in his hands nervously, he cannot look her in the eye. She heard from one of the locals, an early riser, that he saw Matt Tillman leaving the livery before daylight, two days prior.

"Yes, Miss Kate, he was here."

"And the supplies?"

"For him, but I do not know where he went." The hostler is nervous under her staring eyes. "Perhaps Wylie Palette knows, he brought the list for the supplies."

"Was he hurt?" She glares at the man.

"He has a wound, but it wasn't serious."

"Why, Mister Perkins, didn't you tell me he was here?"

"If you could have seen his eyes Miss Kate, you would know. He scared the by jiminy out of me." Perkins shakes his head. "I don't know Miss Kate. He's changed since he came back, cold and hard as nails. I personally don't want any part of him."

"Hogwash, he's just been through an ordeal that most men shudder from. No, Mister Perkins, Matt's fine."

"Yes Ma'am, if you say so."

The Indian horse carries Matt toward his home range. Eager to escape the confines of the stable, he plunges through the snowdrifts, his nostrils flaring, and his body full of energy. Matt points him into the westerly winds. He bypasses the Gorman spread and climbs high into the mountains, heading for the pass that leads into Arapaho Country. He has to push the horses hard because the snow will soon close the passes, making it impossible for him to get through.

On the second day, he tops out on the upper pass and looks down upon the Arapaho range. Now, all he has to do is find the village of Fox Tails and Yellow Bonnet. He knows they have to be somewhere in the lower valleys, but which one? Everything is encased in snow, nothing ventures out. Occasionally, he sees a pack of wolves following him at a distance, but they are too smart to come within range of his Henry.

There is no letting up to the snow. Matt figures he might have to give up finding the villages, and hunt for a place to hold up for the winter. Coming out on a small hilltop, he blinks from the glare of the sun shimmering off the snow. Down below, shrouded in wood smoke, is the conical shapes of an Arapaho Village.

Easing the horses down the snow covered trail, Matt levels off at the base of the hill and splashes across the small, half-frozen stream that feeds the valley. Only the more adventuresome of the villagers are out, to see him ride up. The rest are inside, out of the cold.

Greeting each person he meets, he knows he has been recognized, as not one person shows any sign of fright. A large figure emerges from a tepee wrapped in a buffalo robe. Matt recognizes Yellow Bonnet and he pulls the horses to a stop. Raising his arm he speaks the one word of Arapaho he knows, and steps down from the Indian pony.

Fox Tails walks up, as Matt is shaking hands with Yellow Bonnet. "The Iron Man comes to see his friends, the Arapaho."

"Greetings Fox Tails and Yellow Bonnet, my friends." Both men can see the haggard look on Matt's face, and they can tell, by his subdued voice, he traveled far. Motioning for Matt to enter his lodge, Yellow Bonnet speaks quickly to several young men standing around and they start to unload the little bay horse.

Removing his heavy sheepskin coat, Matt takes a seat to Yellow Bonnet's right, the place of honor for a welcomed guest. The large ornament pipe is brought forth, and the men each take several puffs from it, before passing it on to the next one. Matt is cold, tired, and wore out from his long ride. The warm air inside the lodge lulls him into almost nodding off.

"Yellow Bonnet says it is good to see the Iron Man, and have him into his lodge," Fox Tails says, after the pipe ceremony is finished.

"It is good to be here."

"Why have you come?"

Matt looks at each of the men, "I wish to winter with you until the cold times are finished. There has been much killing and I wish to have peace now."

Fox Tails nods. "Then you are welcome here."

"Thank you."

Yellow Bonnet studies Matt closely then speaks. "The Iron Man is welcome here as long as he wishes, but what about the whites? Do they look for you for killing the other whites?"

Matt shakes his head. "No one looks for me."

"We will fix you a place to live, your own lodge."

"My friends, I would like to have a place away from the village, where I can be alone." Matt waits until Fox Tails finishes translating. "I need to be alone."

"It will be as you wish," Yellow Bonnet says. "Now, you will sleep here while the women prepare a place for you."

Matt does not know how long he slept. The warm and comfortable robes lulled him into a deep slumber. When he awakes, it is dark outside and the village is quiet. The snow stopped and he can see the stars through the smoke hole.

From the soft snores inside the lodge, Matt knows he is not alone. Slipping into his boots, he finds his tobacco pouch and eases through the rawhide opening of the lodge. The cold outside is penetrating, he didn't put on his coat, and his wool shirt is not much protection against the frigid air. Rolling a smoke, Matt walks over to where one of the outside fires still burns and squats down beside it. Several village curs surround him in hopes of getting something to eat. Drawing on his smoke, he studies the quiet peacefulness of the village. The snow comes down quietly and blankets the lodges, it is indeed peaceful here. Perhaps he can forget and bury the past.

The next morning Matt awakes again to the women of the village laughing and calling out to one another across the snow covered ground. Matt slips on his sheepskin and ventures outside. Smelling the cook fires, he remembers he has not eaten in a while and is famished. Looking around for his packs, he spots them piled up, under several buffalo robes. Retrieving his old battered coffeepot, he fills it with fresh snow and sits it heating on one of the fires.

Yellow Bonnet and Fox Tails walk up, and Matt offers them a cup of coffee. Both men seem to know what it is and thank him. A comely squaw, who Matt figures is Fox Tails' woman, hands them steaming hot plates of corn cakes and buffalo ribs. The buffalo tastes wonderful, but Matt has to force himself to eat the cakes, whatever they are.

"We have made you a place," said Yellow Bonnet.

"Thank you my friends," Matt replies, as he reaches inside his coat and pulls out three cigars, he had on the list that the hostler picked up for him.

"A white man's favorite past time after he finishes a meal."

Yellow Bonnet and Fox Tails watch as Matt lights his cigar and they do the same. The smile spreads across each of their faces as they smoke. Matt looks around the village. Each person is busy, taking care of their own chores. Everyone is in a good mood, enjoying themselves. Why can't the whites be the same?

"It is away from this place, by itself," Fox Tails says. "Maybe too far for your safety."

"Who would dare bother me here in Yellow Bonnet's Village?"

"Perhaps raiders from the north or perhaps someone else. Yellow Bonnet, has many enemies."

"Where is this place?"

"There, maybe a mile." Fox Tails' thin finger points down the stream. "Yellow Bonnet says he will have some of the young warriors bring your packs there."

"No need," Matt stops them. "These I bring as gifts to my friends the Arapaho people."

Fox Tails nods. "Iron Man does not have to do this."

Matt looks toward the village, "this I know, but I want to."

"We thank you Iron Man. Our people are poor since the whites put us here. Your gifts will be welcome." Yellow Bonnet smiles at Matt.

"Where are my horses?"

"With the horse herd; they are safe."

"Good, I return the pony you gave to me and I will only need the small bay horse."

Later that night, in front of Yellow Bonnet's lodge, the people gather and Matt produces the packs and opens them. Blankets, mirrors, cooking pots, and combs, everything he could think of, he brought with him. He will be in the village for a long time and he wants good relations with them. Standing beside the packs, he lets each person, by age, pick the present they want.

As the last of the presents are distributed and the people go to their lodges, Matt picks up a long package that he was saving then follows Yellow Bonnet and Fox Tails into the lodge. Sitting down, Matt waits until the traditional formalities are finished. He hands out cooking pans and a coffeepot to Yellow Bonnet's family, and a large wooden handle butcher knife to Fox Tails' squaw. He purposely saves the warrior's gifts for last.

Both Yellow Bonnet and Fox Tails sit stoically, trying their best not to look at the two long bundles that lay at Matt's feet. Matt thinks they remind him of two young boys on Christmas morning. Finally, with their curiosity about to get the best of them, Matt picks up one package, handing it to Fox Tails and hands the other to Yellow Bonnet. Both men study the wrapping paper that covers the bundles. Neither man apparently ever saw wrapping paper before. Finally, Fox Tails tears into his and looks at the gun case tied on the end by a leather thong. Untying the strap, the warrior pulls forth a Spencer Carbine, the same as Hob carried.

Fox Tails emits a cry of delight as he holds the rifle in front of him. Yellow Bonnet finally quits admiring the wrapping paper and opens his gun case. The Spencer's were used, but in almost new condition. Although they are accurate and dependable, most cowboys and hunters replace them with the greater firepower of the Henry. Handing both men a sack of shells, Matt watches as they open the cloth sacks and let the bullets trickle through their fingers.

"In the morning, I will show you how to load and shoot them."

Fox Tails runs his hands over the weapon. "You have done us a great honor, Iron Man, how can we ever repay you?"

"Tomorrow, I will go to the lodge you have prepared for me, and there I wish to be left alone, I have much to think about."

"That is all?"

"That is all," Matt answers. "I only wish to be alone."

"A woman to cook for you, maybe?"

"No."

"Then, it shall be as you ask." Yellow Bonnet flattens his hands out.

True to his word, Matt is up at daylight. First, he has to teach Yellow Bonnet's woman to use the coffeepot and the bean grinder, so he can get a cup of coffee. Afterwards, he steps outside, where a bunch of warriors are assembled to see Matt fire the rifles. Fox Tails' throws his chest out and tells everyone his friend, Iron Man, gives him the rifle because of his great friendship. Among the Arapaho, this is indeed a great honor.

Pointing out a small Pine, fifty yards distance, Matt takes Fox Tails' Spencer and shows both men how to load it. Then, sighting in on the tree, he fires. Snow flies up, two inches to the left of the tree. He hears the moan of Fox Tails disappointment when he misses, and shakes his head, pointing at the rear sight of the rifle. After adjusting the sight slightly, he has the warriors watch him load, and again take aim at the tree. This time, when he fires the tree shakes sending snow falling to the ground and bark flying.

A yell of triumph comes from the watching warriors. Handing the weapon back to Fox Tails, he tells him to load and fire again at the tree. The first shot goes very wide of its mark. The second is no better, but with the third try, after Matt's tutelage, bark again flies from the tree.

Yellow Bonnet's Spencer takes several rounds to sight in, but finally, Matt lets the warrior fire the rifle, and with the first round, the target explodes. Explaining to the men they need to preserve their shells as much as they can because there will be no way to resupply them. Matt nods and starts up the stream toward his lodge. Trudging through the snow, alongside the frozen stream, Matt looks up at the snow-capped mountains and nods his head. It is indeed peaceful and serene here, and that is what he wants. The hide lodge sits back in the trees, out of the wind, and away from the stream so it will be safe from flood when the snows melts in the spring. Matt wonders, will he be here in the spring?

This is what he wants, to be alone and try to forget everything, before he returns to the Elkhorn, if indeed he does return at all. Everything he loves or almost everything is gone now. No, he still has the boy Michael, and Hob, April, and their boys. Everything is not gone and he thinks of Kate. Should he return now, before the passes close for the winter? No, he needs time to ease his wounds and forget Jessie. No, he will never forget, unless the bitterness and rage inside him is dealt with, he will not be fit to live with. He will stay the winter and maybe Kate will understand.

CHAPTER 15

After her visit with the hostler at the livery stable, Kate paces the store, thoughts of Matt racing through her head. Why didn't Perkins tell her when Matt was there? She could have talked to him, and perhaps persuaded him to stay. He saw so much death during the war, why did these killings upset him so much? Where did he go? Maybe to the Elkhorn, but she does not think so. The supplies Perkins picked up for him were more like trade goods for Indians. She wonders did he go west to find the Arapahos, and why? Why did he not stop to see her? She knows he cares for her or did he lie the night of the dance? He could have at least stopped long enough to explain. Why is he so troubled?

Cussing Perkins again, she hollers for Bailey. She has to know if he is all right, was the wound worse than that idiot at the livery knew? Why didn't she go over to the livery earlier this morning? She blames herself as much as Perkins. Matt was gone two days before she started thinking about the strange supplies Perkins ordered, then she heard Wylie Palette was seen over at the livery before he left town. What is going on?

"Yes Sis?" Bailey comes from the storeroom.

"Go over to the saloon and see if there are any Gorman riders in town. If they aren't, tell Russ Williams I need to see him as soon as he can come."

"What do you want that drunken old buffalo hunter for?" Bailey looks at her as if she lost her mind, but he can tell she is upset over something, and you do not cross big sister when she is mad.

"Get!"

"He'll just stink up the store like last time."

"Young man."

"Yes Ma'am, I'm going."

Abigail stocks groceries and watches as Kate paces back and forth. It is almost dark outside, and the clouds are building up for another heavy snowstorm. All the customers already left, heading home to sit around the fire and eat a good hot supper. This is definitely a night to stay inside. The winds already start to pick up.

Bailey enters the store, a disgusted look on his face. "He's on his way, stinks to high heaven, and there are no Gorman riders in town."

"Thank you young Mister Howard and I'll thank you to keep a civil tongue in your mouth while Mister Williams is in here. Do you understand me, young man?"

Bailey shrugs and starts for the back. "It's your nose." He just had to have the last say in this matter, as he detests Williams.

Kate watches as the big buffalo hunter lumbers across the street. A big man, almost six and a half feet tall, with a bristling black beard, and long grayish black hair covering his shoulders. The buffalo coat he wears would weigh most men down, but Williams carries it like it's a feather. A powerful man, and a man that, to say the least, does not smell too sweet. Nevertheless, he knows this country better than anyone, except maybe Jim Cloud and the Indians, but Cloud was twenty miles away on the lower Elkhorn. Russ Williams is her only chance.

Entering the store, he makes the boards groan under his weight as he walks to where she is waiting.

"The boy said you wanted to see me, Miss Kate."

"Yes I do, Mister Williams." The man does smell, but he removes his hat in her presence. At least he has good manners around a lady. Although rough when under the influence of spirits, he always treated her and Abigail with the greatest respect.

"I've got a job for you," she said quietly.

"Yes Ma'am."

"I need you to ride out to the Gorman Ranch and take a message to Wylie Palette for me. It's very important."

"Right now, tonight? Ma'am we've got us a bad one coming." The man looks back out the window, then back to Kate.

"I'll pay you twenty dollars Mister Williams, if you'll go tonight.

You're the only man that can get there without getting lost."

"Yes Ma'am, I expect that's true, and I could sure use that twenty dollars."

"Can you make it? I don't want you going if you can't."

The big man hesitates. He needs the money, but he is wise to this country and the storms that can trap a man. "I reckon I'll buck the tiger. I've been out in worse than this."

"I'll have a letter for Mister Palette as soon as you're ready to ride." She hands him the twenty-dollar gold piece. "Thank you, Mister Williams."

After the man leaves, Bailey steps from the backroom. "I sure don't envy him, that ride tonight."

"It's important," Kate looks at Bailey, "or I wouldn't ask Mister Williams to go."

"Shucks, I know that Kate. All I said was I wouldn't want to be out in this mess for anything tonight." Bailey shrugs. Perhaps he misjudged the man.

Kate quickly fills two sacks of food for Williams, and a grain sack of corn for his mule. As a second thought, she goes behind the counter and pulls out a dusty bottle of Kentucky Bourbon.

She looks at it and smiles, her father's favorite, he liked a nip now and then. Placing it under her arm, she starts for the door.

"Really Kate, you'd do anything for Mister Tillman," Abigail frowns, seeing the bottle under Kate's arm.

Kate turns back on her little sister. "If a woman wouldn't do anything for her man, she's not much of a woman in my book."

Stepping out on the front porch and into the north wind, Kate smiles as Williams rides up on his huge, Missouri bred mule. The animal is as big as the man and with hair just as black. The mule's huge head always amazes Kate. She tells Williams he can drink out of the bottom of a five-gallon bucket and still see something coming down the road.

Williams always laughs that big laugh of his, and replies, "It's big alright, but look at all them brains it takes to fill it."

Kate feels guilty. She wants to know about Matt, where he is, and if he is safe, but to ask a man to go out in this weather. The sky already starts to spit sleet and ice, and the north wind can chill a man to the bone in a matter of minutes. "Mister Williams, perhaps you should wait until tomorrow."

The big man laughs, his huge shoulders shaking. "Now don't you worry, Missy. Old Maynard here will get me there and bring me back. He brought me through a lot worse times than this. Don't you fret yourself none."

"I imagine you have, but you don't have to go."

"I have to. If I back out now, well Ma'am, I'd be the laughing stock of town."

"Oh I doubt that, Mister Williams, but I thank you. I fixed you a bit of food and some corn for your Maynard." She hands him up the sacks.

"Well, Miss Kate, I'm a thanking you, Ma'am." The big man lets out with his trademark booming laugh. "I'll be back in a day or so."

"Oh Mister Williams." Kate smiles as she hands him the bottle. "For the chills."

"You're truly an angel, my lady." Williams studies the label on the bottle and grins. "You're a darlin', Ma'am."

Kate watches as Williams and the mule head north, out of Elk Springs and into the bitter cold wind. She stands there shivering until he is engulfed in the swirls of snow and sleet starts to fall. The man has to be at least sixty years old, and few can match him in brute strength. She wonders what he could have been like when he was a young man. She heard rumors of his escapades as a mountain man, but no one speaks about them, or dares ask him anything about his past.

Going back into the store, she breathes a sigh of relief. Tomorrow she will know where Matt is, that is, if Palette knows.

It's midnight by the time Williams fights his way through the heavy snow that falls harder with each mile he rides. Barely able to make out the huge barn at the Gorman Ranch, he dismounts and pushes open the big door leading into it. Feeling along the wall, he finds the coal oil lantern on a nail and strikes a sulphur to it. Several horses and two milk cows stare sleepily at the sight of the big man and mule, flaring their nostrils at the strange smell.

Leading Maynard to an empty stall, he strips his saddle and gear from the mule and closes him inside. Scooping him some corn and a couple of pitchforks of hay, Williams carries his bedroll and saddle to a corner of the barn where the ground is piled with hay. Williams smiles as he pulls out Kate's sack of food and the bottle she gave him.

"Man needs to fortify himself against this weather." He chuckles, holding up the bottle of whiskey. Licking his thick lips, he pulls the cork. Halfway through his second swallow, he hears the squeak and moan of the big door as it opens and lets in a cold draft of wind.

"Close that door, you dang ninny, are you trying to freeze a man to death in this weather?" Williams laughs, recognizing the tall frame of Pauly.

"Russ Williams, is that you or an old grizzly bear?"

"Pauly, I swear you can smell a cork a mile away."

"Russ, you old rogue, I seen the light through the window, and figured you for horse thieves out to steal my milk cows."

"Mighty handsome milk cows they are." Williams looks at the two Jersey Cows in the corner of the barn. "Light somewhere and take a swig of this, old hoss, it's the real thing, Kentucky Bourbon."

"Peers to me, like a bottle of Skeeter Jackson's watered down, washtub mixin' to me," Pauly looks dubiously at the bottle.

"Well, Pauly, I can see right now, your peering has gone bad. This, my friend is the real McCoy; I'll guarantee it or my name ain't Russell Beanpole Williams."

"Russ, I swear." Pauly shakes his head. "What are you doing out here, in this weather?"

"Well now, I'll tell you, I needed a friend to share this here good drinking whiskey with and I just naturally thought of old Pauly."

"You did, did you?"

"Well, to tell the truth, no. Sit down and I'll fill you in on why I'm out here." Williams hands the bottle to Pauly as he finds a seat in the hay. "Don't reckon you'd believe me if I said I was lost?"

"Hardly."

Cutting himself off a chaw of tobacco, Williams pops it in his mouth and takes the bottle back. "Well Miss Kate sent me out here with a letter for Mister Wylie Palette."

"In this storm?" Pauly asks incredibly.

"Here I am." Williams offers Pauly the plug of chewing tobacco.

"Huh uh, that stuff turns my stomach." Pauly takes another pull on the bottle. "What's she want with Wylie?"

"Didn't ask, tweren't none of my business."

Pauly looks to where Maynard was happy and content, eating his corn, and shakes his head. "If it weren't for old Maynard, the sun would be bleaching your old bones and you know it."

"For a fact, I do." Williams laughs. "But if it weren't for old Russ, the injuns would have already ate him a time or two, but I've got to admit, he's better at finding his way home than a compass."

"Well, Wylie's up at the main house asleep." Pauly takes another pull from the bottle. "Reckon it'll keep till morning or you want me to wake him?"

"It'll keep, but this jug won't. Sit a spell and we'll do our dangest to fight it to a stand still." Williams laughs.

"You know Russ, old Wylie's changed since we all found out he's Vickie's brother, and since he came back from down south with Tillman."

"How's he changed?"

"Well I can't rightly put my finger on it, but he has. He's not arrogant or pushy anymore. I think he's lost his mean streak or maybe he's grown up."

"You don't say, Wylie Palette gone soft." Williams gets serious for a minute.

Pauly raises the bottle. "I wouldn't want to push him too far but he's not looking for trouble. He works right along with the other hands."

Williams stuffs another big wad of tobacco in his mouth and chases it with a swig from the bottle.

Pauly refuses the offer of tobacco and instead, he rolls himself a cigarette. Drawing on the strong cigarette tobacco, he tries to kill the taste of the whiskey.

"Never could figure a man ruining the taste of good drinking whiskey with one of them infernal cigarettes.

"What about your chaw?"

"Wonderful, pure dee wonderful. Kinda flavors the taste a mite."

"Nope." Pauly refuses the bottle. "Why don't you come to the bunkhouse where it's warm and sleep tonight?"

"Nope, thank you ever so much, I've got me all the comforts I need. Besides, what would Maynard think of me, deserting him like that?"

"Well we wouldn't want to hurt Maynard's feelings." Pauly stands up a little unsteady. "See you in the cookhouse at sunup for breakfast."

Williams rolls up in his bedroll and settles into a big hay pile with his buffalo coat pulled over him. Patting the almost empty bottle of whiskey, he grins, "yep, all the comforts of home, thank you Miss Howard."

Palette always has breakfast with Vickie, at her insistence then heads for the cookshack to have his final cup of coffee with the crew. Pauly is the foreman and even with Palette back, nothing changed, he still ramrods the outfit. Stepping out onto the front porch, he hears an awful braying and racket coming from the barn. Only Russ William's mule can set off a racket like that. Wondering what Williams is doing here, Palette heads for the cookshack. Sure enough, as he enters the door, he recognizes the huge shape of the old buffalo hunter and mountain man, sitting at the table.

"Our guest comes first." The cook sets a huge platter of steak and potatoes in front of the big man. "First, I said," as he slaps one of the men across the hand with a spoon, as he tries to grab a biscuit.

Ward jokingly complains, "Cookie, we ain't got us enough beef on this range to fill up that big galoot."

Williams only grins, taking the kidding in stride, as he downs another biscuit. He is use to it; no matter where he goes, someone is bound to tease him about his size.

Looking out of the corner of his eye, he sees Palette enter and sit down. Finishing his breakfast, Williams washes it down with a hot cup of black coffee then stuffs a cut of tobacco in his mouth.

"Mighty fine vittles, old hoss. You ain't lost your touch none." Williams nods at the cook.

"Thank you very kindly, Mister Williams," the old cook smiles, then frowns looking toward Ward. "This younger generation, just don't appreciate good cooking." Ward gives a good-natured laugh.

"We appreciate it alright. We just don't get it."

Williams spits into a spittoon, making it ring. "You should have been with us back in the thirties son, your cook there could fix up the best beaver tail or buffalo tongue in the mountains."

"You two rode together back then?" Ward is suddenly interested.

"Sure did; us two, Gabe Bridger, Kit Carson, Beckworth, and all the rest, and young'un, I tell you, your cook," Williams points. "was the best, bar none."

"Well, I'll be." Ward is shocked.

Pauly only grins and bites into a biscuit. Williams can tell some windies, and the young ones are forever, believing him. The cook, whose name was actually Ambrose Green, came out here straight from the big war.

Looking down the table at Palette, Williams studies the gunman a minute. On two different occasions, they came close to having trouble, but both times, it stopped for one reason or another. Pauly was right, the fire and cockiness is gone from the man. Williams knows Palette is still dangerous as a coiled rattler, but the meanness was replaced somehow with a calmness, he can feel.

"Got you a letter here, Wylie." Williams stands and walks to where Palette is sitting. "Sure must be important."

Palette takes the letter. "Alright Russ, thank you, I appreciate you coming all the way out here with it."

The big man nods, then shrugs into his heavy buffalo coat and heads for the door. "I'll wait at the barn if'n you want to send one back with me. I'm grateful for the grub."

Wylie slits open the envelope with a table knife and pulls out the letter.

"Mister Wylie Palette, Dear Sir, I understand you rode into Elk Springs in the company of Matt Tillman. Could you please tell me his whereabouts? I am very concerned, as I was told he was wounded. Signed, Kate Howard.

Wylie studies the letter, while rolling himself a smoke. Leaning the coal oil lamp toward him, he lights the cigarette. Tillman said he wanted to be left alone, until he could get his mind straightened out, whatever that meant. Should he tell her or keep Tillman's location a secret, as he promised he would do? Passing through the door, he refolds the letter and puts it in his pocket. He heard Tillman and the woman were close. Flipping his spent cigarette into the snow, he walks toward the corrals.

Entering the barn, he finds Williams brushing Maynard down, all the while talking to him.

"Russ, you're welcome to lay up here until the storm blows itself out."

"Thank ye, no. Me and old Maynard best be getting along, we told that girl we'd bring her your answer today."

Wylie walks over to the mule. "I didn't know he was this big up close."

"Nigh on to seventeen hands, big for a mule. His papa was a Missouri Mammoth Jack, and his mammy was a Percheron work horse."

"How much you figure he weighs?"

"I'd say close to thirteen fifty or thereabouts."

"Wylie grins. "He's a big'un alright. Russ I want to thank you for coming out with the letter. It takes a good man to buck this weather."

"And a good mule." Williams adds. "You gonna tell the girl?"

"I guess you know what she wants to know?"

"No, but I can guess. She's sweet on this Tillman feller and wants to know where he is."

"Yep."

"He's probably out at his new ranch, don't you reckon? Where else would he be in this kind of weather?"

"No, she knows he didn't go there."

"How?"

"She's a woman. She knows."

Williams slides his bedroll behind the saddle and lashes it down. Sliding his Henry into the boot, he looks to where Wylie is trying to make up his mind. Flipping his rein over the mule's neck, he starts for the door.

"Hold up a minute Russ." Wylie pulls the envelope and a pencil from his pocket and hastily scribbles something on the back. Handing Williams the letter, he reaches inside his coat and pulls out another gold piece.

"No thank you Wylie, I've done been paid."

"The drinks are on me then, next time I'm in town."

Williams grins. "Now you're talkin'."

He was never, until now, a friend of Russ Williams, but watching the big man ride out into the storm, because he gave a girl his word to return, he has to admire the man.

Hob sits by the fireplace in the small cabin, smoking absently on his pipe. Jacob, Isaac, and the smaller Michael, wrestle playfully on the bearskin rug. The boy had been frightened and withdrawn. Now, with April mothering him like a sitting hen, and the two older boys to play with, he finally come out of his shell, and once again, is as playful as a young one should be. He never once asks about his parents. Hob figures he saw everything and there is no need to ask, or he is still too young to understand what happened.

Hob's mind isn't really on the boys, or his pipe, and it hasn't been, since Palette's visit. With little work to do, and with the heavy snows finally upon them, Hob sits around and wonders where Matt is, and if he is okay. His mind is on searching for him, but where, this is a big land, filled with mountains and valleys. It would be like looking for a field mouse in a meadow. No, he will just have to wait.

He rides over to the lower Elkhorn with Tin Cup, to ask Cloud's advice, but he already knows what it will be, when they rein up outside the big house. Cloud and May Bell greet them on the front porch and usher them in, out of the cold. Cloud is healing but far from being up to a long ride in search of Matt. Cloud listens as Hob tells him everything Palette told him, about the supplies and Matt being wounded.

"He's gone to Arapaho country, I'll bet my bottom dollar on it."

"Why?" Tin Cup warms his hands by the stove.

"That's the only likely place he can go, believing the Arapaho would honor his wish to be left alone. That's where we'll find him or he'll find us."

"Can we get through this time of year?" Hob asks.

"Maybe, I don't know without trying, but if I were you I'd let him think on it a little while before going after him."

"Is he safe there?"

"He's safe from the Arapaho anyway, cannot say about any other tribes that may come in to raid, but I doubt any will be out in this weather."

Hob and Tin Cup have dinner then say their good-byes and mount. Cloud follows them to where their horses were fed in the barn. "I'll ride with you Hob, whenever you say."

"Thank you Mista Jim, but I guess you're right, we'll wait a spell."

The ride home is cold. Neither man speaks a word as they climb the mountain trail back to the Elkhorn. Hob only stops long enough to check on the stallion and his mares. Now that the General and his men are all dead, Hob turns the horse back out on the open range. Occasionally, the stallion brings his mares in to the ranch for a good feed of corn, but mostly he keeps them in a sheltered valley, west of the house. Hob has the crew haul hay out to them twice a week.

After supper, he taps his pipe out in the fireplace then walks outside and looks off to the west, over the mountains. "You take care of yourself old friend, and I'll be along soon as the passes clear." Hob mutters to the wind as he makes his way toward the barn.

Kate whirls, as Williams steps through the door, late in the afternoon. Hurrying toward him, anxiety crossing her face, she smiles when he pulls the letter out and hands it to her. Turning the envelope over, she reads the words Palette had written.

"Miss Howard, he's in Arapaho country, give him some time and he'll be back." Wylie.

Kate studies the writing several minutes then looks up at the big man. "Come into the kitchen, Mister Williams."

Pouring the big man some coffee, she notices how he makes the furniture look so small. Turning the envelope over once again, she reads the words. "Give him time." Looking across the table at Williams, she reaches for her cup.

"Wylie says he's in Arapaho Country."

"Yes Ma'am, that's what he told me at the ranch."

"Why, Mister Williams?"

"Wylie says he was tore up after killing that Ferguson boy, and just wanted to be by himself."

"But, it was self-defense, I don't understand."

"No Ma'am, you would have to be in his shoes to understand something like that." Williams takes her hand. "He'll be back in time, Miss Kate."

"I want him back now, Mister Williams."

"He's a grown man, he has his pride." Williams looks down at the floor. "Let him keep it."

"Are you saying I shouldn't go?"

"No Ma'am, I don't really know what I'm saying, but if I were you, I believe I'd wait a spell and give him some time to forget."

Kate stands and walks around the table. She is amazed, even though she is standing the man is almost the same height as she is. Neither speaks, as her troubled mind tries to sort out what she should do. What would be right for her and Matt? She wants him home. Should she go after him? "Mister Williams, will you take me to Arapaho Country?"

"Miss Kate!"

"I will pay you, whatever you ask."

"Miss Kate I can't do that, the passes are probably closed and the snow is getting deeper by the day. I'm not on real good terms with them Arapaho after that big fight we had at Green Meadows, a couple years back."

"Mister Williams."

"Yes Ma'am."

"Will you take me or do I go alone?"

"No Ma'am, I won't take you, and you can't make it alone."

"Very well, Mister Williams, thank you for your services." Kate dismisses him.

"Miss Kate, he's a real man, give him time."

"I can't just sit here and worry about him."

"There's no need for you to worry, Miss Kate."

"Wouldn't you, if you were in my shoes?"

Williams studies her for several minutes then nods his head. "I never spoke of this to a living soul and I want you to keep it to yourself. When I was young, a mountain man had himself a squaw that he put quite a store by. Injuns killed her. The young man hunted down and killed plenty of injuns and then he went off by himself to be alone. Your man needs time alone Miss Kate, time to forget and to let the meanness leave him. From what I've heard about Matt Tillman, he's a real man."

"I know he's a real man, he's my man Mister Williams, and I'm going after him."

"You'll need Jim Cloud for this trip."

"Will you go get him for me?"

"I thought he was badly wounded?"

"Just tell him to come in when he feels like going to Arapaho Country."

"Yes Ma'am, give me a day to rest my mule. He ain't no youngster anymore. Me and him both are kinda long in the tooth."

The following day, Russ Williams makes the ride to the lower Elkhorn to give Jim Cloud Kate's message to come into Elk Springs whenever he feels like riding. The snows came early, with a vengeance, and the roads are impassable by wagon. Only a horse and a man with a tough constitution would dare the trails for any distance this time of year. Most of the ranches and smaller homesteaders laid in their supplies for the winter. Occasionally, a warm Chinook wind blows in, but even then, the roads can be hazardous.

Williams, astride his big mule, returns with the news Kate wants to hear. As soon as his shoulder heals a little more, Cloud will ride into town. The days seem to drag for her, even though she keeps herself busy with the store. A month passes, the sun shines occasionally, but the drifts are worse this year than people have ever seen them. Kate frets and several times, she starts to speak to Williams again about taking her. She knows it is no use, the trails and especially the passes are closed until spring. Even the cowboys from local ranches rarely venture into town with the nasty weather. Kate knows it is pointless, but every day she watches for Jim Cloud to come riding down the street. Bailey and Abigail stay completely out of her sight when they can. How many times can they clean the store shelves?

Saturday morning, the sun shines bright, and warmer for a change. The wind stays calm, and icicles hanging from the eaves are even dripping onto the street.

Kate is busy with a customer, does not bother to look up as the door opens and closes. Jim Cloud and May Bell stand looking at her from the doorway.

Walking to the counter as she finishes with the customer, Cloud clears his throat. "Miss Kate."

She is astonished. "You're here, both of you." Rushing from behind the counter she hugs May Bell and grabs Cloud by the arm.

"It's us alright. Sorry we took so long, but this weather has been the worst I've seen in years." Cloud smiles at her.

"How is your shoulder? Russ said it was giving you problems." Cloud hugs May Bell. "With this little nurse, it's as good as new."

Kate rushes them into the back kitchen and sits them down at the table. "I'm glad Jim. How have you two been out at the ranch?"

Cloud grins. "It was a little rocky until the boys decided I was the boss.

Now everything's working out just fine."

"I'm glad for you. Have you seen anybody from the upper ranch?"

"Matt's not there Kate, if that's what you're asking, and no I haven't seen anybody since Hob and Tin Cup visited over a month ago."

"Russ told you what I wanted to see you about?"

"That's why I'm here, well that, and one other reason." Cloud grins and squeezes May Bells hand.

Kate looks at the two of them and smiles. "No."

"I'm afraid, yes," May Bell answers. "We've come to get the preacher to marry us, if you'll let us use the store tonight, and I can get someone to stand up with me."

"Certainly you can use the store, and Bailey will be more than happy to be your best man." Kate is elated.

"It's about time we were married," Cloud became serious. "May Bell might become a mother."

"Russ didn't tell me." Kate smiles. "I'm so happy for both of you."

"No, he didn't know."

"Jim, I have to go find him, I just have to." Kate changes the subject. "Do you understand that I have to go?"

"You mean to Arapaho country?"

"Yes or where ever he is."

"And you want me to take you?"

"I'll pay you anything."

Cloud frowns. "You know better than that, but it's too hard a trip this time of year for a man, let alone a woman."

"I don't like to beg, Jim."

"I'll go find him."

"No, he's hurting, and I've got to go for his sake." Kate pleads with her eyes. "He might not even see you but he'll talk to me."

"How do you know?"

"I know, he hasn't changed that much."

"We'll talk about it more tonight." Cloud stands up. "I'll leave May Bell here with you while I go speak to Preacher Willis."

Cloud leaves the store and walks across the street toward the saloon. Looking inside he sees Russ Williams at a back table, talking with some town loafers. Stepping back outside, he continues down the street to the preacher's house. Knocking on the door, he removes his hat when the preacher's wife answers the door.

"Why Jim Cloud, we haven't seen you since the funeral." The woman smiles. "How's your wound?"

"Fine Ma'am." Cloud quickly tells her what he wants and she whisks him inside. Preacher Willis comes from his study and shakes hands. Quickly explaining what he wants and that he would like the wedding to be tonight, Cloud thanks the preacher and retreats up the street.

Entering the saloon, he finds Williams by himself this time. Pulling up a cane-backed chair, he orders two whiskeys and shakes hands with the big man.

The barkeep brings one glass of whiskey, looking sternly at Cloud. "Jim, I like you, but you know the rules about selling whiskey to Indians." The saloon man quickly retreats to wait on other customers.

Williams pours half the whiskey into his glass and laughs.

"I'm getting hitched tonight." Cloud announces.

"You're what?" Williams exclaims.

"I am, little man, and you're invited." Cloud grins. "But, Maynard can't come. I don't think Miss Kate would like it."

"I'll be there." Williams downs his whiskey. "But, that's not the only reason you're here?"

"I need you for a job, providing of course you and that danged mule are not too old," Cloud laughs, slapping Williams on the back.

"Don't tell me, she talked you into it."

"Yep, she's mighty persuasive."

"When do we leave?"

"I'll take May Bell back home tomorrow. If the weather holds, I'll be back the next day and we'll pull out."

"What about the passes up in the high country?"

"We won't know until we get there," Cloud frowns. "If we don't take her, she's bound to get someone to go, and for enough money, somebody will."

"What's the pay?"

"Corn for Maynard and good sipping whiskey for you."

"Done." Williams laughs and grabs Cloud's hand, almost squeezing the blood out of it.

CHAPTER 16

Matt looks into the small mirror, the face looking back at him, he hardly recognizes. He never wore a beard, but it has been two months since he last shaved. Dressed in deerskin pants and shirt with his feet encased in leather moccasins, he looks like one of the old mountain men of years past. Looking over to where his clothes hang from one of the lodge poles, he suddenly makes up his mind and he is ready to go back.

Stepping outside, he looks up the creek toward the village. Not a footprint shows in the snow. Yellow Bonnet kept his word, not a soul came by or bothered him since he arrived. Occasionally, he goes to the village without seeing anyone.

He occupies his days by hunting and skinning out his pelts. The small game is plentiful here in the mountains. The Indians quit hunting for skins to trade, as the price was so low it was not worth the trouble, but it keeps Matt busy with something.

He killed several deer and a few elk, which he took into the village and hung on the cross poles for the people. In payment, the women of the village mysteriously left moccasins and the clothes he is wearing, inside his lodge when he was away hunting.

Picking up his rifle, Matt starts toward the village then stops and reenters his lodge. Pulling out several cigars, he turns back toward the village.

Fox Tails is the first to see him walking along the creek and waves.

Seconds later, he is surrounded by villagers who are all glad to see him. Yellow Bonnet steps outside to see what all the commotion is about. If he did not know who Matt was, he wouldn't be able to recognize him.

The white man is gaunt from walking the mountains, but in good shape, and Yellow Bonnet can tell the man is finally at peace. The smile on his face, and the swing to his step, shows he found the peace he was looking for when he first came into these mountains. This white man is different from others. He respects the Indian and their ways, and as the warriors saw, he was terrible in battle, braver than the grizzly bear.

The sun is shining today and the snows cease. Yellow Bonnet waits for Matt and Fox Tails near his lodge. "It is good to see the Iron Man again."

With Fox Tails translating, Matt tells the big warrior it is good to be back with the people. Sitting on robes, outside the lodge, Matt hands out cigars to several of the warriors. He waits until they light them, before lighting his cigarette. The cigars from the store are a little stronger than Matt enjoyed.

"You brought the village much meat and we thank you," Yellow Bonnet said.

"How can we repay our friend?"

"I have been repaid. You let me stay here and your women made me these fine clothes." Cigar smoke drifts around the fire, outside the lodge. Many of the warriors want Matt to tell tales of the war. The big guns, the huge armies, and the numbers of men killed fascinate them.

"Iron Man, are there so many whites that so many can be killed?" A young warrior asks curiously.

"Yes, the whites are like the leaves on the trees, they are mighty warriors, but worse, the Indians have what they want, my friends."

"What would that be?" Yellow Bonnet asks. "The land of our ancestors?"

"The land, yes they are hungry for land, but this is what they will risk dying for." Matt produces a handful of gold nuggets.

"Yellow iron." Fox Tails leans forward and takes a piece of the gold.

"They will kill their own mother or brother, to possess gold."

"Why, you cannot eat it, wear it, it is useless."

"The white man trades this metal for horses and food. It makes him rich and it also makes him crazy." Matt tries to explain and make them understand. "You must never let the whites know you have this metal in your mountains."

Yellow Bonnet nods his head. "The Iron Man does not want this yellow iron?"

"No, I have found what I came for. Now it is time for me to go back to my people but I will return to hunt and talk with you." Matt tosses the gold into the ashes of the fire.

"Do you go back to your home to the east?"

"Yes, as soon as the passes clear."

"We will be sad to see you go."

"I will be sad also, but it is time."

Yellow Bonnet waves his arm and two young boys lead three mares forward near the fire. "These are for you, to replace the ones the bad whites killed."

Matt stands and walks over to the mares. They are as good as the ones he had lost. Once again, his mind returns to the horse ranch he imagines and thinks of the last few months. With mares like these, and the stallion, the Elkhorn will raise the best Cavalry horses the army could want.

"I thank my friends."

Matt returns to his lodge after eating with Yellow Bonnet and his family. Fox Tails walks with him part of the way. Neither man speaks much, enjoying the peacefulness and quiet of the mountains.

"When will you leave?" Fox Tails asks again.

"As soon as the passes clear."

"That may be a long time." Fox Tails motions at the snow laden mountains. "If the Iron Man wants to leave, he can ride as far as the passes and then walk on the big shoes like the rabbit does."

"You mean a snowshoe?"

"We can make you some, but it will still be a difficult journey, my friend."

Matt did not think of making snowshoes. He knows the Indians use them in the north, to go hunting when the snows are deep, it keeps the elk and deer huddled helpless beneath the cedar breaks. He didn't see any in the Arapaho village, but apparently, Fox Tails saw them or know of them.

"Good." Matt nods. "We will start tomorrow."

"These rabbit feet are hard to walk in if you do not know them," Fox tails explains. "They tire a man."

"With your help, we will make some tomorrow."

Fox Tails nods and with a wave, he starts back toward the village.

Matt watches him go. He made good friends among these people and he is glad they are his neighbors.

Entering his lodge, he pulls several fox pelts toward the fire. Sorting through them, he keeps only the blemish free ones and sets the others aside. He wants the women of the village to make Kate a coat and he wants it perfect. Tomorrow, he will return to the village and trade his coffeepot to one of the women to make the coat. He has no further use for it since he is going home.

It is almost dark when Matt gathers his Henry and starts for the mountains to check his rabbit snares. He is enjoying himself for the first time in a long while.

Returning to the lodge after nightfall, he is tired from his long walk. Tonight he will sleep peacefully. Rolling one last cigarette, he sits and watches the embers of the fire. Finishing, he tosses the butt into the flames and rolls into his robes.

Matt awakes with a start from something that makes him wide-awake. Throwing the robes back, he slips into his Moccasins and steps outside. From the village, he can hear screaming and war cries of the warriors. Racing to get his clothes on and grab his weapons, Matt sprints from the lodge and runs toward the sound of battle. He is in good shape and his legs carry him quickly over the snow toward the village.

Only the shadows of moving bodies, rolling on the ground in mortal combat, are visible in the gloom. Matt cannot tell the Arapaho from the invading enemy. A short warrior runs screaming at him from behind a lodge and Matt fires. The force of the bullet knocks the man back, into the side of a lodge. Two more fall to the Henry as Matt races toward Yellow Bonnet's lodge.

The big warrior is fighting with an enemy on the ground. Matt swings the Henry, caving the man's head in. Pulling Yellow Bonnet to his feet, they race together, toward the horse herd, where most of the fighting is taking place. Most of the enemy warriors are retreating, taking many of the horses with them. Yells of anguish rise above the village, as women and children find their family members dead.

Matt and Yellow Bonnet can only stand helplessly by, as they listen to the hoofbeats of the enemy. It is morning before they can catch enough horses to pursue the fleeing warriors.

Matt shrugs his shoulders and looks at Yellow Bonnet. "Utes," is the only word Matt understands.

Walking back into the village, Matt watches as the squaws built up the cooking fires. He can see several of the enemy warriors, lying about, where they had fallen.

Fox Tails rides up on a horse he was able to catch. "They were Utes on a horse raid," the warrior says as he dismounts.

"I didn't think they would come with the snow so deep," Matt says, looking at Fox Tails and shaking his head.

"They are mountain people. The snow does not bother them." Fox Tails shrugs. "The women say you killed three of them with your rifle gun."

Matt shakes his head, so much for peace and quiet. Even here, in these secluded mountains, people fight for one reason or another.

Suddenly, one of the squaws runs up to Yellow Bonnet, screeching. The tall warrior hurries off behind her.

"It is his woman. They have killed her." Fox Tails speaks quietly. "Now they will feel the wrath of Yellow Bonnet."

Matt rolls a cigarette and sits down next to a fire. The villagers are slashing on one enemy that was found still alive. It amazes Matt how the man does not utter a sound as he is sliced to pieces by the women.

Finally, the village quiets, except for the wailing of the women inside the lodges. Matt finds the coffeepot he gave the dead woman, beside one of the fires, and pours himself some coffee. Morning will come, but there will be no sleep tonight.

At first light, they round up and herd several horses into the village. Yellow Bonnet is issuing orders and picking out the warriors to go in pursuit of the raiders. Fox Tails leads a horse and hands the rope bridle to Matt.

"I go for ammunition and my coat," he speaks to Fox Tails and rides toward his lodge. Something catches his eye as he rides down the creek. Stopping, he makes out the shape of a wounded enemy warrior, crawling through the trees alongside the trail. Matt watches the man a minute then sights his rifle and pulls the trigger.

Several warriors race their horses toward the sound of the shot. "It seems there will be no peace and quiet, anywhere he goes," Matt thought, as he rides toward his lodge.

There were at least fifty horses taken from the village. The others were scattered through the surrounding timber in an attempt to keep the Arapaho from following. Fox Tails figures at least thirty of the enemy attacked the village. They find seven dead bodies so at least twenty or more enemy warriors are ahead of them.

The pursuing Arapaho are outnumbered by at least two to one, with only nine riding horses having been caught. All the assembled warriors agree Matt should go along. They witnessed the power of his spirit in battle and that bolsters their courage.

Matt hasn't ridden bareback since the days of his youth but he did not forget how. The pursuers carry nothing but their weapons. They will travel fast to run down the killers of their people. The Utes are heading northeast, into their own hunting grounds. The Arapaho will have to catch up to them quickly. If they get to their village, they will have to give up the chase.

Matt looks at Yellow Bonnet and the hard set to his face. He does not think the warrior will give up. Many Utes will die to avenge his woman; of this, Matt has no doubt. The morning is new, and the pursuers have all day to follow their trail. A warrior called Long Nose is in the lead. He, Matt is told, is the best tracker in the Arapaho Nation. Yellow Bonnet does not intend to lose the killers of his wife.

Matt heard little gunfire in the early morning fight, only his Henry and the two Spencers, he gave Yellow Bonnet and Fox Tails. That means there is no possibility of a long-range ambush. With the numbers in favor of the Utes, they can attack the following warriors with great expectations of winning. The Utes are brave warriors. They will turn and fight, if the Arapaho close in on them.

Matt can see the tracks in the snow, where the warriors traveled into the Arapaho land afoot. Fox Tails informs him of the way enemy warriors always went after horses. That way, they are less likely to be seen and would be able to handle a greater number of horses on their return trip home.

Yellow Bonnet stops the pursuit at noon, allowing the horses to catch their wind. Long Nose rides back to them, excitedly talking to the big warrior. Fox Tails looks to where Matt smokes a cigarette and nods.

"Him say enemy close, maybe over there." Fox Tails points his chin at a far mountain range. "Him say we catch up quick, if we hurry."

"Why does Yellow Bonnet wait then?"

"Him think, maybe a trap."

"What will he do?"

"Yellow Bonnet will fight, but he want horse not tired."

After several minutes pass, Yellow Bonnet nods, and Long Nose rides back into the lead. Tracks are spotted showing where a warrior was watching them from the tree line. Yellow Bonnet only grunts, as his horse circles the tracks then he follows Long Nose up the steep trail. Matt motions to Fox Tails and both men push their way in behind the big warrior. If an ambush is coming Matt wants the rifle fire up front, to help break the attack.

Again, the Utes pulled out, giving up their ideas of attacking the smaller column. Matt knows they are just waiting for a better spot to converge from both sides. With their superior number of men, he knows the enemy wants to fight, as they will gain several more horses, plus more glory. After the long pull up the mountain, Yellow Bonnet calls for a halt again. Matt can see the trail leading down into the valley.

"There we fight," Fox Tails points and grins.

"How do you know?"

"Fox Tails smart Indian, Iron Man watch 'em, we fight there," the warrior grins, as care free as if he is going hunting.

Yellow Bonnet arranges the warriors on both sides of the trail as they bottom out, onto the valley. Matt leads one group, while Fox Tails leads the other. Yellow Bonnet rides right down the middle. It is indeed a good place for an attack. They hardly reach the middle of the flat meadow when Ute warriors come screaming from the woods on both sides. The Indian pony Matt is riding is young and he never heard gunfire before. The loud popping of Yellow Bonnet and Fox Tails rifles, have him lunging around so bad, Matt cannot sight on the onrushing warriors.

Dismounting, he kneels and takes careful aim at the nearest rider. The Henry smacks against his shoulder and the warrior flips backward from his horse as if a giant hand hit him. Again, Matt takes aim, and another warrior falls.

Fox Tails and Yellow Bonnet both manage to knock a warrior from his horse, breaking the charge of the Utes.

The Utes turn racing from the valley with several of the hot bloodied Arapaho in pursuit. The race is quickly over. Yellow Bonnet knows they can never catch the enemy, as they are mounted on the best horses of the Arapaho herd and they are not tired.

A small horse nickers out in the valley and Matt grins as he recognizes his little bay. Riding over to where the warrior fell, Matt dismounts and grabs the reins. "Well Stumpy, it's good to have you back. I guess them Utes know a good horse when they see one." Matt mounts the little horse and rides back to where the others wait.

They killed four men and retrieve several of their herd. Still Yellow Bonnet is not satisfied. Matt wonders, with the death of his woman, if he will ever be satisfied. Well, he knows exactly how the man feels.

The chase lasts through the night and into the next afternoon. The enemy warriors are switching onto fresh horses from the herd and are not slowing down. Yellow Bonnet is furious. He wants to come face to face with the killers of his woman. They are nearing the mountains that are the beginning of the Ute hunting grounds. To go further is to endanger the rest of the trackers and Yellow Bonnet knows it. If the Utes come out of their mountains in numbers, they could run down the Arapahos on their tired horses, easily.

Yellow Bonnet reluctantly calls a halt in a stand of woods and dismounts. Calling his warriors around him, he looks off to the north. Fox Tails translates for Matt.

"Him say he go on, send horses and men back."

"He's going alone?"

"That's what him say," Fox Tails shrugs. "Him mad. You gottum little weed?"

Matt pulls a cigar from his pocket and hands it to the warrior. Striking a sulphur, he lights it then rolls himself a smoke. Shaking his head, he remembers the same words coming from his mouth only a couple months ago. Ironic, he thought, he is in the same situation again. For a man seeking peace, he seems to find trouble waiting for him.

"Tell Yellow Bonnet the Iron Man will go with him."

"Him say, maybe you go home."

"No, I'll go with him." Matt nods. "I'll go home when this is over."

"Him say you no owe him, you save his life two times now."

"I'm going."

"Then I go too," Fox Tails informs Yellow Bonnet.

Nodding, the warrior hands his lead rope to another warrior, and trots off to the north, afoot. Matt looks surprised, but shakes his head and follows. Long Nose makes up the fourth man of the party, as they travel at a slow trot on the trail of the Utes. The rest of the warriors leading the horses turn toward home.

Yellow Bonnet makes sure his men keep their tracks well away from the trail of the horses. Somewhere up ahead, a lookout will be posted to see if they still follow and he wants to skirt around this man. They spot the lookout riding toward them at almost dark. Yellow Bonnet hides the men and lets him pass. Less than an hour later, he comes back in a lope, heading for the main body of Utes. Yellow Bonnet motions them forward.

After traveling all night, Matt is exhausted when the big warrior stops at almost daylight. Ahead, he can make out the smoke of a campfire. Spreading his hands, Yellow Bonnet motions them forward.

The Utes were told the Arapahos quit the chase and are returning home. Busy putting on their finery and paint, to make an impression on the waiting village, they are unaware of the danger creeping toward them.

Matt counts fifteen warriors, standing about laughing and eating. They have no idea of the trouble awaiting them.

Three rifles fire at almost point-blank range, killing three Ute warriors. Screaming, the others lunge for their weapons as the Henry kills two more. Again, all three rifles speak as the Utes try to retreat toward the horse herd. Finally seeing the futility of retreat, the remaining warriors charge them. Matt drops two more with his pistol and the enemy warriors are on them. Fighting hand to hand, the Utes finally give up and try to make a break, but it's too late. The rifles drop them, one by one, as they run across the open ground.

Matt watches, as the Arapahos scalp the dead warriors and then he helps round up the herd. Yellow Bonnet does not know how far the Ute village is, but it cannot be too far. The dead Utes were putting on their war paint for a triumphant return to their people.

Turning the horses back toward their village, the Arapahos watch fearfully behind them, expecting the enemy to return at any time. Matt rolls a cigarette and grins at Fox Tails. "Yep, this sure is peace and quiet," he muses.

Chapter 17

As soon as the "I do's" are over and the few guests at the wedding leave, Cloud has Kate and Russ Williams sitting at the kitchen table, discussing their trip into Arapaho lands. Cloud will take May Bell back to the Elkhorn first and check on everything. After that, he will meet Kate and Williams at the upper Elkhorn Ranch. He already sent a rider to fetch Tin Cup back to the lower Elkhorn to help run the ranch in his absence.

Kate draws up a list of supplies and Cloud reads it off to Williams, as Russ cannot read. Cloud explains everything to Kate, making sure she understands if they cannot get through the passes, they will turn around and abandon the trip until the spring thaws. Kate, with a frown, agrees to the proposal, since it is the only way to get Cloud and Williams to go forward with a venture they figure is foolhardy, at the least.

"Miss Kate, are you sure you won't change your mind?" Williams worries. "You being a girl and all, this will be a rough trip for a man in good weather."

"Russ, you gave me your word. If I get Cloud to go then you will go."

"I did?"

"Well, you practically did. Anyway, if we can't make it, well, we'll just turn around."

The rest of the evening is spent with a dinner party for the newlyweds and the few remaining guests. Bailey pulls out his father's old fiddle and plays a few dances. His eyes almost pop out when Williams asks Kate to dance. The big man is actually graceful on his feet, and Bailey can hardly believe it. He even took a bath and put on clean clothes.

When Kate tells him how splendid he looks, he smiles and laughs.

"Maynard probably won't recognize me in the morning and won't let me anywhere near him."

The party lasts until almost midnight when everyone begins to leave, saying their good-byes and congratulating the newlyweds. Kate is tired but she is also elated. She is finally going to look for Matt.

Cloud and May Bell ride a few miles with Williams and Kate before they turn toward the Gorman Ranch. Cloud's mind races at the thought of the undertaking ahead. He will take May Bell home and cut across the mountains to the upper Elkhorn. He still does not like the idea of taking Kate into Arapaho country, but he just does not have the heart to refuse her, and she will not listen, even if he did. He will probably get a good cussing from Tillman, but he caused this by running off.

At the cut-off, Cloud and May Bell wave and ride on, looking back once as they disappear from sight. He mounted Kate on a good mountain horse from the livery. Cloud grins, next to Williams and Maynard, she looks like a midget on a pony. He worries but he knows Kate is a good rider. He saw her riding the livery horses before, but she is not tough to the saddle. This is going to be a long, cold, and hard ride.

When Kate and Williams ride into the Gorman Ranch, Vickie insists they come in for coffee and warm up before they ride the rest of the way to the Elkhorn. Kate thanks her and dismounts. She wants to speak with Wylie Palette and thank him for the letter he sent.

"So you're really going?" Palette cannot believe it.

"I'm going." Kate looks him squarely in the eye.

"Tillman's a lucky man."

"I don't know about that Wylie, but I'm going after him, lucky or not."

"Yes Ma'am, I see you're definitely set in your ways." Palette looks over at his sister. "Sis, you've got Pauly here, I think I'll ride along and watch."

"You find something amusing?" Kate sees the grin come across the gunman's face as he heads toward the barn.

Palette saddles his grey and pulls on his sheepskin overcoat. Looking over at Kate and Williams, he doffs his hat and bows. "I'm ready when you are."

Almost three hours later they pull into the yard of the Elkhorn. Hob greets them in the yard as they arrive. He looks Williams over and nods. Few times in the past, he has met a man bigger than himself but now one stands before him. Ushering them into the cabin, Hob introduces Kate and Williams to April and the children. Kate bends down and picks the bashful Michael up in her arms.

"He looks like Matt."

"Yes Ma'am he do." Hob agrees.

April pours coffee for the three cold riders as Rollie appears at the door, offering to put their horses in the barn and feed them.

"You can put the mule in the barn, young feller, but don't try to unsaddle him," Williams laughs, downing a piece of April's cake. "I'll be along directly."

"Yes Sir," Rollie laughs. "I've done heard about your mule."

April refills their coffee. "Miss Howard you'll stay up at the big house tonight. Hob already has it warm for you. Mister Palette and Mister Williams will stay in the bunkhouse, if that's alright with you'uns?"

"That'll be fine April."

"You'll take breakfast here with us or I can bring it up to you at the big house." April sits the heavy coffeepot back on the wood stove.

"I would enjoy having breakfast with your family," Kate answers, smiling at Michael.

"Mister Cloud will probably be here first thing in the morning." Hob says. "He'll probably want you'uns to pull out as soon as he gets here."

"We'll be ready." Williams downs the last of his coffee and stands up. "I reckon I better go see after Maynard as I don't want his feelings hurt."

"You stay here with me Miss Howard and we'll talk, maybe you can help with supper," April said, trying to make Kate comfortable.

"I'll stay, April, on one condition."

"Yes Ma'am."

"I hope we're going to be friends and my name is Kate."

April laughs and nods as Michael climbs up into Kate's lap.

Running her fingers through the boy's thick black hair, Kate looks into his dark eyes. He leans up against her and smiles, touching her face with his small hand. "April, tell me about Matt. I know you've known him all your life, he told me so the night of the dance."

April nods. "Okay Miss Kate, we'll talk."

Cloud rides in two hours past daylight, as Hob predicted. Tying his horse to the barn corral, he walks down to the cabin. The morning is cold, but no snow is imminent and the sky is bright blue, predicting a beautiful day for traveling. Cloud finds everyone, except Williams, huddled around the small breakfast table. April pours him a cup of coffee, as soon as he pulls out a chair and sits down.

"Well, how's it feel to be a married man?" Palette kids him.

"Great, you should try it sometime."

"I would indeed, but the only problem is, the only woman I want is fixing to run off to Indian country and probably get scalped."

"That could be a problem alright." Cloud looks at Kate and laughs.

"Ya'll ready to ride?"

"Ready as we'll ever be."

"Let's go." Cloud finishes his coffee and walks to the door.

Another surprise follows as they walk to the barn. Hob has his horse saddled and is going with them. Cloud looks at him and nods his head. He already figured the big man would go with them.

"Them injuns gonna think the whole army is coming after them," Williams jokes, as he leads Maynard from the barn.

Cloud walks close to Williams, out of earshot of the others. "Russ, you ride drag and watch out for the lady. If anything happens, anything at all, you take her and head for home."

"I'll take care of Miss Kate, don't you worry yourself about that. Just get us across the mountain in one piece."

"I'll do my best."

The five riders start out, heading due west for the Arapaho lands, riding single file. Cloud is in the lead with Palette, then Hob, and finally Kate, with Williams bringing up the rear. Cloud makes it clear before they pull out of the Elkhorn headquarters that he is in charge, or he is out. No one argues. They know this is a dangerous undertaking for them all. A blizzard could hit any time. They only have provisions for ten days, only enough to get them there and back with no delays.

Everyone is aware of the risks involved but nobody wants to back out. Each has his own reason for going. Williams is doing it for Kate, he really does not know Tillman. Hob is going for his friend and Cloud does not know why Palette decided to make such a hard ride. He knows for sure, why Kate is going and Cloud himself is going, not only because she asked him, but also because Matt was a friend to him. The necessity of it is unreal to Cloud as he figures Tillman will come in at first thaw or when he decides to. Nevertheless, Kate wants him back now. She is indeed a strong willed woman.

The trails past the lake are not as bad as Cloud feared but the mountain trails and passes are still ahead of them. It will take at least another day or two before they know if they can make it through. Cloud tells Williams to let him know if Kate needs to rest, but so far, she is holding up well. He figures she would. There is no way she will ask for any special favors and take the chance of the men using her for an excuse to turn back.

Night camp finds them on the foothills of the steep trails leading to the first of the mountain passes. Cloud finds a good shelter area of heavy cedars and pulls into it. All the horses are tied on a picket line, army fashion, except for Maynard, who is tied off by himself. Horses not used to mules are a bit skittish of them at first and Cloud does not want to contend with any runaway horses. Breaking out the oats, Williams and Hob tie on the feed bags, while Palette and Cloud build a fire and cut cedar boughs for their beds. An extra packhorse was brought along just to carry the horse feed.

Kate has the coffeepot boiling and side meat cooking, when the men come in and pile their bedrolls and saddles around the fire. Passing out cups, she pours the men their coffee and returns to her cooking.

"Say, if old Matt knew how good this coffee is, he'd be heading back this way already," Palette brags.

"We'll get an early start in the morning, soon as the horses are fed and watered." Cloud announces, rolling himself a smoke.

"How many days will it take us, Jim?" Palette asks.

"Depends." Cloud looks up at the sky. "If it doesn't snow, or we don't have too much trouble on the passes, we'll be there day after tomorrow."

"And if we do?"

Cloud looks at Palette then at Kate as he answers. "We'll turn back like we agreed."

No guards are posted, as Cloud does not figure on any problems this side of the high pass into Arapaho country. There, he will start posting a night guard, until they reach the safety of Yellow Bonnet's village.

Morning finds them riding up the rocky mountain path, leading out of the valley. The snow isn't as bad as Cloud figured it would be. The trail was swept clear by the strong north wind that had been blowing. Another clear day dawns, and Cloud figures, with a little luck, they will be in Arapaho lands by dark.

Kate did not realize just how cold the back of a horse could be in this weather. Her teeth are about to start chattering, when Williams rides up beside her and wraps her in an extra buffalo robe he tied on Maynard. The hide is a shock to her. Never has she felt anything so warm. Almost immediately, buried deep in the robe, she begins to warm up. Peeking out from under the robe, she looks back at the big man and smiles. Even her cold feet are beginning to warm.

How the men keep from freezing she does not know, but they seem to be making it fine. She wonders what it's going to feel like at this altitude when it starts to snow and the wind starts blowing.

Cloud pulls up to look at the pass ahead. He can see the snow piled deeply between the rock walls. Motioning for Palette and Hob to follow him, he has Williams and Kate stay behind and build a fire. Riding into the canyon pass, Cloud pulls up and dismounts.

"How far is it through there?" Palette asks, dismounting beside Cloud.

"Hundred yards or so, but only this short space will be deep. We'll have to break trail afoot before we take the horses in."

Palette nods. Cloud has to admit, the man is game for anything. He does not worry about Hob either, as the man doesn't know the meaning of fear. Having Palette hold the horses, Cloud breaks off two straight cedar limbs, and hands one to Hob as he starts forward, feeling his way in the snow.

He knows the soft snow can pile six feet deep in places, enough to smother a man if he sinks under and it swallows him up. Tying a short piece of heavy rope, he brought especially for this purpose, between him and Hob then Cloud starts forward feeling his way slowly. The first stretch of snow is only twenty-five yards long. Cloud buries up to his waist several times, causing Hob to pull him back. Both men, stamp the snow down under them as they make passes back and forth, until Cloud figures it will hold a horse. Palette relieves Cloud, and starts walking back and forth until he has packed the path as hard as he can get it.

It takes almost four hours, but the worst part of the trail should be passable. Cloud only needs to lead one of the pack animals forward and see if he can make it over their beat down path. First, Hob, Palette, and he has to rest their legs, which feel like lead weights from all the exertion they put forth. Sipping on the coffee and smoking, Cloud looks over at Kate and grins.

"You know Kate? I'm half a mind to tell Matt what he's fixin' to be in for."

"Why, Mister Cloud, whatever do you mean?" She laughs coyly.

Rested, Cloud stands up, grabbing the lead rope of one of the packhorses and starts back toward the pass. Hob follows to convince the animal going through the small path is better than balking. Several times the horse buries to his knees before he can lunge forward and regain his footing on solid ground. Finally, they are through the first heavy drift. Another fifty yards ahead, they will face the same problem again, but this time the snow is not as deep or quite as wide. By sundown, the men give out from taking turns beating a path in the soft snow, but they grin at one another, knowing they are through the pass. The worst is over and all the horses are on the Arapaho side of the mountain.

Cloud is spent and hurriedly directs the men into a natural shelter of boulders with a large rock overhang. By the time Williams has the fire going, and Kate has made coffee, the men have the animals fed and picketed for the night. Palette is going to feed Maynard, but the mule has his mind set on biting Palette, rather than eating, causing Williams to let out with a laugh.

"Better let me tie the bag on Pilgrim, unless you want to come up short some fingers."

Palette only grins and walks to the fire. "Only a crazy man would put up with an animal that ornery," he mutters.

Cloud laughs, "They're two of a kind, don't you think?"

Hob nods. "We had us some of those critters back in Virginia, most cantankerous things that were ever born. Most was like him, a one-man animal, but if they were good ones there's not a horse any better."

"Are we through the drifts now?" Palette asks.

"Might be one more, small place, about a mile down, but I figure we've got it made now." Cloud puffs on his smoke.

Supper finishes, the men sit around, enjoying the warmth and cheer of the fire, a feeling only tired, exhausted men can feel. Cloud is surprised the snow wasn't deeper on this side of the pass, but the wind kept it blown free of the trail. Tomorrow, when they get down lower, it can be different.

"We'll reach Yellow Bonnet's village by noon tomorrow, if the weather holds," Cloud announces, as he looks up at the darkening sky.

The wind switched around, coming from the north, and it got colder all during the afternoon. Cloud worries, as he still has to get to the village, find Matt, recross the mountains before more snow falls blocking the pass, and return home.

Russ Williams keeps looking at the sky also. "Boys, we could be in for a bad storm tomorrow, old Maynard has one ear cocked down, and he's seldom wrong."

"What in tarnation are you babbling about Russ?" Palette looks at the big man.

"Well, I can't rightly say, but this weather could turn bad."

"On account of that blasted mule of yours has got one ear turned down?"

"I always thought mules could only hold one of them long ears up at a time?" Cloud has to get in on the fun.

"You're right, that's true enough, but old Maynard there just ain't your typical run of the mill mule." Williams looks over fondly to where Maynard is contentedly chewing on his ration of oats. "No siree bob, he's a blue-blooded, fine bred Missouri mule. You might even say he's an aristocratic mule."

"What is an aristocratic mule for pete's sake?" Palette wants to know.

"That, my ignorant friend, is a mule whose pappy came from England, and who lived in the King's own stable. Yep old Maynard there is from a long line of aristocrats."

Palette rolls his eyes. "That there mule is from England? Bull."

"Not him, you ignorant Irishman, his pappy was from England."

"Alright, alright," Kate laughs. This close to the Indian village and Matt, she is not going to let anything, especially a mule, spoil her good spirits.

"What you got behind your back, Missy?" Williams rises on his elbow, curious.

"If you two will quit arguing about Maynard, I've got you a bonus for getting us over the mountain." She holds up another bottle of her daddy's fine Kentucky Bourbon. "But, you can only have one cupful each."

Williams smacks his lips. "You're right Jim, Mister Tillman's gonna have his hands full with this little lass, to tease a thirsty man that way."

Kate laughs, "Isn't a cupful better than none at all, Mister Williams?"

"Yes Ma'am," he laughs. "Being as you put it that way."

"That's better."

"What about Hob. He don't indulge in the finer things in life. Maybe I could help him out with his share?"

Cloud's predictions were right. They reach Yellow Bonnet's village a little past noon the following day. As soon as they ride into the village, he knows something is amiss. Women are still wailing, and many have cut their hair, and blood is running down their arms where they hacked themselves in mourning for their dead. Signs of a fight and bloody spots on the ground show there had been a battle of some kind.

Many warriors, recognizing Cloud, gather around the riders. All are armed and ready for battle. Cloud dismounts and looks around at the smoking village and the dead bodies of the Utes that hadn't been moved.

"What has happened, my brothers?"

"Our enemies, the Utes, raided our horse herd and killed many of our people, including the squaw of Yellow Bonnet."

"Where is Yellow Bonnet?"

"He follows the raiders to punish them, for his woman's death."

"Is the white man, called the Iron Man, here?"

"He was here, but now he rides with Yellow Bonnet and Fox Tails."

Cloud studies the faces of the warriors, and looks to where Kate still sits her horse. "How many warriors are with Yellow Bonnet?"

"We had only nine horses, so seven warriors are with him and the Iron Man."

"This woman is tired. Can she have lodging until I return?"

"We will give the woman lodging. Where do you go?" An older warrior asks.

"Yellow Bonnet may be in trouble if he goes too far into Ute hunting grounds. I go to help him fight our enemies."

"We will protect her with our lives."

"I thank you, my brother. I will leave the bearded one with you." Cloud nods his head at Williams.

"We know this one. He was our enemy many moons ago." The old Chief Singing Wind glares at Williams.

"He is a friend of the Iron Man now and our friend too. He will fight for the Arapaho if he is needed."

The old Chief nods. "He was a dreaded enemy."

Cloud turns to where Hob, Palette, and Williams wait. Explaining quickly, he steps to where Williams and Kate sit. "Russ, I need you to stay here and protect Kate. Will you do this for me?"

"You have my word. No one will harm a hair on her head."

"Thank you, my friend."

"I'm going!" Kate sticks out her chin.

Cloud looks down at her. "No Ma'am, you're not, now do as Russ tells you, or I'll tie you up myself."

"Alright, I'll stay here."

Five more warriors round up horses and follow Cloud north out of the village. The snow just starts to fall as they disappear from the village. Keeping to a slow trot, to save their horses, Cloud pushes them steadily until sundown. Pulling into a grove of trees, he dismounts and ties his horse.

"We'll rest here two hours then we'll push on."

"In the dark?" Palette asks.

"In the dark."

The sun is beginning to break in the east when Cloud pulls them up for another rest. Far below them, runs a long narrow valley, almost five miles across. A warrior holds his hand to his eyes and points. Cloud can only make out small specks in the early morning light.

"There they are?"

Mounting, the riders push their horses through the swirling snow as hard as they dare on the slippery trail. On the last knoll, before leveling out onto the valley floor, Cloud pulls up and studies the oncoming horses.

The same warrior points again. "There."

Cloud looks across the huge valley to where the warrior points. At least fifty or more of the enemy are coming hard on the heels of the horse herd. The warriors, pushing the herd, are running the tired horses as hard as they can, aware of the danger closing in on them. Cloud pushes his horse hard to the bottom, racing him full out, across the valley. Bypassing the oncoming horses, he turns his horse and pulls up beside Matt. Herding the horses into the trail leading over the mountain, Cloud hollers for the men to dismount and spread out across the trail. Placing everyone with rifles behind rocks and other places of concealment, he tells the warriors with bows to back them up, if any enemy gets past the rifles. Sending two warriors on toward home with the horse herd, Cloud shakes hands with Matt, turning to await the oncoming enemy.

"Good to see you, Hob, Wylie." Matt grips the men's hands and laughs.

"I thought you were looking for some peace and quiet," Palette grins.

"I guess there's no such thing."

Six rifles roar, as the Ute horsemen ride into range. The unexpected clash of the rifles and five of their warriors falling from their horses temporarily discourages the onrushing warriors, causing them to slide their blowing horses to a stop. Again the rifles roar, this time unhorsing four more warriors. With a scream of fury, the Utes charge the small band, hidden behind the rocks.

The rifles do their deadly work, as warrior after warrior slides from his horse. Finally, the maddened warriors retreat from the roar of the rifles and the arrows coming at them.

Stopping out of rifle range, the Utes sit their horses and taunt the Arapaho to come out of hiding and fight like men.

Yellow Bonnet reloads the Spencer, and mounts his horse. Matt puts his hand on the big warrior's arm and shakes his head. Fox Tails and Cloud walk over to their horses and mount.

Matt looks at Hob and Palette and shrugs.

"Well boys, looks like we've been invited to another dance," Matt says as he mounts the little bay.

Palette grins at Hob. "Sounds like it's gonna be a real shindig and this time I'm able to dance a jig or two."

Hob only shakes his head and looks at Matt.

Yellow Bonnet leads his Arapaho braves, along with the two white men, one half breed, and one black man, out to face the Ute warriors across the valley. Spreading his warriors out into a long line, Yellow Bonnet sits and watches his enemies across the snow covered valley. Now, with the dead Utes lying everywhere, the odds are even now. With a scream, Yellow Bonnet slaps his horse and races madly toward his enemies. Fox Tails is right beside him as their horses race neck and neck toward the Utes.

Matt and Palette's Henrys are spitting death among the bunched, Ute warriors, as they clash into their ranks. Yellow Bonnet has gone completely berserk as he fights his way through the enemy line and turns his horse back to fight hand to hand with his hated enemy. Matt fires until his rifle hit on an empty chamber. Using the rifle as a club he unhorses several Utes.

As sudden as it began the fight was over. The Utes cannot stand against an enemy that fights like demons. Matt looks around. Bodies are strewn everywhere around him. Looking over at Hob who is, as usual, at his side, he nods.

Hob looks at all the dead Ute warriors and grins. "Almost like the war, isn't it?"

Matt agrees, "Almost."

Two Arapaho warriors had fallen in the fight. Fox Tails took an arrow in the leg and Palette has a bad slash on his shoulder. Yellow Bonnet chased the Utes across the valley and returns in triumph. Cloud explains the big man's honor has been restored and his dead squaw has been avenged.

Capturing the loose horses, the Arapaho place their dead across the back of two, and follow the horse herd back along the mountain trails toward their village. Cloud does not mention Kate, as they ride slowly into the village. Williams comes riding up on Maynard, grinning like a boar coon. Cloud introduces Matt to the big man and motions Williams to be quiet.

Pulling Williams off to the side, he whispers to the man. "Where is she?"

"She's waiting in Mister Tillman's lodge downstream a ways." Williams grins. "She doesn't know he's back."

Cloud nods. Riding over to Matt, he coughs. "Say Matt you got any tobacco? I could sure use a smoke."

Matt feels in his pocket and frowns. "Sorry Jim, I'm fresh out."

"How about in your poke?" Cloud pouts. "I sure need a smoke, bad."

"Okay, I'll be right back." Matt has no idea what Cloud is up to, only that he wants a cigarette. After all the man did for him, tobacco is little enough to do for him.

Matt lopes the little bay down the creek and pulls up at his lodge. Dismounting, he is about to enter when she steps out of the lodge. Recognizing him, she throws herself into his arms.

"Matt." She ran her hands over his face, pulling his head down to meet hers.

"I guess it's time for me to come home."

"Yes Mathew Tillman, I believe it is." She smiles up at him.

The End